Praise for the

"*Yes, Justin* is a very powerful novella showing ... heal troubles within a couple, who at its core loves each other."

— Victoria, *TwoLips Reviews*

"...a feel good story that will leave you happy to have read it."

— Penelope, *Kinky Book Reviews*

By My Side
A Recommended Read! "...an absolute joy to read. I literally could not set this book down..."

— Lea, *BlackRaven's Reviews*

"I could not put this book down once I started to read *By My Side*. This is one I will be reading again."

— *BDSM Book Reviews*

Out of My League
"The warmth, compassion and desire that emerge between Kaelen and Mia are explosive enough to rock the pages."

— Shannon, *The Romance Studio*

"...a very sensual read..."

— *You Gotta Read Reviews*

Loose Id®

ISBN 13: 978-1-62300-169-8
SAFE WORD: OASIS
Copyright © October 2012 by Loose Id LLC

Cover Art by Valerie Tibbs
Cover Layout and Design by April Martinez

Publisher acknowledges the author and copyright holder of the individual works, as follows:
YES, JUSTIN
Copyright © November 2011 by Michele Zurlo
BY MY SIDE
Copyright © January 2012 by Michele Zurlo
OUT OF MY LEAGUE
Copyright © February 2012 by Michele Zurlor

All rights reserved. Except for use of brief quotations in any review or critical article, the reproduction or utilization of this work in whole or in part in any form by any electronic, mechanical or other means, now known or hereafter invented, including xerography, photo-copying and recording, or in any information storage or retrieval is forbidden without the prior written permission of Loose Id LLC, PO Box 809, San Francisco CA 94104-0809. http://www.loose-id.com

DISCLAIMER: Many of the acts described in our BDSM/fetish titles can be dangerous. Please do not try any new sexual practice, whether it be fire, rope, or whip play, without the guidance of an experienced practitioner. Neither Loose Id nor its authors will be responsible for any loss, harm, injury or death resulting from use of the information contained in any of its titles.

This book is an original publication of Loose Id®. Each individual story herein was previously published in e-book format only by Loose Id® and is a work of fiction. Any similarity to actual persons, events or existing locations is entirely coincidental.

Printed in the U.S.A. by
Lightning Source, Inc.
1246 Heil Quaker Blvd
La Vergne TN 37086
www.lightningsource.com

Contents

Yes, Justin
1

By My Side
81

Out of My League
183

YES, JUSTIN

Oasis: Adult Fantasy Fulfillment

ADVERTISEMENT

Think about what you want more than anything in the world. It isn't out of reach. Oasis is an adult fantasy fulfillment service that specializes in making your dreams come true. Anything from a weekend getaway with someone you love to an erotic encounter with a stranger—or strangers—can happen. Call us today and make your fantasy a reality.

*Oasis reserves the right to reject any application for any reason. Oasis is not an escort service. We match people on the basis of their fantasies and arrange for those fantasies to be fulfilled. Fantasies are fulfilled at the discretion of management.

Case 1

I want to be the only thing a man thinks about. I want him to master my body and my soul.

Chapter One

Justin rose early, as he always did, and watched the woman sleeping next to him. Trish, his wife, didn't stir even though shafts of soft light penetrated the cracks in the curtains. He wanted to lift her nightgown, pin her hands over her head, and wake her up by thrusting deep into her sleep-soft body.

Her eyes would be bleary and dark in this half light. She would stare at him in wonder for a second, and then she would surrender to his will and his passion. It would be like it used to be when they were first married and they couldn't get enough of each other.

Over the past two months, he'd frequently entertained this fantasy, and the blame lay solely with her. Perhaps the idea of holding her down wasn't new, but the idea that he could wake her up and take what he wanted hadn't crossed his mind in more years than he could remember. Given the number of times she'd pushed away his questing hands, it just didn't seem consensual anymore.

That was before he saw her questionnaire.

In it she had clearly stated that she didn't want him to ask for sex. She wanted him to remove the choice. Though why she would turn him down when she wanted it too presented a paradox he was only just beginning to understand.

Rolling from bed, he took his morning wood into the shower and entertained himself with the fantasy of fucking his captivating wife of fifteen years. This would be the last morning he let her sleep undisturbed. She wanted him to let loose his dominant nature. He would do it for both of them.

A half hour later, dressed in comfortable jeans and a cotton shirt, he headed to the kitchen to make breakfast. He broke out eggs, milk, cheese, and bread. Mikayla, their oldest, loved the way he made cheesy scrambled eggs. She would whisper that she liked them better than Trish's, but he knew the truth. Trish hated eggs and refused to make them.

Bacon sizzled, and the toaster let out a *ding*. A small tug on his shirt caught his attention. "Where's Mommy?"

He ignored the twinge of guilt in his gut. Of course she wanted Trish first thing. Trish got them up each day, snuggled them until they were awake, bundled them off to day care, and then picked them up after a full day teaching music to six hundred elementary students. She made dinner whether or not he was there to dine with them. And when he worked really late, she tucked them into bed at night. She'd tucked them in last night while he had been at his last Oasis class.

Of course, she thought he had been working late.

"Mommy's sleeping. She has a big day ahead of her, so we'll let her sleep and surprise her with breakfast." He crouched down and held his arms open for a hug.

Mikayla blinked at him, and then her sleepy brown eyes opened a little more. She smiled and snuggled into his shoulder. He lifted her and stirred the eggs.

"I made your favorite, baby."

"Daddy, I'm not a baby. I'm going to kindergarten next year."

He grinned at her indignant tone, which conflicted with the way her entire body relaxed into his hold. "You'll always be my baby, Kay-Kay."

"Hannah's the baby."

Every inch her mother's daughter, Mikayla wasn't going to cede the point.

"Yep." No sense in arguing. She'd realize sooner or later he'd never change his mind.

Footsteps sounded in the hall. His family was waking up. Trish appeared, still clad in her rumpled nightgown. Hannah hung from her neck like a baby koala.

He smiled, but he wondered if it reached his eyes. "Good morning, ladies."

Trish frowned. "I thought you had a trip today."

She was pissed at him. Though she didn't say anything about all the late hours and business trips, they grated on her nerves and wore down the foundation of their marriage. He'd learned a few things from reading her questionnaire, both things she'd disclosed and things he inferred. She had all but come out and said she felt like a single mother, not the sexy, desirable women who occupied his fantasies in the shower every morning.

Negotiation. The introductory BDSM class Oasis had required him to take for the past six weeks—part of the fantasy-fulfillment process—had emphasized negotiation as the solution for every problem. Want a quickie in the morning? Negotiate terms for when that would be acceptable. Want her to not wear underwear to bed? Negotiate terms for when that would happen. Want her to stop pretending like nothing was wrong with their relationship? Negotiate terms for conversation.

They never talked about anything. Even when he'd told her he had a conference to attend this weekend, she hadn't shown much of a reaction. She hadn't even pressed her lips together in an attempt to hide annoyance.

Sometimes, learning to dominate and discipline seemed like marriage counseling. Talk it out, talk it out, talk it out. In a scene, he had to know what she did and didn't want. He had to be in tune with her desires without asking to make sure.

That was where his confidence wavered. Sometimes Trish seemed like a stranger in his bed, a woman who mothered his children and made dinner. He often left before she woke up and came home after she had already been there for hours, an incidental character in their family dynamic.

Ten years ago, he knew how to touch her. He knew how to look at her to make her blush. He could get away with fingering her in the movie theater, her soft moans disguised by the loud cacophony from the action flick he'd chosen for just that reason.

Now, he wasn't certain he would be allowed to hold her hand in the theater. He didn't even know if she liked action movies anymore, much less if she liked to get action at the movies.

She frowned and turned her attention to the kids, a sure sign of displeasure. Perhaps she thought he hadn't listened to her question.

"I don't have to leave until ten. I wanted to let you sleep late. You won't be able to tomorrow." He didn't mention that she wouldn't be sleeping late because he would be waking her up for sex. That definitely wouldn't go over well. Hopefully, this weekend would change both their attitudes.

She turned away, but not before he saw the guilt in her eyes. He doubted she would get in the car with him later. Her fantasy began with being blindfolded and kidnapped by a stranger she didn't get to see. Not the safest way to start a scene, but he didn't care to argue that point, either. He would be the one kidnapping her, so she would be safe.

"My parents are taking the kids for the weekend." Her attempt to fling that as a challenge didn't quite make it over her shoulder. He heard the subtext. A good husband would clear his schedule and spend some quality time with his wife.

Just wait.

After breakfast, he headed to the bedroom to double-check his bag. She wouldn't follow him. That would open her to the possibility of an intimate moment, and she had long ago stopped taking emotional chances with him. If he wasn't so absent, she would feel closer to him. If he felt closer to her, he wouldn't be absent so much. One problem fed the other, and it was ruining their marriage.

He sipped his coffee and made sure his overnight bag had all the things Oasis had told him to bring. They would provide many items, but he wanted to make sure he had the flogger he'd used in practice all these weeks.

Training on the leather-covered mannequins with sensors that provided digital feedback hadn't been nearly as nerve-racking as practicing on a real person. Men and women, attending the Oasis class so they could fulfill their fantasies and the fantasies of whomever they were matched with, had offered their bodies as fodder to help the doms in the class hone their skills.

Of course, he'd spent some time under the lash himself. It made him seriously question whether or not

Trish knew what she had been asking for when she filled out those detailed questionnaires describing what she wanted in a dom and what she expected in a scene. After those sessions, talking with submissives had opened his eyes to what they gained from the experience.

They found it sexually exciting, but more than that, they hungered for the peace that came afterward. They craved knowing someone cared enough to give them the pain and pleasure they needed. They basked in the closeness it generated.

Justin wondered why they couldn't make one of those questionnaires for a marriage. Check the box if you expect your husband to take out the trash, make enough money to take an expensive vacation twice a year, attend every one of the kids' soccer practices, spank you before sex.

The instructor-counselors at Oasis had assured him that she wanted this. She had initiated contact and detailed her fantasy. Part of him hated that she hadn't shared her fantasy with him. *"Communication often breaks down this far into a relationship when people are in the habit of taking one another for granted. Talk it out."*

Next he triple-checked to see if he had a butt plug. Never in a million years would he have considered using her ass for sexual purposes. Perhaps he lacked imagination, but it had never seemed like an option. The answers on her questionnaire made it clear she not only considered it an option—she demanded it be exercised.

And now that he knew it was on the table, he fantasized about the experience. That part of the class had contained a theoretical discussion and a demonstration that made him want to go home and try it on Trish right then and there. But he hadn't, because it would blow the surprise of the scenario she had so painstakingly crafted.

He brushed his teeth and steeled his nerves. She wanted this. He wanted this. Finding that invitation from Oasis in his in-box had changed his life. He didn't know how they came up with the idea to contact him, but he thanked his lucky stars they hadn't paired her with another person whose wish happened to match hers. While he would never have thought to contact a place like Oasis—or do half the things she'd put on the questionnaire they'd handed him at that first training session—his wife had. Someone there had recognized her cry for help and sought him out.

At first, he had been upset that his wife wanted to cheat on him. Then he realized her description of the guy she wanted to dominate her matched him perfectly. Reading her answers, he had been surprised she didn't ask for someone with a scar on his left knee and a right earlobe that was a little smaller than the left. She didn't want some nameless, faceless stranger. She wanted him.

Well, she was going to have him. And he was going to have her.

He kissed his girls good-bye and stifled a growl when Trish turned her cheek to him, denying him the pleasure of her lips. That was the last time he would allow that kind of behavior. Knowing she wanted him to push her on these issues gave him all the permission he needed.

He put his suitcase into his car and headed for the rental place to change his SUV for the one Oasis had reserved for their trip. It would give Trish time to settle the girls at her parents' house and walk to the pickup location.

* * *

Oasis had sent her a list of items to bring along in the bag they'd provided. She couldn't bring her own purse, not that it mattered. It was full of receipts and to-do lists, evidence of the life she wanted to escape.

She rummaged through the bag to make sure everything was there, locked up the house, and walked the three blocks to the main road bordering her subdivision on the north side. The sun shone brightly in one of those wonderful spring days that made her want to run barefoot in the grass. She wore jeans and a tank top, as per the instructions, and tennis shoes.

She didn't feel sexy or desirable. She didn't feel like anything other than the thirty-six-year-old mother of two who could no longer wear the same sizes she had when she was a teen. A sigh whooshed from between her lips as she stopped at the appointed location. The strip mall boasted a pharmacy, a sports bar, and a quick oil-change station. She stood on the narrow sidewalk between the pharmacy and the road, keeping the pale brick wall at her back.

A black SUV stopped on the road in front of her. Patricia held her breath. The instructions said he would be driving a black SUV. She wondered what he would look like, this mystery man whose fantasy matched hers.

The light turned green, and the SUV turned the corner and disappeared. Patricia's shoulders drooped, an outward sign of her nervousness and disappointment.

Suddenly, the world went black. A hand clamped over her mouth to muffle her impending shriek. Her heart beat fast, but she willed her body to calm down. This was what she wanted. She had asked to be kidnapped by a dominant stranger. He was going to spend the weekend using her body for his pleasure.

The paperwork she had filled out specified the kinds of things to which she consented: kidnapping, bondage, spankings, and a whole host of sexual things she had always wanted to try. These were things she had been too ashamed to share with Justin. Even if he still cared for her sexually, he wouldn't understand this side of her desire.

"Patricia?" The gruff voice sent shivers down her spine. His chest pressed against her back. He was roughly the same size and build as Justin, just as she had specified in her application.

His hand remained over her mouth. Wordlessly, she nodded. Her head didn't move all that much, but she knew he felt the motion of her confirmation.

"I'm going to release you. Don't turn around or move until I tell you to do so. Do you understand?" He whispered the words in a sexy, husky voice.

A thrill ran from her belly to her pussy. She craved this kind of danger. She nodded again. He removed his hands.

Light flooded her eyes, blinding her to the empty road in front. She took a deep breath through her mouth, and the darkness returned. This time, a silky blindfold pressed against her forehead and cheeks. He adjusted the elastic strap behind her head.

"Can you see?"

Patricia shook her head. No light peeked in from any point. The swatch of silk hugged the curves of her cheeks and molded to the bridge of her nose.

"I'm going to guide you to the car. Follow my directions exactly. From this point forward, you are slave, and I am Sir. The safe word is 'oasis.' Do you understand?" He spoke this directive in a gravelly whisper, telling her things she already knew. She had chosen the safe word and the terms by which they would be known. He had obviously studied the paperwork.

She wondered if he would ever use his real voice. The force and strength weren't disguised, but she still wanted to hear what he really sounded like. "Yes."

"Yes?" Now he growled.

It did the trick. "Yes, Sir."

Without using more words than necessary, he guided her to the car and helped her inside. Strong hands aided her in securing the seat belt. He leaned across her, and Patricia inhaled his clean scent, looking for any clue that might tell her something about her mystery man. From the few times he'd brushed lightly against her, she knew she liked his build, but she wasn't able to discern anything more.

The door closed, blocking out the distant sounds of traffic. The opposite door opened, then closed. Patricia listened to the small noises that indicated his movements as he latched his seat belt and started the car.

Silence filled the SUV. No music played on the radio to distract her from thoughts about what might happen in the next few hours. Minutes stretched. The dull sounds of other cars faded, and she guessed they were heading out of the city.

She hoped to God he wasn't going to murder her and dump the body. Oasis promised thorough background checks. They had certainly checked out every aspect of her background.

Nothing about this man seemed overly dangerous or threatening. Though his voice had been gruff and low, he didn't sound cruel, and he had been gentle and courteous as he loaded her into the car. She wished she could see his eyes. The eyes revealed so much of a person's soul, and Patricia had always found herself attracted to eyes. Her husband had gentle blue eyes. She used to get wet just looking into his expressive baby blues. How long had it been since she had taken the time to actually look at him?

"Take off your shoes and socks."

The directive, like the ride, was quiet and controlled. This man exuded strength, which she liked. However, her panties remained dry. Her body didn't respond the same way as the myriad heroines in her favorite erotic novels. So far, the experience interested her. Except for that first moment, no sense of excitement had rushed through her veins. She had thought waiting would increase her sense of anticipation, but she found waiting while blindfolded to be highly overrated as a method of increasing anything other than her frustration and impatience.

Patricia toed off one sneaker and then the other. She peeled away the plain white ankle socks.

She wiggled her toes against the floor mat. It was clean, scratching gently at the bottoms of her feet.

"Good girl. Lose the jeans."

Patricia hesitated. "We're in public."

"No talking, slave. Remove your jeans or you will be punished."

She knew they were well outside of the city limits. She knew the countryside boasted very little population. The chance of anyone seeing her was slim to none. Still, she couldn't bring herself to unbutton her jeans. Nobody but Justin had seen her naked in more years than she could remember. She wasn't young and svelte anymore. Two pregnancies and the passage of years had left their marks.

More than that, Patricia wanted Justin. This fantasy was doomed from the start because Justin was the only man she wanted to see her naked, to touch her, to kiss her. She couldn't do this. The fantasy had sounded so wonderful on paper. Oasis promised the fulfillment of her deepest desires—but her deepest desires involved her husband.

Tears soaked the back of the blindfold, pressing hot against her eyelids. "I can't do this."

Silence greeted her declaration. This fantasy belonged to him as much as it belonged to her. Patricia's heart beat faster. What if he didn't let her out of her agreement?

"Please take me back. I can't do this." She choked on the words and begged with every fiber of her being.

"No one is around, slave. No one will see you but me."

There was something in his throaty whisper, something familiar that reminded her too much of Justin. Her heart broke as the reality of what she was doing crashed into her consciousness. She was cheating on Justin. She was cheating on the man to whom she had pledged her fidelity and love. Her tears came faster.

"Oasis. I can't do this. I'm married. I love my husband. This was a mistake, a huge mistake. I don't know what I was thinking." She didn't care that he heard her sobs.

The car slowed, and Patricia breathed a sigh of relief as she anticipated the U-turn that would take her home. She could be back before Justin ever knew she was gone.

Gravel crunched under the tires as the car stopped. Patricia yanked away the blindfold. It wasn't that she wanted to see this mystery man as much as that she wanted to apologize for ruining his fantasy.

She turned to him and gasped. Unreadable blue eyes stared at her. Tiny, familiar laugh lines edged them, though no smile lit his face. His lips were drawn tight against his teeth in an almost grimace. Several expressions—anger, hurt, determination—suggested themselves, but nothing definite manifested.

"Justin."

"Trish."

Humiliation and shame fought to be her dominant emotion. "I'm sorry. I don't know what I was thinking. I don't know why I did this." She reached for her socks.

"Leave them."

The hard edge to his voice halted her actions. "You have every right to be mad at me."

He turned to stare at something near the steering wheel. "You were planning to cheat on me."

She had nothing to say to that. A denial would be appropriate, but it would be a lie, and she had already apologized.

"It's my fault," he said. His strong, confident voice came out quiet and subdued. "I work late all the time, and I'm frequently gone on the weekends. I leave you alone a lot. You joke about being a single mother, but it isn't a joke, not really. When I stand back and I look at my role in our family, I don't see that I'm necessary."

She had to interrupt him. "You're necessary, Justin. The girls love you. They miss you when you're gone. It's just that they're so used to you not being around."

Patricia trailed off, having made the wrong point. This was another thing to add to the list of ways in which they no longer communicated. Everything she said always came out wrong.

His long fingers were splayed across his thighs. He pressed the tips hard against his muscles there, rendering the skin around his nails a bloodless white. "When I found out what you were planning, I was so pissed at you."

She held her breath and tried not to look at him. Anguish burned her insides.

"But then I thought about it from your perspective."

Something in his voice changed. He traced the seam on the side of his jeans, and she knew his anger had fled.

"I'm not having an affair, Trish. I've never even thought about having one. I can't remember the last time I made love to you. We haven't had sex in months. I miss it, but I'm not looking elsewhere."

She had wondered about his fidelity so many times, but she had always avoided thinking about what it meant for their relationship. The idea of him with another woman made her feel numb inside. She had been too afraid of the pain to face the issue head-on. The sad state of their relationship was a painful topic, but she knew Justin needed to have his say. She owed him that much.

"When we decided to have kids, we promised each other that our relationship would always come first, that we would make a point to communicate with each other. We haven't done that, not really."

She knew what he meant. Telling him the times and locations of their daughters' soccer games wasn't conversation. It was small talk, filler. It was all they had.

He played with the locking mechanism on the keychain dangling from the ignition. She watched him from the corner of her eye. "When I saw your answers on the questionnaire, I was a little shocked. Mostly, it made me sad." Now he looked at her, piercing her with those eyes she never could resist. "I wondered why you never told me you wanted those things, but then I realized the answer was pretty obvious."

Patricia closed her eyes against the judgment she knew was coming. The things she had asked for on her application were kinky and a little perverted. She had needed to look up some of the items on the Internet. In order to fill in the survey, she'd had to learn the difference between a flogger, a tawse, and a single-tail. Terms like "butt plug" and "anal beads" were no longer vague images in her head. Even nipple clamps came in a variety of styles she never would have imagined. In fifteen years, Justin had never indicated an interest in any of those things.

While filling out the questionnaire, the veil of anonymity had acted as a protective barrier. She didn't care if strangers judged her. She only cared about Justin's opinion.

"Are you going to divorce me?"

He stared at her for too long. His silence and lack of reaction made her squirm. She hadn't meant to ask that question. She didn't want to give him that out.

Finally, he shook his head. "No, Trish. I don't want to live my life without you. I would kill the man who touched you, but I would never give you up."

She sagged with relief, but her body trembled uncontrollably. He clicked the release on her seat belt and pulled her across the console and onto his lap. She pressed her face into his shoulder, and he smoothed back her hair. It had been so very long since he had held her like this. The sweetness of his care made her shake harder. He stroked her until her tremors subsided. Then he just held her against him.

"I can't tell you how relieved I was when you asked me to take you home. Truthfully, I was surprised you got in the car with me in the first place. I honestly thought you'd chicken out way before now." He murmured the words against her temple. The caress of his lips against that sensitive patch of skin made her yearn for far more than she had a right to expect.

The laugh that forced its way from her chest was of the bemused variety. "I only got into the car because when you blindfolded me, you pressed your chest against my back and I, well, you felt like you."

Justin grasped her chin, tilting her face to his. The kiss was gentle, full of tenderness and regret. Though he had said he would never let her go, Patricia wondered where this fiasco left the state of their marriage.

When the kiss ended, she shifted, trying to avoid the awkwardness of the situation. The futility of the effort struck her. She gathered courage and asked the question she should have asked when she tore the blindfold off to see him sitting in the driver's seat. "Justin, what are you doing here?"

She expected him to shrug or feign indifference, but steely determination glittered behind his eyes. "Oasis contacted me. It took them some time to convince me it was for real, but once I saw the paperwork, I realized they knew you wanted me. It was pretty obvious."

She nodded, a little overwhelmed by their perceptiveness and the lack of anger in Justin's response. "What now?"

His smile was too cocksure. "The way I see it, we paid for a rental car and a nice cabin in a remote area with a wicked-looking dungeon decor, and the kids are with your parents. You take back that safe word, and I'll carry out my end of the bargain."

Shock rendered her immobile. Finally, she lifted her head and leaned back to look up at him. He was a half foot taller than her, and the height difference hadn't completely disappeared because she was sitting on his lap. She let her eyes drink in the lines and contours of the handsome face she knew so well. "Justin, you're not into any of that stuff."

Now his grin turned wicked. "Oh honey, Oasis made me take classes in the finer points of bondage and sadism for the past six weeks. All those nights and weekends when you thought I was working late, I was attending beginner dom classes specifically tailored to pleasing the sub they had selected for me. There are so many things I want to do to you, most of which never occurred to me before I saw your questionnaire."

He ran his hand from her knee to her hip and back.

Patricia bit her lip. "Are you sure about this? I don't want to ask you to do something that doesn't turn you on."

He palmed her breast. Heat penetrated the tank top and the thick layer of her bra. "It turns me on, honey. The idea of having you tied up, your ass in the air with my handprint all over it, begging for more definitely does it for me."

She swallowed. "Will you punish me for this?" She didn't elaborate.

He nodded, a brief, swift acknowledgment, though his eyes never left hers. "I'll teach you to even think about letting any man but me put his hands on what's mine."

With that, he pinched through the fabric, rolling her nipple between his fingers. Patricia yelped even as the pain dissipated and pleasure radiated in its wake.

"Tell me you want this, Trish. Tell me you want to belong to me. Tell me you want me to use your body, to torture you for my own pleasure until you sob and beg for release."

Cream soaked her panties, generated from a combination of the pinch and his description. She took a deep breath. "Yes, Justin. I want to belong to you. Only you. I take back the safe word."

He eased her back into the passenger seat. "Stay put."

Patricia watched as he exited the car, biting her tongue in an effort to remember her place. This was a completely new side to this man she had married all those years ago. A stranger wore her husband's body and sported a devious smile she hadn't seen in far too long.

He came around the front of the SUV and opened her door. "Come here, Trish." He held out a hand to help her from the high seat.

Patricia looked at the gravel on the shoulder of the road and then at her bare feet. Then she glanced at Justin, hoping for a reprieve. She found no mercy there. Still, she hesitated.

With an impatient growl, he lifted her from the seat and shoved her against the outside of the back door, pinning her with his chest and hips. A thrill ran through her body, sending heat to her core. She hadn't realized her forty-year-old husband was still strong enough to sling her around like this. He looked good, but he hadn't been to a gym in years. She knew her eyes were wide, and she made no effort to temper or hide her reaction.

The gravel beneath her feet was not an issue, because he barely let her toes graze the ground.

"You need a lesson in following orders, my sweet slave. That's twice now."

Her mouth dropped open. "Twice?"

He kissed her, crushing her lips to his and forcing his tongue between them. He established mastery and control. Patricia's knees turned to jelly, and fire raced to her pussy.

He cupped her mound through the thin denim covering her lower half. His heat fed hers. She moaned, a sound he captured in his mouth. He rubbed the heel of his hand against her pussy. Patricia ground against the pressure, soft cries issuing from deep in her throat.

Justin loosened the button on her jeans and lowered the zipper. He shoved his hand down her pants. This pair of jeans was made from a soft, stretchy material. It offered no resistance to what he sought.

He delved beneath her sopping underwear, sliding his fingers into her wetness so deep he lifted her back onto her toes. Short cries of pleasure poured from her, swallowed by Justin's endless kiss.

At long last, he pulled his lips away. He stared deep into her eyes as he pulled his fingers away, taking that glorious heat with him.

"I told you to take off your jeans, my little slave."

Patricia glanced to her right, taking in the long stretch of road behind them. She shifted her gaze to the left. No other cars or people were in sight. No mailboxes dotted the road to indicate anyone lived nearby. She pleaded anyway. "Justin."

His smiled chilled her to the bone and sent shivers of excitement shooting along her veins. "I like the way you beg, slave, so I'll overlook the fact you didn't call me Sir."

He bent at the knees, pushed his shoulder into her stomach, and scooped her up. She heard the door opening. The soft upholstery of the backseat cushioned her fall as he tossed her inside. It didn't take but a moment for him to peel away her jeans and underwear. He tossed them to the floor.

Patricia shivered. Cool air brushed over her sensitive, heated skin. Before she could process the look in his eyes, Justin turned her onto her stomach and pulled her so that the lower half of her body dangled from the edge of the seat. Anyone approaching from behind Justin would be able to see her bare ass. Immediately, Patricia felt the heat of a blush staining her cheeks. She wasn't as fit as she had been when they met. Her ass was wider, and it sagged a bit. She had no idea if he still enjoyed the view.

He pressed one hand between her shoulder blades, holding her down. With his free hand, he smacked the fleshy part of one cheek. Shards of pain bloomed. Patricia jerked in response, instinctively trying to escape. He used more force to keep her in place.

Another blow fell, this time on the other cheek. She cried out in protest even though the sting of his first strike was now radiating through her body as pleasure.

Wetness rushed to her pussy. She had been moist before, but now it trickled down the insides of her thighs.

Justin rained blows on her ass. They came faster and faster, spreading heat in their wake. Her hips jerked, and her ass rose to meet his hand, greeting it with courage and enthusiasm. Some of them fell close to her pussy. Her loud cries pounded in her ears, and she dug her fingernails into the seat.

The unfamiliar stimulation confused her body. She wanted him to stop, but at the same time, she thought she would die if he didn't continue. She wanted to feel his thick cock filling her pussy, his hips and thighs slapping against the sensitized flesh of her ass and upper thighs as he fucked her hard.

At last it stopped, and she found herself lifted and cradled in his arms. He scattered kisses on her face, spreading the fresh tears she hadn't known she was crying.

She was so close to orgasm, yet she felt completely relaxed.

"You okay?" His question was muffled in her hair, but it couldn't disguise his tension.

She nodded.

He put her back on the seat, facedown with her legs hanging over the edge. Was he going to resume the spanking? Her ass and the tops of her thighs were on fire. Maybe if he did this a lot over the next year, she would learn to take more than this. For now, she had reached her limit.

"Justin, please. I'm sorry."

He chuckled. "Glad to hear it. When I give you an order, I expect you to obey immediately and without question."

Patricia sniffed. Part of her wanted to dare him to try to get away with this at home. The rest of her desperately wanted this fantasy. She held her tongue.

Another blow landed on her sore cheek. She yelped. He growled. "You will respond with 'Yes, Sir' or 'Yes, Justin.' Unless you're gagged, I expect a response."

"Yes, Sir." Patricia tried it out. It didn't feel right. "Yes, Justin." That felt much better.

He dug around in a duffel bag she hadn't noticed on the floor. She watched from her perch on the seat. The single bag she had been permitted to bring was there as well.

She couldn't see exactly what he found. She waited, knowing she would find out eventually.

She felt Justin smear a cold cream over her abused skin. The heat lifted a bit. She hoped it would ease the soreness, but not nearly as much as she hoped he would relieve the ache in her pussy. The punishment and his display of dominance was doing exactly what she had fantasized it would. She needed to be fucked in the worst way.

Then his hand was gone. She felt him moving around behind her, but she didn't dare raise her head to peek. Her poor ass couldn't take much more discipline.

She jumped when he pried her cheeks apart and touched her anus. In all the years they'd been married, he'd only ever done that accidentally. Each time, they had ignored it completely. Before she could figure out his complete intention, he eased a slippery finger inside.

"Relax, Trish. This is just the beginning. I need to stretch you a bit before I can fuck you here."

She sucked air and forced herself to breathe evenly. It neither hurt nor burned. The sensation was unfamiliar but pleasurable. He had never once indicated an interest in her ass. Well, not like this. "Justin, you don't have to do this if you don't want to."

His amused chuckle was answer enough. "I never thought you would let me. When I finish with you, my lovely slave, you won't be able to sit for a week."

He withdrew his finger, returning a moment later with more lube and a second digit. Patricia wondered exactly how he would exact his revenge for her contacting Oasis. She also wondered if it was okay that the thought of all the ways he would punish her put her that much closer to orgasm.

"Spread your legs a little wider and relax. I'm not going to rush this."

After doing as he directed, she closed her eyes and concentrated on the things she felt. Her body hung from the backseat of an SUV, and she wore absolutely nothing on her lower half. A tingling heat spread over the areas where he had spanked her. Every few seconds, a strong spring breeze ripped through the interior of the car, ruffling her hair and emphasizing the contrast between the hotness of her ass and the coolness of the air.

And her husband had at least three fingers in her ass. He thrust them in and out, stretching and pulling, working the lubricant into her sphincter muscle. A vision of him thrusting his cock into her ass, while she struggled to stay on her hands and knees, ripped a quiet whimper from her.

Justin's cock wasn't too short or too long. He was perfect that way. He fit into her pussy as if he was made to be there. Their first few years together had been filled with sexual marathons. Having kids had changed their sex life far more than either of them could have anticipated. It wasn't the fault of the children; it was just that Patricia and Justin had never figured out how to balance those things. In the end, the kids took precedence.

Patricia missed waking up to the feel of him thrusting inside her. She missed the taste of his semen.

Justin's hand left her back. There was no need to hold her down anymore. She wasn't going anywhere, and she had no intention of protesting. He slid those free fingers along her slit until he found her clit. He pinched it sharply. Liquid heat shot from her pussy to her belly button. She gasped, the sound loud in the silence of the empty road. The strength went out of her knees, and she was grateful for the seat holding her up.

He rubbed her clit, stroking it the way he knew she liked. She rocked her hips against his hand in time to the thrusting in her ass. A long, low cry began in the back of her throat. The largest orgasm in over a decade loomed in her future.

Justin pulled out.

Patricia whimpered.

He fished something from his bag. From the corner of her eye, she saw him wipe his hands off. Too weak to raise her head and too smart to speak without permission, Patricia mourned her almost-orgasm silently and kept her body still.

The next thing he pulled from his bag of tricks was a butt plug. Patricia had spent a lot of time researching them online, and she knew they came in various sizes. The size to which Justin now applied lubricant was not the smallest size. It was medium. In terms relative to what had previously been shoved up her ass, it was huge. However, if she compared it to the circumference of Justin's cock, it was definitely smaller.

"This is going to hurt, Trish. Feel free to scream."

Scream? His fingers hadn't hurt. Oh sure, there had been a little bit of pinching and burning, but it wasn't enough to be considered painful. She had enjoyed it.

The tip of the toy nudged the tight muscle guarding her entrance. "Take a deep breath and let it out slowly."

She did what he asked. When she breathed out, he pushed in, and it felt like something far larger and harder than what she had seen him pull from the bag. Her exhalation turned to a sharp cry. It did hurt.

He circled his palm over her lower back, massaging in a way that calmed her down. "Relax, honey. That was just the tip."

The tip? "You gotta be kidding me."

He chuckled again. The sound was beginning to wear on her nerves. A minute ago, she had been close to orgasm. Now she felt like her asshole was on fire. Just when she thought she was going to give in to the urge to say something nasty, she felt his finger on her clit again. Her waning desire flared to life, and she moaned.

She wiggled her hips, thrusting to grind her pussy against his palm. He pushed the plug farther into her each time she rocked back. The painful pinch and burn morphed into something sweet and tart.

The largest part entered her bottom, and he stopped playing with her clit. Patricia cried out in protest.

"You can't tease me like this, Justin. I'm going to die if you don't let me come."

He moved her body, drawing her up until she stood on the gravel strip between the road and the grass. Patricia's vision swam as she struggled to deal with the conflicting sensations running rampant in her body.

"Tell me what it feels like." The timbre of his voice was low and smooth.

It was on the tip of her tongue to ask him if he was considering shoving a butt plug up his ass, but she refrained. They could save that for later. For now, he was in charge. She was just beginning to understand the full weight of what it meant to be a submissive, to give herself completely over to another person. She loved Justin, but she had never surrendered to him. All of their sex had been about mutual satisfaction.

She was intensely grateful that Justin was there. This would not have worked with anyone but the man she loved with her whole heart and soul.

"I feel full. I feel..." She stopped, and the heat of another blush stole up her neck. She looked down, focusing on his gray tennis shoes. A silver stripe ran along the side, tapering at the toe. She had bought those for him when he indicated an interest in resuming jogging, but she hadn't known he wore them.

He lifted her chin, his firm grasp guiding her to face the steel in his eyes. "No, Trish. None of this. You will not hide from me, and you will not censor your thoughts and feelings. That is what got our marriage in trouble in the first place. I don't blame you. I do it too. It stops now."

He had never before used this domineering tone with her. A wave of desire further weakened her ability to stand. She gripped his arm. "I feel like I belong to you. I feel possessed, sexy, loved. I feel alive for the first time in years."

Justin enveloped her in his arms. He smoothed his hands down her back and kissed a path along her temple and forehead.

"Good," he said. "I want you to feel like that. You do belong to me, Trish. You are mine. You are sexy, and you are loved."

Complex emotions, things she didn't want to analyze or face, burned near her heart. She gripped him hard, trembling with the force of her emotions, and he held her until it subsided. Then he released her.

"We need to get going." He spread a towel on the passenger seat and buckled her in, never once offering her the option to dress.

The seat kept the plug firmly planted in her ass. Justin eased the car back onto the road. The vibrations of the tires on the road magnified and thrummed in her ass.

"Play with your clit," he said, breaking the silence. "I want to hear you come."

"Yes, Justin." She was wound so tight, it wouldn't take long.

She dipped her fingers into her juices and swirled them around her clit. Not bothering with a slow build, she set a fast pace and climaxed in less than a minute.

Resting her head back against the seat, she smiled and closed her eyes. "Thank you, Justin. I needed that." She couldn't imagine how he was holding out. The bulge in his jeans hadn't diminished as he drove.

"Don't stop."

Her eyes flew open. They had tried this kind of thing before, only to stop when her overstimulated clit couldn't handle more. "I need a break."

He slammed on the brakes. She braced one hand on the dashboard and both feet on the floor. "What the hell are you doing?"

Too late, she saw that this was no time to berate him for his driving skills. He grabbed the back of her head, fisting her hair in his hand, and pulled her close to him. Passion possessed the kiss until he seemed to get himself back under control. He released her, and once again he exited the SUV.

Butterflies ran races in Patricia's stomach. The skin of her ass burned and tingled. Would he spank her again? She wasn't sure she was sufficiently recovered from the last one.

The back door opened and closed. Her door opened. With a swiftness she hadn't thought he possessed, he handcuffed her wrists to the head support. She watched, fascinated, as he wrapped a soft strap around each leg just above her knees. They fastened with Velcro. When he secured the straps to a steel pole, she understood what he was doing. This device would keep her legs spread.

Next, he produced scissors and proceeded to cut away her tank top and bra. Now she was completely naked. Anyone who saw the car would be able to see her breasts.

He must have seen she was about to protest. "Not a word, Trish. You've already earned two punishments. I'm okay with giving you as many as you need. You will learn that you are mine. You belong to me, and you will do what I say, when I say it, and exactly how I want it done."

Recognizing the steely determination of the man who had relentlessly pursued her in college, she shut up.

He sucked one of her nipples into his hot mouth, biting and stretching it to a taut point. He pulled a pair of tweezers from his pocket and pinched the wet peak. Patricia yelped as it tightened, and she realized the tweezers were actually a clamp. Electric desire shot from her nipple to her clit.

He repeated his actions on her other breast. Patricia arched her back, seeking more of this new kind of stimulation. When he finished, Justin stood back, admiring his handiwork. Twin clamps, attached to a chain, dangled from her nipples. Every breath she took caused a tiny tug that sent sparks to her clit. He had ordered her to masturbate, and she hadn't complied. Now her hands were cuffed to the seat behind her head. She begged silently, knowing he wasn't in the mood to hear anything she had to say.

Justin reached for her pussy, feeling for her hole. She closed her eyes, secure in the knowledge he would find her clit soon.

She was wrong. When he abandoned her again, he left behind a small object lodged in her vagina. He held up a remote and gazed at her with a triumphant grin.

"Punishment time, Trish. You'll learn to do as you're told eventually." He pressed a button, and the tiny vibrator hummed to life.

The vibrations were small, not enough to bring her to orgasm, just enough to keep her on the edge. This was going to be a long drive.

Chapter Two

She was quiet for the most part. Every now and again, a little whimper would escape. She was being very, very good, but he didn't necessarily want that from her. Something had driven her to contact Oasis, something more than his absence from their marriage. There was no way she was going to tell him voluntarily.

Besides, he hadn't spent all those weeks taking BDSM lessons from Oasis to squander this opportunity. Too many nights, he had joined her in bed and talked himself out of tying her to the headboard and waking her up. His innocent wife had no idea of the things he wanted to do to her. She had no idea of the desires she had created with that damn questionnaire she'd filled out.

If she had just been honest with him instead of confiding in strangers who ran a fantasy fulfillment service, they could have taken those classes together. He could have practiced on her. He would have acted out each and every one of her fantasies and thrown in a few he'd developed, and their relationship wouldn't be so tenuous. They wouldn't be struggling with how to share their wants and desires with each other.

The kind of openness and communication they could have established in those classes couldn't help but bleed into other aspects of their relationship. Perhaps that was what had drawn her to this in the first place. Perhaps she saw BDSM as a way to fix the source of the problems in their relationship.

Justin sneaked a quick peek at Trish. Her soft brown curls, just long enough to brush against the tops of her shoulders, bounced into further disarray. He loved her curls. He had annoyed her on more than one occasion by playing with them. He liked to pull on one until it was as straight as it could be and then release it, taking great joy in watching it bounce back into place.

Trish hated when he did that. She also didn't care to be called Trish. He was the only one who ever got away with it. She once said it sounded right coming from him.

She had an amazing body that only seemed to get better with age. It was curvier now. Her hips were wider, a result of two pregnancies. She sagged in a few places, but that seemed to matter to her far more than to him. He wanted to touch and taste every inch of her, to convince her that her beauty still captivated him. He knew she didn't consider herself attractive anymore.

When she said she felt sexy, it had taken every ounce of his self-control to refrain from letting loose with a victory yell.

He hadn't lived up to her expectations in the past few years, but she hadn't been honest about her discontent. They would begin working on that now. He aimed to begin making up for his part of the problem this weekend. Trish deserved better. She deserved to have all of him.

He wondered how she would take the news when he told her that he had taken a voluntary demotion to free up his time. It meant less money, but he didn't honestly think she would care about that. Frowning, he squelched the urge to swear out loud. He hadn't even thought to consult her about taking a demotion—though then she would have wondered where he went two nights each week and every other Saturday afternoon.

She whimpered again. He checked her out. Her cheeks were flushed, nearly as red as her backside. In a million years, he'd never thought the act of spanking his wife would make him so hard it hurt. Every time he shifted, the abrasive denim of his jeans torqued his need up another notch.

He dialed up the remote. Her body jerked, and her eyes flew open. She turned her head, regarding him with wide eyes. He grinned back at her and turned on the radio.

Her whimpers turned into desperate squeaks. She strained to close her legs, but the bar between her knees prevented that from happening. Her arms moved, her back arched, and she yanked at the handcuffs.

"Justin, oh, Justin."

He loved the way she said his name. At home, she never used it. She almost never spoke directly to him. She sent the girls to him instead. *"Go ask Daddy to start the grill. Go ask Daddy if he has to work this weekend."*

He loved being a father. He loved that his little girls looked so much like Trish. They both had her kind soul and generous heart too. She was a giver, his Trish. He hadn't understood what that meant until the second week of bondage classes when the instructor explained that most submissives were givers. As her dom, it was his job to make sure she got what she needed, sexually and emotionally.

The noises she made grew louder and more urgent. He reduced the speed of the small egg he had placed inside her.

She groaned and shifted to look at him. "You're going to kill me this way, aren't you? You're going to tease me until I die from frustration."

He wanted to stop the car and fuck her, but he didn't. She had to accept the fact that he was the boss. Besides, GPS put their destination at only fifteen minutes away.

The small opening announcing the narrow road to the cabin wasn't more than a brief break in the tree line. The ruts in the driveway caused both of them to rock back and forth. Justin braced himself with one hand on the door. Trish moaned loudly.

He glanced over again. The way her elbows bent next to her head obscured the expression on her face. He liked the way she looked, bound and helpless, completely at his mercy. Well, the road's mercy, at any rate. Judging by the noises she made, her pleasure intensified as the car bounced over the ruts.

She sighed when he stopped in front of the cabin. Leaning forward as far as she could go with her hands bound behind her neck to the headrest, she peered at it through desire-heavy eyes. She licked her lips. He noticed they were drying out from all the panting she had been doing. He made a mental note to see to them while he bathed her.

"It's small."

He knew what she was thinking. Given how much money they had both paid for this "vacation," they had expected a larger place. From the specs he had seen, he anticipated three rooms: a kitchen/living room, a bedroom, and a five-star bathroom. The living and sleeping areas would be equipped with bondage equipment. The brochure promised a multitude of equipment, a selection ranging from a St. Andrew's cross to a simple flogger. For the bathroom, it had boasted a jetted tub and a massage table, everything he would need to properly care for his slave. The kitchen would even be stocked with their favorite foods, which they had listed in the detailed questionnaires they'd filled out.

"Don't worry about it." Images of his lovely wife in full slave mode floated before his eyes. He had been masturbating to this fantasy ever since he responded to the call from Oasis and agreed to be trained as her dom. "You'll spend most of your time chained to the bed or kneeling at my feet."

When she didn't respond, he swallowed his trepidation and looked at her. Those dark brown eyes stared at him speculatively, and he knew she was wondering how this would change their relationship once they returned home. Justin didn't have an answer for her. That was one of the things they were going to discuss while they were here.

"Are you going to untie me?"

He grinned. "Eventually." Without elaborating, he leaped from the SUV and went around back to grab their bags. She hadn't brought much. He had specified that she bring no clothing with her, save what she would wear to return home.

He disappeared inside. Trish could wait in the car for a bit longer. He had been hard for too long. If he didn't take himself in hand, he was going to fuck her before he got her inside the cabin.

It was as he expected. The door opened to the combination living room and kitchenette. One wall showed two open doors. One door led to a bathroom. The other led to the bedroom.

Justin looked around for a bit, taking in the decor. Dark wood, leather, and polished chrome made up the bulk of the furniture. It wasn't to his taste, but he found it perfect for this weekend. Every single piece sported places to tie his slave. He could bend her over the back of the chair and bind her wrists to the arms. He could splay her on the coffee table and secure her in a variety of positions. An assortment of whips and other implements hung from the walls as featured decorations. There were no pictures, only mirrors.

His cock jerked, pulsing painfully as he pictured her lying spread-eagle on the table while he ate dinner. He could lick her between bites. He could hold ice cream to her clit, and she wouldn't be able to escape.

Justin dropped his suitcase onto the bed and loosened his pants. He knew this relief would only be temporary.

PATRICIA SQUIRMED, TRYING to move the egg closer to her G-spot. She didn't know if she wanted to be angry with Justin for leaving her in the car with this damn tiny vibrator buzzing away inside her. This was exactly what she had asked for in her fantasy—a man who controlled her pleasure and bent her to his will. This wasn't something she had always wanted, and this wasn't something she would want all the time, but how she wanted it now!

She yanked on the handcuffs and tried to move her knees, but like her attempt to move the egg, nothing happened. A huge smile stretched her lips. Oh, she loved this, loved that it came from Justin.

All of a sudden, the speed of the vibrations increased. She moaned loudly, the singular sound filling the silent interior of the SUV. The orgasm was close. She knew she should open her eyes to see if Justin was near, but she couldn't find the energy. She tried to subdue her reaction, but her body wouldn't cooperate. It jerked and twisted. The seat belt was the only thing stopping her hips from rising to thrust against the empty air. The climax came, washing over her body without quite sating her need.

Good God, she wanted another spanking!

The vibrating ceased, and she groaned. Next to her, the door opened, bringing with it the cool rush of spring. She hadn't realized how much the car smelled like sex. It took all of her energy to turn her head.

"Beautiful," he said. "Simply beautiful."

He freed her knees first. The seat belt came next. Blood flooded back into her nipples as he eased the pinch of the clamps. The pins-and-needles feeling made her gasp and writhe. She wanted to call the sensation painful, but it wasn't. It was uncomfortable, unsettling, and smacking of promises yet unfulfilled. She ached to feel the heat of his hands or his mouth around them, but he showed no signs of doing that.

He retrieved the egg before seeing to the handcuffs. When he helped her from the car, every muscle in Patricia's body protested. She had forgotten about the plug filling her ass, but now she was completely aware of it.

"Come," he ordered. "I've run a bath for you."

He led her to the bathroom. She wanted to take a moment to look at the cabin, but he pushed her forward. The flow of water from the tap pounded a steady beat, calling to her from the bathroom.

"You can see it all later. I'll give you a half hour alone, Trish. Don't take out that plug, and don't masturbate." With that, he closed the door.

She stared at the solid piece of wood. At first, she marveled at the changes in her husband. He had always been so kind, treating her with respect. They were equals in all things. Now… He still treated her with respect. There was more kindness in him, but there was also a ruthlessness to him, an iron will that made her thighs weak.

Gradually, her musings faded, and she noticed the door. A steel bar hung from leather straps that must have been secured on the other side. Manacles dangled from it. Eye hooks were placed strategically down the door. If she were chained to the manacles, a rope could be threaded through them to bind her waist, her knees, and her ankles.

She blinked away the vision of herself bound there, awaiting Justin's pleasure or his torture. Perhaps both.

In addition to a tub large enough for two, the bathroom sported a massage table.

Steam wafted from the water filling the tub. She turned off the faucet and eased herself into the water. Cream coated the insides of her thighs, and sweat made other parts of her sticky. She wanted to be clean for Justin. Not since her wedding day had she so wanted to floor Justin with her appearance.

She washed and ran fresh water. Her time was almost up. Maybe he would join her in the tub. Maybe he would bend her over the side and fuck her. Maybe he would tie her to the door. Desire flared, and her hand crept lower, caressing her thigh before finding her soft folds. She pressed her clit. The little nub was already hard and ready.

"I told you not to do that."

Her eyes flew open. She hadn't heard the door. Her body was submerged to the shoulder, meaning she could only feel the cool air he brought on her face.

She smiled the most inviting smile she could muster. "I was just thinking about you."

He pressed his lips together. Instead of feeling defensive, as she usually felt whenever he displayed this expression, she felt the tingle of anticipation.

"Stand up and let the water out."

She did as he commanded, flipping the lever for the drain with her toe. He wrapped a towel around her and lifted her from the tub. She reached to take the towel from him so she could dry off, but he shook his head.

"No, Trish. You belong to me. I'll take care of you."

He patted her dry, and then he turned to the array of after-bath products on the counter. They were hers. She hadn't noticed those before.

"Lie on the massage table, facedown."

The table had a place for her face to rest. She did as he commanded. He traced paths down her arms, across her shoulders, over her back and legs. There was no continuity to his pattern. He explored, leaving gooseflesh in his wake. Patricia shivered.

"I'm going to take out the plug. I need you to relax."

A tug and it was gone. The sensation of fullness disappeared, leaving her feeling abandoned and empty. The wet sound of lotion being pumped caught her attention.

Not once in fifteen years had he ever attempted to do anything like this. As he rubbed in the cream, his hands massaged and caressed. It was as erotic as it was tender, as sexy as it was sweet. Patricia felt truly loved and cherished for the first time in far too long.

"Turn over."

He paid the same attention to the front of her body, lingering over her breasts, kneading them with care.

When he finished, she felt like liquid. She could assume any shape he wanted. She would do anything he commanded. He brushed his finger over her lips, rubbing in her favorite lip balm.

"Spread your legs, slave."

The narrowness of the table required her to bend her knees and drop her legs over the side. She liked that he called her "slave." It was another name only he could use.

He teased her folds with the same gentle pressure he had used on her back. Wetness smeared where he touched. The massage had done its job.

"So wet, my slave. So wet for me."

She wanted him to press harder, to thrust his fingers inside and fuck her with them. He withdrew, and she held in a whimper of protest.

He held his wet fingers to her lips. The musky scent of her arousal filled her nose. "Open, slave. Lick my fingers clean."

Patricia had never done anything of the sort before. Sure, she had given her share of blowjobs, but this was different. Uncertain as to whether or not she wanted to know her flavor, she opened her mouth. He slid his fingers inside, fucking her mouth with slow, even strokes.

His eyelids fell to half-mast. She recognized the telltale sign of his arousal and sucked harder. The sweet-tart taste of her cream didn't matter nearly as much as

Justin's reaction. If she could only push him over the edge, he would bend her over the side of the massage table and sink his cock into her empty pussy.

Too soon, he withdrew his fingers. "Well done, slave. You might want to hang on to the table. This is going to hurt a bit."

Adrenaline pumped through her system. Just because she liked the pain didn't mean she wasn't a little afraid of it.

He snagged something from the counter and turned his attention back to her pussy. "Beautiful," he said. "You know, when we were younger, your pussy was a delicate pink color. Now it's a bit darker. So are your nipples." He glanced up at her face. "It's sexy as hell, Trish. I've never told you that before, but it is."

Heat suffused her neck. She had noticed the changes, especially after each pregnancy, but she never knew what he thought about them. Part of her had wondered if he found her less attractive because if it. Now she knew.

A gentle pinch on her clit chased all thoughts from her head. He was doing something she couldn't see with the item he hadn't shown her. The pinch grew sharper, squeezing her clit painfully. She yelped.

"You'll get used to it, my slave. Just like the nipple clamps." He grinned and tweaked one nipple, turning it into a hard peak. "We'll get back to those later."

Her nipples were still sore from their earlier imprisonment. He took her hand and tugged her into a sitting position. The pinching feeling shifted, and now something pulled as well. Moisture flooded from her pussy, and she knew she would leave behind a wet spot when she stood.

"It's weighted, my sweet. Whenever you move, you're going to feel it. Stand up and bend over the table. It's time for a bigger plug. I plan to be able to fuck you there before you fall asleep tonight."

He snagged something from a contraption on the counter. It took her a moment, but she recognized a bottle warmer.

Justin squeezed gel onto his fingers and disappeared behind her. She felt the gentle press of his fingers on her anus as he massaged the gel into the muscle.

Her clit throbbed, both in yearning for the same kind of stimulation and in protest over the clamp with its weights pulling down.

"Breathe in and out, my slave. This one is going to hurt a bit more."

Trish took a deep breath. As she exhaled, he pushed an impossibly large object into her ass. Her muscles stretched, but the bath and the lube had done their jobs. It didn't hurt at all.

She heard water run as he washed his hands. Trish remained still, her gaze glued to the back of this familiar stranger.

He dried his hands on a towel. "Stand up, slave."

The fullness from before had nothing on what she felt now. As she straightened, every nerve ending in her pussy screamed as the full effect of the weights combined with the sensations in her ass. She gasped.

He crossed his arms and assessed her with a critical look in his eyes. "Dinner is ready. Afterward, I'm going to make you scream and beg."

Patricia had no idea how to respond to that. Even if she had made it this far with a stranger, she wouldn't have felt the tingling anticipation set free by the trust she had in Justin. "Thank you, Sir."

Dinner wasn't what she expected. Justin had cooked pasta with a white mushroom sauce. He directed her to a chair. Given the amount of lubricant and wetness seeping from her, she was relieved to see that he had covered it with a towel.

He served her when she expected things to happen the other way around. Patricia always served him when he made it home for dinner. Because she was the one always home, she was used to serving the kids. Taking care of Justin had become a natural extension of the work she already did.

She looked up at him as he set a full plate in front of her. "Thank you, Justin."

His mouth curved in a pleased smile, and she realized he was pampering her this way to make a point. While she might be his slave this weekend, he would be the one taking care of her. She hadn't felt this cared for since the early years of their marriage. Tears pricked behind her eyes.

They ate in silence for a little while, both of them satisfying their stomachs before they moved on to address more complicated hungers.

"I'm going to be following the guidelines you laid out in your questionnaire, Trish. If there's anything you want to change, now is the time to do it."

When she'd filled in the answers to the hundreds of questions in that questionnaire, visions of Justin had filled her mind. Those answers were tailored to suit Justin and nobody else. She saw that now.

"No, Justin. I trust you. I want to please you." The throbbing in her clit had reduced to an occasional twinge.

Though he hadn't fastened the clamp very tight, she knew it would hurt anew once he removed it. She shifted in her chair, and the plug moved deliciously inside her.

He sipped his water and watched her. "I can't do all the things you want in one weekend. We'll have to work up to some of them, anyway."

Patricia held the belief that preparation for anything new resided completely in her mind. Perhaps Justin wasn't ready. This was the first time for both of them, but Justin had the job of seeing to her well-being and dishing out the punishments.

Still, they were both on new ground here. He was learning her body in an entirely new way, and it would take time to do it well. When they had first begun sleeping together, he had taken the time to find those special spots that could trigger the reactions he wanted. If this was how Justin wanted to proceed, then she would trust his decisions. She nodded.

"Before we leave, we need to talk about where this goes from here. We can't go back to the way things were before."

He didn't have to finish his thought. Patricia knew they were headed for divorce or a life filled with complete unhappiness. She didn't want either option, not when she knew they could be so blissfully happy together. They had been that way once, and they could do it again.

"Yes, Justin."

He cleared away the dinner plates. She watched as he rinsed and loaded them into the dishwasher. When he dried his hands and turned toward her with a dispassionate expression, adrenaline coursed through her veins. This was it; this was the moment for which she'd yearned.

She wetted her lips.

He crossed the room. The muscles of his thighs straining and bunching under the fabric of his jeans caught and held her attention. When he stopped, she stared at the bulge between his thighs. She'd always considered Justin's dick the ideal size. It filled her mouth and her pussy perfectly. She couldn't remember the last time it had been in either place. He'd better do something productive with it pretty damn soon.

"Stand."

She struggled to her feet, clenching her sphincter so she wouldn't lose the plug. She had grown accustomed to it, and Justin had used a lot of lubricant. Despite her best effort, it nearly slipped out. Oblivious to her struggle—or perhaps ignoring it—Justin captured her lips in a searing kiss, plundering his tongue inside to master her that way.

Trish melted in his embrace, submitting completely. She followed his lead, participating in the kiss enough to reciprocate but not enough to take over.

When the kiss ended, he held her against his heaving chest. She felt like no boundaries existed between them. He twisted his fingers in her hair, tightening to pull lightly. Trish mewed, breaking the spell.

Justin turned her around and pointed her toward the living room area. The entire decor indicated a dungeon. Even her dining chair had contained places where rope or bindings could be attached. With his hand on the small of her back, he guided her to a piece of equipment she knew to be called a St. Andrew's cross.

The heavy wooden structure featured cuffs attached to eyelets. Justin ran his hands over her skin, caressing from her shoulders to her feet. When his forays led him back up her body, he lifted her right arm and secured the padded leather cuff around her wrist. He tested the tightness by slipping a finger between her wrist and the cuff. Then he did the same thing with her left arm.

"How does that feel, Trish? Tug on them a bit. See if they dig into your wrists too much."

She tugged as hard as she could. The wide cuffs dug in a bit, depending on how she moved her hands, but she didn't find it to be unreasonable. "It's fine, Sir."

He swept her hair out of the way and planted a string of kisses along her neck and shoulder. A couple of strategic pulls of her hair told her he had put it up in a ponytail, shortening it enough to keep it off her shoulders.

"Widen your stance."

Trish hesitated. If the plug slipped out, she would be mortified. The sharp sting of a smack on her ass got her moving.

"I owe you two punishments, Trish. You will do what you're told immediately and without question."

One for not listening and one for touching herself in the bathtub. She knew the rules. Oasis had sent her a list, and they'd required her to pass three quizzes on them in the past two months. She wondered whether or not Justin had been made to meet the same requirements.

"I'm sorry, Sir." She spread her legs and prayed the plug stayed put.

Justin ran his hands down the outsides of her legs and up the insides. When he reversed directions again, he secured the cuffs to her ankles. "I'm going to whip your back, Trish. I know you indicated an interest in having your breasts and your pussy whipped, but that's something we'll save for when you're a little more used to being whipped."

She sagged a bit in relief, transferring a bit of her weight from her feet to the cuffs holding her wrists. The fantasy of being whipped had brought her to a self-induced orgasm many times, but she'd never actually heard falls whistling through the air or felt the sting of them against her skin.

He continued to move his hands over her skin lightly, coaxing every nerve ending to the surface. She shivered and tried to lean into the heat emanating from him. A maddening few inches separated his chest from her back, but the restraints prevented her from moving.

When he reached under her, she whimpered. The lips of her labia had already parted because of her wide-legged stance. He fiddled with the clip on her clit, opening it and lifting it away. Blood rushed to that tiny bundle with a vengeance. She cried out at the pleasure-pain mix and arched her back to escape. Her body went nowhere. She half wished Justin would touch her clit, massage it until the strange sensations disappeared, urge it toward pleasure. Unfortunately, his hand had dropped away.

She felt him near her, and she knew he watched her reaction. She neither tempered nor prolonged her reactions, giving him honesty with every inch of her being.

She felt the plug ease from her ass. Mortified, she gasped and hoped he didn't hold it against her. The electric feel of him disappeared, and she heard the sound of running water. Relief rushed through her as she realized she had heard no thump to indicate it had fallen. Justin had removed it.

With him gone, though he was just across the room, she relaxed against the smooth wood of the cross. She hadn't recognized the tension created by the impending promise of a whipping. That promise hadn't vanished, but she saw that Justin wasn't going to hurry it. He was going to make her wait. She didn't think he intended it as a punishment. Oasis guidelines had demanded a clear identification of a punishment prior to its administration.

The slap of bare feet on wood announced his return. Reaching under her, he zeroed in on her clit with an accuracy that came from familiarity. He pressed hard. She yelped.

"Sore?"

The swollen nub throbbed under his finger. "Yes, Justin."

He traced a circle around her clit. Shivers raced through her body. "Sensitive?"

"Yes, Justin." She struggled to form words because she knew he would add to her list of punishments if she didn't respond.

He plunged two fingers into her slick wetness, thrusting against her sweet spot. He fingered her hard. Cries and pleas poured from her mouth, but he didn't vary his pace. No matter, the tension coiling inside her didn't need much more to burst. Just before she fell over the precipice, he stopped.

"Punishment number one, my sweet slave." He leaned over her shoulder, pressing his bare chest against her back, and she watched him lick her juices from his fingers. "No orgasm."

He kissed a path down her back, drawing his fingertips lightly over her skin. Tiny tingles feathered from each point of contact. He worshipped the rounded cheeks of her ass before making a return trip. By the time he nibbled at her earlobe, her whole body shook.

Justin always had the power to make her tremble, but so much time had passed since they'd done more than grope each other in the dark. She had forgotten how good he was with his mouth.

"We're going to start slow, Trish. Feel free to cry out as loud as you like. I won't stop unless you use the safe word. Say it for me now."

She breathed in through her nose, using the deep breath to gather her courage. "Oasis."

"Good girl. Tell me you want this."

She needed this. "I want this, Justin. Please whip me."

The heat of his chest moved away. She heard the slap of the flogger against something. His jeans? She couldn't tell, but she was proud that she hadn't flinched, and she didn't flinch again when he tested it a few more times. She knew Justin too well to think he'd start without any kind of warning.

Soft leather brushed across her shoulders as he trailed the falls along her skin. He teased her back where he had sensitized the skin just by kissing it reverently. Shivers made her body jerk, but the cuffs buckled to the cross held her in place.

"So responsive. My Trish, always so responsive." He stepped back, taking the softness of the falls with him. "This shouldn't hurt yet, honey. Relax into it."

That he kept dropping the whole dom demeanor didn't upset Trish in the least, and it didn't ruin the fantasy. Having him here, administering her whipping, far outstripped any of the fantasies she'd imagined. The fact that he behaved the same way he always behaved around her meant he was comfortable with what they were doing, and she hoped that meant he would want to continue this at home.

The first slap of the whip startled her away from those happy thoughts. The sting she had read about in all those novels was curiously absent. He had said it shouldn't hurt, but she didn't really think he would know one way or another. She couldn't quite decide what it felt like.

Another blow fell. They came rapidly, but they didn't hurt. If anything, it felt a lot like a massage. Trish relaxed into the rhythm as he moved up and down her back. Before too long, he extended his territory to cover her ass and thighs. By the time his whip dropped away, she felt liquid.

Hot cream dripped from her pussy, but the urgency she thought she would feel wasn't there. If he took her down now, she would be ripe for making slow love, not for quick, hard fucking.

His fingertips trailed down her back. Where he always felt a little like fire touching her skin, he now felt like ice. She shivered.

"How are you doing, Trish? Your skin is the loveliest shade of pink."

"I feel relaxed. A little floaty." Her words came out slow and a bit slurred. Now that she thought about it, she felt like this after having a drink or two. Justin always teased her about being such a lightweight.

He laughed softly. "Good. This next part will feel different."

An eternity seemed to pass before anything happened, but she knew only moments elapsed. Her relaxed state played with her mind, messing up her sense of reality. Vaguely, she wondered if this was the subspace she'd heard so much about.

The falls of the whip whistled through the air, but she paid them no mind. Though they hadn't made this sound last time, her groggy brain didn't see a real difference. Once the falls landed, her back definitely distinguished the sensation. Tendrils of fire raced along every place those falls struck and pulled her far away from the nice, relaxed place Justin had sent her.

Stunned, Trish couldn't cry out. The whip fell again and again, alternating on each side of her back. She lost count of how many times he struck her, but the fire traveled down her back, over her ass, and onto her thighs. He whipped her hard everywhere he had massaged.

Her relaxed muscles screamed in protest, a loud sound that hurt her ears. Gradually, the noise died down, and she realized those screams had come out of her mouth. True to his word, Justin neither stopped nor slowed down.

She writhed, trying to escape the blows, but the cuffs on her wrists and ankles held her still. Because he had spread her legs and arms so wide, she couldn't even wiggle from side to side.

"Please, please, please." The plea fell from her lips, but she didn't know if she wanted him to stop or to keep going. After all, she'd asked for this. She'd nearly destroyed her marriage in order to experience this. Perhaps she had this coming.

The burn and the pain morphed into something different. Her distorted sense of time wouldn't tell her exactly how gradually it happened. One moment, she struggled to not scream the safe word. The next moment, a profound sense of peace blanketed her body and soul.

She didn't know when the whip stopped, but eventually, she found herself enfolded in Justin's arms. A cool cloth pressed to her eyes, and she realized she'd been crying.

"Let it all out, Trish. You keep too much inside." He ran his fingertips down her side in an odd caress, avoiding her back.

An overwhelming sense of helplessness always made her answer "Oh" when he told her he had to work late or over the weekend. Sometimes he texted her, and she didn't even have the chance to say that much. When he did that, she responded by not texting back.

Now, she let loose everything. Perhaps being in his arms when he was her dom wasn't the right place to air her grievances, but she did it anyway. After all, he had asked.

"I hate when you work late. I hate when you work all weekend. I wouldn't mind if you had something every now and then, but right now all you do is work. If you were having an affair, I could see how you would be gone so much, but you're not. You're actually working, and I can't tell if it makes me angrier to know that or not."

He said nothing while she spoke, but he continued holding her in his arms, and the area of his caresses widened. He trailed light tracks of fire over her back as he moved his hands there. She shivered, shuddering in his arms, and he kissed her temple.

"The girls keep asking why you don't come to their soccer games, and I'm getting tired of telling them you won't be home for dinner. I'm so angry with you, Justin. I'm angry, and it hurts. I never wanted to be mad at you like this. I love you, but we can't continue like this."

"No, we can't." He wiped some tears from her cheeks. "You can't keep holding everything in. You were ready to go off for a weekend with a stranger rather than talking to me about what's bothering you. If Oasis hadn't contacted me, this would have destroyed our marriage instead of bringing us closer together. I know I can't keep going on thinking I'm doing what's best for our family when I've never asked you what you want. We take each other for granted. We've stopped seeing one another as people and started defining each other by function."

He feathered his lips across hers and cupped the base of her skull to tilt her face. He deepened the kiss, apologizing and promising without words. She wanted the words, but she didn't feel like she could demand them. Since they were just beginning to renew their relationship, she could accept this for now. There would be time for words later. beginning to

At last, he broke the kiss. "A few weeks ago, I took a voluntary demotion. I won't be working evenings or weekends. Any extra time I've spent at work since then has actually been spent with a dom from Oasis who taught me how to give you what you want."

She hadn't seen a change in his paycheck, but she couldn't deny his skill with a whip. He hadn't had that skill before.

"They owed me a crapload in bonuses. I insisted on getting those now. We won't see a change in income for another month. But you'll have me home a lot more, and I think I'd like to keep you in instead of taking you out."

Completely forgetting her role, she gasped. "Justin, what do you mean you took a demotion? You worked hard to get as far in that law firm as you have."

He shrugged.

She smacked her palm into his shoulder. "Don't you think you should have discussed this with me first?"

He seemed surprised at her reaction. "I thought this is what you wanted."

"I do, but I..." She didn't want him to resent her when he failed to realize his dream of making partner in the next two years. "Damn it, Justin. This whole trust and honesty thing cuts both ways. It's your job, but it affects our lives."

"I'm sorry. You're right. I didn't think about it in those terms. It can be temporary if that's what you want. This is something we can discuss tomorrow, honey. Right now, I can't get this image of you out of my head. You're tied to the bed, spread open, waiting for me to exercise my will on you."

As he spoke, he moved her closer to the door to the bedroom. Through the opening, she spied the massive bed and the network of hooks in the ceiling.

"Go lie across the bed, on your back. Legs up, knees bent, hands behind your neck."

She arranged herself on the coverlet. He hadn't asked her to clear away the bedding. The soft down conformed to her shape, cradling her even as it increased the intensity of the heat radiating from her entire backside. She scooted so that her pussy was close to the edge of the bed. Justin would want complete access.

He followed a short time later. He'd removed his shirt before he whipped her, and his skin glowed softly from the exertion. She watched as he finished undressing, folded his jeans, and placed them on the dresser. His boxers and socks followed.

Trish admired the way his hard cock jutted from his body, curving just enough to always reach her G-spot. He closed the distance, moving to stand where he had an unobstructed view of her pussy.

Her shoulders hurt a bit from having put so much of her weight on them when she had been on the cross, so she folded her hands over her abdomen. It also served to hide the roundness and stretch marks.

Justin lifted a brow at her position. "My shoulders are sore," she said. Her insecurities lay just behind her explanation. "I'd rather not lift my arms just yet."

"Then you may put them by your sides. Don't hide what's mine from me."

She obeyed. At least she was on her back. That helped a bit, though it did nothing to keep her breasts from sliding sideways. Glancing up at Justin made all those self-deprecating thoughts flee. The smoldering look in his light blue eyes showed a man who liked what he saw. She didn't know how, but his cock grew even harder.

Roughly, he grasped her hips and pulled her to the very edge of the bed. Her feet fell over the side, and her bottom half dangled from the bed. He pushed her knees farther apart, lined his cockhead up with her entrance, and sank into her welcoming wetness.

Trish couldn't remember the last time he'd fucked her. She couldn't remember the last time he'd gazed at her with a predatory gleam in his eyes. She gasped at the fullness, loving the way he fit perfectly inside her body.

He thrust his hips, fucking her fast and hard. With each thrust he bumped against her sore clit. It hurt, and it felt good, and she struggled to adjust to the contradictory sensory information. Just when she acclimated to his frenzied pace, he stopped, withdrew, and wiped himself off with a wet cloth.

Trish waited on the bed, not moving from the way he left her, because she had no idea what he planned.

"Get on your knees."

She scrambled to obey, dropping down onto the hardwood floor and kneeling with her knees spread wide. She clasped her hands behind her back. The position thrust her breasts forward.

Justin stood before her, the purpled head of his cock inches from her lips. "Open your mouth. I want you to take me slowly."

She always liked giving head to Justin. The texture of his silky-smooth penis and the salty taste of his semen combined in her mouth to make her feel possessed. Submissive. Yes, she had been yearning for this feeling the whole time. She had just lacked the experience to know the extent of what she wanted.

She licked him and barely refrained from asking to use her hands. If he wanted her to, he would ask. He knew her skill set.

He eased just the head past her lips. She sucked and swirled her tongue around to lap up the tiny beads of precum. As he worked himself deeper, she relaxed her jaw and tilted her head a bit. He liked to fuck her mouth. He liked when she remained still and let him thrust at his own pace.

She sucked to the rhythm he set and drew her tongue along the sensitive underside of his cock. He sank into her farther than he'd ever tried before.

"Swallow, Trish. I want you to take all of me."

On his next thrust, she did as he commanded. His cock pressed into the sensitive tissues in the back of her throat, bringing tears to her eyes, but his moan and the shudder of pleasure that ran through him made the discomfort completely worth it.

He thrust several more times and withdrew just when she became used to the rhythm of his deep thrusts. She sat back on her heels and guessed at the game he played.

Grabbing a bottle of water from the dresser, he took a drink and handed it to her. Suddenly aware of her thirst, she gulped the rest of it and handed the empty bottle back to Justin. His carefully neutral expression and the light glinting from his hot eyes unnerved her. She fidgeted under his perusal.

"Sit still, Trish. You'll have an orgasm when I give you one, not sooner. Misbehaving will only get you into trouble."

Her chin came up. Had whipping her been a punishment, or was the way he played with her now a punishment?

He chuckled softly and set the empty bottle on the dresser. "Relax, Trish. I'll always let you know when I'm punishing you. Like now. Cup your breasts. Lift them for me."

She did as he asked, and he dropped to his knees in front of her. She didn't expect a kiss, but he grasped her head and held her still while he plundered her mouth. Moisture dripped from her pussy, running down her thighs in a silent plea.

When he ended the kiss and settled back, she noticed the delicate chain in his hand. Nipple clamps. Damn. They were still sore from earlier.

Dipping his head, he took one nipple in his mouth. He sucked hard and rolled the little nubs against his teeth. She cried out, but he didn't stop. A vise clamped around her breast, and it took her a moment to realize she squeezed her own flesh in her hands.

The sharp pulls of pain radiated through her body, mingling with the feeling of fire that covered her back, thighs, and ass. He thrust two fingers into her wetness, and she struggled to remain upright against the push and pull of the different pressures he exerted on her.

His talented, knowing fingers found her sweet spot immediately. He switched nipples, torturing the other while he drove her to the brink of madness. One more thrust.

"Please don't stop."

She begged, but he had withdrawn again.

"Punishment, my love. No orgasms for bad slaves."

She whimpered in protest. "You're going to kill me with wanting."

In response, he pulled her nipples, stretching them until she cried out. He didn't bother to show her the simple clamps he'd used last time. He just slipped them on and tightened them down. He didn't make them as tight as last time, but she was much more sensitive now, so that much pressure would be too much stimulation.

He stepped back and watched her face, looking for something. She peered back at him, waiting expectantly. Despite what he said about no orgasms, she didn't really think he'd leave her hanging. They'd come a long way toward reconnecting today. They couldn't sustain that momentum without multiple orgasms. He'd already delivered several, and Trish knew this was only the beginning. The gleam in Justin's expressive blue eyes told her that he'd developed a taste for domination.

He pushed to his feet, his knee crackling as he stood. "Crawl to the bed and bend over the side."

She didn't like that order, but she complied without arguing or asking after his knee. Bent over, her tender breasts pressing into the mattress, she waited for her master to decide her next sensation. With an impatient nudge, he kicked her feet apart.

"Don't move, Trish. Not one inch." He reached between her legs, parting her swollen slit. He massaged her pussy with her own cream.

Trish writhed, and a stinging swat landed on her ass. Sweet pain radiated from the contact. She jumped and cried out, involuntarily trying to escape.

"Mine, Trish. You belong to me. You'll take what I give you, and you'll be still when I tell you to be still." Justin rained blows on her ass, spreading them evenly over both cheeks. Tears came to her eyes, and she squirmed, unsure whether she wanted this much stimulation. She didn't want to disappoint Justin. Her desperate, primal urge to please him couldn't be denied.

All of a sudden, the sensations converged, blooming into a pleasure unlike anything she'd experienced. Urgency turned to patience. Peace and the largest orgasm in existence loomed within her reach. She moaned and relaxed into his punishment. "Yes, Justin. Yes. Please don't stop."

He stopped. She whimpered in protest, but she didn't voice her displeasure. "Punishment is over, my lovely slave." His cockhead eased into her pussy opening. His fingers pulled her ponytail from where he'd tucked it under the last loop of elastic. He wound her hair around his hand and pulled her head back.

For the first time, Trish noticed the floor-to-ceiling mirror on the wall next to the bed. Her flushed face stared, wide-eyed with wonder, from the reflection. Behind her, Justin, equally flushed, wore a look of triumphant determination that made her melt all over again, just as she had the first time she ever saw him all those years ago.

With a roar, he buried himself in her channel. She watched, fascinated, as he thrust into her. For a minute, she felt detached from her body. The wanton, well-loved woman in the mirror was a stranger. The man pounding his cock into her looked like the man she'd spent the better part of her life fantasizing about.

"Mine. Mine. Mine." His mantra reached her ears. He claimed her. He owned her, body and soul. Nothing desperate or uncertain remained. For the rest of their lives, they would be together.

"Yes," she said as she jolted back into her body. Heat, molten and hard, made her muscles into a quivering mass. She had no control over any part of her body. Giving in, she put all of her trust in her husband.

Justin reached around and removed each nipple clamp, one right after the other, giving her no time to acclimate. Trish gasped as fire raced to her nipples. Justin only thrust faster. He gripped her hair tighter and pulled harder. She couldn't hold off the orgasm. He'd said punishment was over. In a molten torrent, she came hard. Her pussy contracted, sucking him deeper and laying claim to him the way he claimed her. The waves of lava washing over her body went on and on. The keening cry issuing from the depths of her lungs followed the waves.

He thrust twice more and followed her over the precipice.

Trish lay trapped beneath his weight and made no effort to move him. She didn't want any space separating her from the love she thought she'd lost. Tears gathered in her eyes, a reaction to the preciousness of their love and the terror she had carried for so long but refused to acknowledge. She hadn't wanted to lose Justin. She hadn't wanted to replace him. Terror and desperation had led her to contact Oasis.

She wept for what she'd nearly lost. She wept for the love she had almost betrayed.

Justin lifted his weight from her, his soft cock slipping from the channel he called home. He moved her to lie fully on the bed and folded her in his arms. "I've got you, honey. Let it out. Don't keep it inside."

She choked at his words. "I already cried."

"You always used to cry after having a big orgasm. I hated it, but now I can appreciate what it really means."

Trish struggled to control her sniffles as her tears tapered off. "What does it really mean?"

He pressed kisses to her eyelids and to the wet places on her cheeks. "It means you love the hell out of me and you feel both close to me and very vulnerable. It's a precious gift, Trish. I'll never take it for granted again."

Vulnerable. Yes, she used to feel safe enough with Justin to not mind crying in front of him. When had she begun to hide her emotions? She clung to him until the trembling subsided, and then she fell asleep in the safety and comfort of his embrace.

Chapter Three

She woke from her nap warm and sated. The scent of sex filled the room, reminding Trish of this new side of Justin. For the first time in her life, she thought of herself as Trish, not Patricia—her mother had been relentless in insisting on her full name. From the day she had met Justin, he had shortened her name.

At first, she hadn't liked it. However, when faced with the prospect of alienating the single sexiest man she'd ever met, she had meekly accepted the moniker without correcting him. Over time, she had grown used to it, and now it felt like a punishment when he called her Patricia.

Justin's chest pillowed her head, and her legs were twined with his. She lay listening to his even breath and enjoying the regular rise and fall of his chest. Before long, nature called. Slowly, she raised her head.

"Where are you going?" Justin's voice didn't sound as sleepy as it should have.

She looked up to find his steady gaze clear and blue, no hint of clouds. "Bathroom. I didn't want to wake you."

"I wasn't sleeping." He shifted, and she disentangled her legs from his. "I miss holding you like that. How about we shower together? That's something we haven't done in a while."

"Yes, Justin."

He sat up and grinned. "I like hearing you say that."

Trish bowed her head proudly. She liked seeing his smile. Knowing she'd done something to bring him happiness made her feel almost giddy inside. She headed to the bathroom, and he joined her before too long.

The steady hiss of the shower spray filled the large bathroom. On the counter, Trish found her favorite brush among the bath products Justin had arranged on the counter. Oasis hadn't let her bring many of her own things, but they were here. Justin's thoughtfulness touched deep.

He'd always been thoughtful. Even though he hadn't been home much since the kids had been born, he always remembered the little things. When their eldest daughter, Mikayla, expressed an interest in costume jewelry, he began bringing her eclectic pieces home from each trip. When the tin of chocolate in the freezer ran low, he filled it even though he didn't care to eat it himself.

She had been so wrapped up in the problems in their marriage that she had let herself forget the things she loved about him in the first place. She needed to focus on appreciating what he did well and less on how he fell short. Justin seemed better at not holding her faults against her. She could learn from him.

Trish pulled out her ponytail and dragged the brush through the tangles. In the mirror, she watched Justin reach out to take the brush. "Let me."

When they had first become intimate, he used to watch her brush her hair, but he'd never asked to do it. Surprised, she relinquished possession. After a few tentative strokes, he settled into a rhythm. He followed the glide of the brush through her hair, a soft caress that soothed her and made her feel cherished. When he finished, she melted back into his embrace.

Steam wafted from over the top of the shower's glass doors. He dragged a hand over her ass. "The marks are gone, but it's still radiating heat. How does it feel?"

She knew she would be sore tomorrow, but every protest of her muscles would be a reminder of what they'd shared. "It turns me on when you do that."

He kissed the top of her head. "Good. I have plans for us in the shower." The brush clanked against the marble countertop. With a hand on her hip, he guided her into the shower.

The inside looked a little different from what she expected. The stall shower could easily fit a few more people. Water issued from spouts on three walls. Along the back side, a low bench curved from the plastic surround. A bar hung from the ceiling, and vinyl restraints dangled from it. Justin lifted one of her arms and secured her wrist to the restraint. He repeated the action with her other arm. Warm water soothed her skin from three sides, spraying everywhere but directly into her face. Justin removed one showerhead and brought it closer to wet her hair. He washed it, massaging vanilla-scented shampoo into her scalp before rinsing it away.

While he conditioned it, he washed evidence of sex from her body, and he forced her to watch helplessly as he washed his own body. She wanted to feel the smooth glide of his muscles under her washcloth. She wanted to coax his cock to life and kneel before him so she could show him how much she loved him.

Despite the warm water, her nipples hardened to tiny, pebbled peaks. Her sex swelled, and her mouth produced extra saliva. A whine escaped as her body begged to give him anything he wanted.

Chuckling, he rinsed conditioner from her hair. When he finished with that, he released her arms. Blood flowed through her extremities, tingling a bit in her wrists and fingers.

"Bend over, darling. Put your hands on the bench and show me that pretty little ass."

The way he framed his request startled Trish, even though he had been saying things like that all day. For fifteen years, Justin had avoided saying anything overtly sexual. He'd complimented her appearance in general terms. He'd shown an appreciation for her legs, her breasts, and her ass through touch and looks, not words.

Trish decided she liked hearing him verbalize what he liked. Perhaps some might find it rude, but she wanted her husband to objectify her body. She already knew he liked and respected her as a person. Now she wanted more.

He reached between her legs and found her slick wetness. Not long before, he'd rinsed away her cream. Evidence of her desire wouldn't be denied. It hadn't taken her body long to replace the necessary juices.

"What a hungry little cunt you have, Trish. Would you like me to fuck it?"

Hearing such decadent words in her sweet Justin's low tones made Trish's pussy throb with need. Did she want him to fuck her? Hell, yes. Would he do it if she begged? She had no idea. He definitely liked playing the dom, so he might get off by denying her pleasure. "If that's what you want, Justin."

"You want to give me what I want?" He plunged two fingers deep inside.

She arched her back and willed herself to not move further. "Yes, Justin. I want to give you whatever you want."

He thrust into her pussy, pumping furiously, working her body expertly. She moaned, and he removed his fingers. She whimpered when he left the shower without telling her she could move.

Listening intently, she tried to figure out what he was doing. She shifted her weight and rolled her shoulders. Sliding and clunking sounds came from the other side of the bathroom. He returned before she could piece together evidence from the noises he made.

He pressed his cooled skin to her ass and thighs. A small sound of surprise escaped her lips, but she managed to not jump away. The temperature difference sent a shiver up her spine, but it disappeared quickly as the water heated him again.

The tip of his cock brushed the lips of her pussy. "Use one hand, Trish. Guide me inside you."

Eagerly, she complied. With one hand, she held the weight of her upper body on the bench. With the other, she positioned him at her entrance and pushed back to take him inside.

He thrust, burying himself to the hilt, but then he stopped. The safety of close contact disappeared as he leaned back, peeling his abs and his hips away from her ass. He pulled her cheeks apart. He worked cool gel into the tight ring around her anus, and her pussy quivered around his dick.

"I'm going to fuck your ass, Trish."

Oh, he didn't have to warn her. She knew what he planned to do. Juices dripped from her pussy. She wished he would fuck her there a little too, but he remained still.

He massaged lubricant inside. His cock withdrew. In moments, his thick crown pushed at her sphincter. She breathed out and relaxed.

Justin's cock was much thicker than the plug he'd taken out a few hours ago. The stretching didn't hurt or burn as she'd expected from the research in which she'd engaged via erotic novels. The sensation sent electric tingles straight to her pussy, and that empty channel was becoming a little jealous. It throbbed with wanting.

He pushed further, gently working his cock until she felt his thighs against hers. "Tell me how it feels, Trish."

Why did he keep asking? Did he want her to strap one on and fuck him like this? She shook the snarky thought away and concentrated on what she felt. Anxiety. Yes, that explained why such an immature comment had been her first reaction.

Blood rushed through her body, bringing a sense of anticipation. A sharp slap on her ass brought her out of her head.

"When I ask a question, you will answer it, or you will be punished." He followed up with another slap, but it didn't distract her from the tight growl his voice had become.

Something about the way he talked to her turned her on even more. He hadn't said he expected an answer. He had said she would answer. He left her no choice but to follow his directive. Hot cream rushed from her pulsing pussy.

"Anxious." She amended the first term of description that had popped into her head. She wasn't afraid or nervous. "Like something is about to happen that I'm going to really like, but I don't know exactly what I'm going to like about it."

It was a fair statement since Justin had never fucked her ass before. She had no idea what to expect.

"I feel full inside, but it's very different from when you're in my pussy. The sensations are muted a bit."

He withdrew almost all the way. She felt the ridge of his crown press outward against her muscle. Then he steadily slid back in, burying himself deep. She moved one hand forward to counter his momentum. While his move had given her more sensation, she still waited to feel the same kinds of pleasure she felt when he fucked her pussy, the kind that would push her toward orgasm.

He dug his fingers into her hips as he pumped into her a few more times. She realized she wouldn't have an orgasm like this, and she whimpered at the unexpected punishment.

Justin paused. "Talk to me, Trish. Tell me what you're feeling. I know I'm not hurting you."

No, he wasn't hurting her. "I kinda wish you would," she said. "It doesn't feel like I thought it would. It feels good, like I'm yours to use however you want whether or not I enjoy it, but I honestly thought it wouldn't be very different from when you're in my pussy."

In response, he withdrew completely. The tip of his cock pressed against her anus. Without warning or apparent regard for her ass's near-virgin status, he reamed her.

Sharp bits of pleasure-pain radiated directly to her pussy, and an exclamation of pleasure squeaked from her lips. He slapped her ass, sending more heat where she needed it.

"Like that better?"

"Yes, Justin."

He withdrew and slammed into her again. Tingles prickled up her spine and covered her scalp, blooming into a unique kind of pleasure. She doubted she could orgasm this way, but she definitely had found the joy in anal sex.

She arched her back more, opening to him fully, offering everything she had. He settled into a frantic rhythm, riding her ass hard, taking possession, and forcing her submission. Peace and calm washed over her as she gave her body for his pleasure. Perhaps she wouldn't climax, but she would please her Justin.

"Mine," he said. "This ass is mine, Trish. Play with your clit. I want to hear you come."

"Yes, Justin." She lifted a trembling hand to her pussy. She pinched and pressed, touching herself without mercy. The distraction of Justin fucking her ass, pounding into her so enthusiastically, proved to be too much. He'd ordered her to climax, so she let her hand wander lower. She pushed two fingers into her surprisingly tight channel.

Behind her, Justin gasped, and she realized she could feel his cock through the thin walls separating it from her fingers. She pumped her fingers in and out, caressing them both with a rough touch. Justin's breathing grew ragged, and she reveled in her power.

"Come for me. Now."

His order triggered a storm of reaction. Trish's body bowed into a stiff shape. Her back arched, writhing under an onslaught of feeling that robbed the bottoms of her feet of all sensation. She screamed her climax, coming harder and longer than she ever had before. Behind her, Justin pumped into her. Hot jets of semen bathed her insides, and he only pounded harder. The orgasm went on and on and on.

Her elbows couldn't hold their locked position, and she collapsed. Her consciousness didn't fade, but her comprehension of the world wavered and shifted. She felt Justin's strong arms holding her tight. He sat on the bench, cradling her to his chest. The staccato rhythm of his heart beat time against where her hand rested. Warm water washed over them, helping to keep the shivers at bay.

He tilted her head back and kissed her, thrusting his tongue into her mouth to claim any part of her that might feel it didn't belong to him. As her motor control returned, she tried to kiss him back, but a place deep in her soul only let her accept his mastery of her mouth.

For the first time in a long time, Trish felt all was right with the world.

Chapter Four

Morning sunlight streaming through the trees outside dappled a pattern over the objects in the room that made the details difficult to see. Justin blinked away the fog of sleep and reached for his watch to check the time. They didn't have the cabin for much longer. A noontime checkout heralded a definite end to this unexpected second honeymoon with his beautiful bride.

Less than twenty-four hours before, he had watched from down the street as his wife left their home to meet a strange man. The thought didn't bring the same pain it had the day before, or even the month before, because things had changed between them. Of course, they still needed to talk about how this would all manifest once they got home.

He liked the idea of having Trish as his submissive, but he couldn't keep her naked all the time. He also couldn't expect her to have every decision she made approved by him either. They each brought different areas of expertise to this marriage, and he knew when to cede to her wisdom.

However, he definitely wanted to keep control of their sex life. He could make her wear a butt plug to teacher in-service days. He could spank her before she went to bed. He could intrude upon her time in the shower. He could wake her up for sex every single morning. Good God, he loved morning sex. When they were first married, he used to wake her up every morning, sometimes by plunging his cock into her pussy. Her eyes would open, and her murmured sigh would turn to a gasp. When had she begun turning him down?

His gaze wandered to her still form. The sheet, tucked under her chin, covered her entire body. Her hair lay scattered on the pillow, a ratted mess that held an appeal all its own because he had been the one to muss it.

Whether or not she consented to being his sex slave after this weekend, she was his to command for the next three hours. He wanted to fuck her ass again, but he reasoned that she had to be sore. He hadn't been at all gentle with her the night before. Because she had enjoyed it so much, he didn't regret being rough.

Mindful of the tenderness she had to feel all over her body, he eased the sheet away. She grunted a protest and tightened her grip. A quick glance at the headboard revealed that a set of nylon restraints attached to an eye hook. He unwound them and wrapped one around each of her wrists.

She opened her eyes, a question there that didn't make it past her lips. Her gaze followed the nylon line to the hook in the bed frame. As he knew she would, she figured out the situation quickly. He loved her intellect. Beauty, brains, and a generous heart—his Trish had it all. No way in hell would he let her go.

"Raise your hands above your head and spread your legs."

The restraints kept her hands together. Shades of uncertainty flashed behind her eyes, and he knew she was thinking about things like morning breath or whether her armpits stunk. Justin thought she smelled perfect this morning, with or without deodorant, so he wasn't about to let her go satisfy a few vanity issues.

She lifted her arms and rested her hands on the pillow above her head. She turned a bit and shifted to spread out the way he wanted.

He smiled as a reward and removed the sheet. Her stiff, swollen nipples stood in a silent salute. He tested her soreness with the light flick of his thumb. She inhaled sharply and closed her eyes.

"Sore?"

"Yes, Justin."

He loved hearing her say his name like that. It meant so much more than acquiescence. Every time she said it, she reaffirmed her love for him. Leaning down, he closed his mouth around her areola. This time, her intake of breath indicated anticipation. He let her feel the heat of his mouth.

Her chest rose and fell. She squirmed a bit, trying to thrust her breast farther into his mouth. He pressed a warning hand down on her hip. Immediately she stilled. He switched breasts.

"Please, Justin. Oh, please suck it or lick it or bite it or something."

He lifted his head away from her breast and kissed her on the mouth. He sucked and licked and nipped at her lips and tongue. She responded enthusiastically. Small pleading noises vibrated in her throat.

Reaching down, he wrapped his hand around his dick and dragged it through her slit, coating it with her juices. Internally, he breathed a sigh of relief to find her so aroused. Justin and his morning erection loved having this kind of control over her.

She squirmed as he rubbed the head of his cock over her clit. Before too long, his patience ran out. He thrust into her, deep and hard. She closed her eyes, and her mouth opened to emit little panting breaths. She wrapped her legs around his hips.

So fucking sexy. He didn't bother with finesse or teasing. Morning sex, he decided, would be all about fucking.

Still, he wanted her to have an orgasm. Feeling her silky walls squeeze around him as kittenish moans and squeaks issued from her mouth left him feeling almost as good as an actual climax.

"You'd better get there before I do, Trish. Bad girls who don't climax when they're told get spanked."

Her pupils dilated, and she came hard. Her legs, wrapped so firmly around him, squeezed to the point of pain, and her back arched up from the mattress. Justin thrust once more and followed her over the cliff.

He collapsed onto her breasts. After a minute, the rapid rise and fall of her chest slowed. He lifted his head, a precursor to removing his weight, and saw her brief frown.

"What's that about?" In the past, he would have pretended he hadn't seen her displeasure. It would have only led to some kind of criticism, and that would develop into a full-blown argument. No more.

In a lot of ways, those dom classes were better than marriage counseling. He learned not only why communication was important, but how and when to push the issues.

She blushed, but she didn't break eye contact. "I'm sorry, Justin. I was just thinking I should have held it off because I think I really want that spanking."

Laughing, he planted a firm kiss on her lips and released the restraints around her wrists. Before yesterday, she wouldn't have admitted to anything like that. It made him feel great to know she wasn't censoring her thoughts. "Maybe later, if you're very, very good. Right now, we're going to have breakfast. You have fifteen minutes to get your naked ass to the table."

Her eyes lit. "Or I'll get a spanking?"

Never give a sub the punishment she wants. Give her what she needs. They needed to talk. "No. You won't get breakfast. I already told you how to earn a spanking, Trish."

With that, he left the room. He couldn't take the chance she might do or say something to derail his plans. Fifteen minutes later, she sat on the towel he had spread over a chair. He set a steaming mug of coffee in front of her and served waffles with bacon.

She inhaled appreciatively. She absolutely loved weekend mornings when he made breakfast. It meant time off for her. He had been so busy at work that these mornings had become rare, and she vowed to appreciate them more in the future. "Shouldn't I be doing the cooking?" She bit into a slice of bacon.

"Why?" He sipped coffee and waited for her to verbalize the response he knew was coming.

"Because I'm the submissive."

"You're not a servant, Trish. You're my wife. The fact that you've discovered your submissive side doesn't mean I expect things to change." He meant to assure her that he didn't intend to treat her as a servant. From the way she frowned, he knew he'd said the wrong thing.

He tried again, using plain words. "I mean, I don't find it sexy or fulfilling to have you wait on me. I like to do things for you too. Maybe we've both forgotten what that's like. That's something I want to change."

She stared at her waffles for a minute. Her jaw moved as she ground her teeth. He waited for her to voice her displeasure, to remind him of the reason they'd both forgotten what it was like to have him pamper her, but she merely took a bite of waffle.

"Trish."

She didn't look up from her plate, but she froze in place.

"None of this. We're changing the way we're doing things. I'm working less. We're being honest and talking more."

Now she looked up. "Is that really what you want? I know how much your career means to you. I don't want to take that away. I want you to be happy, Justin."

"I am happy. I want to be with you and the girls more than I want anything else in the world." His chest puffed with an emotion that couldn't be gained through work. Only his family could make him feel like a complete man.

"And now you'll be home for dinner? We'll really have weekends together?" Fragile hope made her brown eyes a few shades lighter.

He nodded, and the pride inflating him from the inside fizzled out when he saw the tears tracking down her cheeks. Rounding the table, he pulled her onto her feet and into his arms. "Don't you want that?"

She buried her face in his chest. "Yes, Justin. I want that very much."

He held her for a few moments, and then he eased her away a bit so he could see her face. "Trish, we really need to talk about how things are going to change when we get home. I would like you to finish eating and get dressed so we can do some negotiating."

* * *

Trish pulled the plain pair of sweats from her bag and pulled a white shirt over her head. Big fish swam in her stomach, churning her delicious breakfast until it threatened to reappear.

Justin had worked so hard to achieve all he had at work. With a demotion, his dreams for a partnership in the law firm would never come true. Part of her felt guilty for making him feel he needed to do this. The rest of her floated on clouds of elation. She missed her husband. She missed the man who laughed and joked, who liked to pick her up and swing her in circles no matter where they were, who gazed lustfully at her breasts and ass. She hadn't seen that man in years.

By the time she made it into the living room, only forty minutes remained until they had to leave their little cabin. Justin sat on the couch in jeans and a white dress shirt. He'd left the top three buttons open. His knee waved restlessly from side to side, and she realized he was just as nervous about the coming discussion.

She paused between the chair and the sofa, wondering where he would want her to sit.

He stood. "I thought we would go for a walk, unless you had strong feelings about staying here."

She nodded, and he held out his hand. The tentative smile on his face grew more confident when she put her hand in his.

They didn't speak as they exited the front door. Justin scanned the line of trees completely surrounding the house, broken only for the driveway. He tugged at her hand. She followed him as they turned left. She hoped to find a trail or something. Not only did she not want to get lost in the woods; she didn't want to have to watch for branches and things. She wasn't exactly dressed for a hike.

A small dirt path became apparent as they moved closer. Trish breathed a sigh of relief. They could walk side by side, holding hands. The narrow path would force them to walk close to each other. She smiled up at him just as he glanced down at her.

"Tell me the truth. What did you think of this weekend?"

This weekend had been the single best weekend of her life. "It was incredible. I don't want it to end, not yet."

"It doesn't have to, honey. It doesn't have to ever end."

She knew they couldn't stay there forever. Plus, she missed her kids. "We don't have much time left here." And he wasn't exactly using it right up until the last minute.

"I'm not talking about here. I'm talking about at home. I like being your dom. I don't want this to stop. I don't want this to have just been a vacation. And there are classes we can take together to explore this new Dom/sub thing."

A small wooden bridge, nothing more than a few planks connecting two banks, appeared ahead. Justin stopped on it and peered at the water in the small brook as it trickled downstream.

The wistfulness in his voice made her breath catch. She didn't want to lose her dom. "The classes sound nice, but Justin, we have two kids. We can't very well do this in front of them."

"No," he said. "And I'm very uncomfortable with the idea of anyone else seeing you naked. That's something only I should see. However, there are things we can do.

Domination and submission aren't just a method of having a sexual relationship. We'll have to feel our way through it and talk about it a lot, especially as we're starting out, but I want to continue."

Trish understood his point. Deep down, she wanted to submit to him. Not in everything. If he told her what to make for dinner or to clean the bathroom, he would face her wrath. But she wished he would take over and tell her what to do in the bedroom or force her to talk about things that bothered her. If he hadn't forced her to talk to him this weekend, all of their problems would have remained bottled up inside her. Years spent repressing her displeasure wouldn't fall away easily. She needed him to push her on these issues. "Yes, we'll have to negotiate all those things."

He brushed his palm over his chin. "About my job."

"You wanted to make partner."

"Not so much. Not anymore. I used to want that, but it's taking too much time away from you and the girls. Being part of my family is more important than making partner. We'll have to cut back on vacations."

She didn't care about that at all. "But we'll be together more, so we won't have to rely on those times as being the only family time we get. Are you sure about this, Justin? I don't want you to wake up ten years from now, look over at me, and regret seeing me there."

He laughed, a choking sound that made her look over to check his breathing. "If I change my mind, I'll talk to you about it before I do anything. I should have talked to you before I did it in the first place. I'm sure about this, Trish. I haven't been more sure about something since the night I asked you to marry me."

A smile tugged at her mouth. He'd done a traditional proposal at a nice restaurant. He hadn't knelt on the floor, and he'd been cocky and confident, two qualities that curled her toes in the most exciting ways. "You were that sure about me, were you?"

"You dropped hints for weeks, and you said yes before I finished asking. I had no doubt you loved me and you wanted to spend the rest of your life with me. Just like now. No doubts." He lifted his brow as if daring her to argue.

"Some doubts." She squeezed his hand. "But we'll discuss those as they come up."

He nodded. "As long as we're talking, I'm okay."

Wind rustled the tops of the trees, and remnants of the spring breeze carried the smell of promise. "What about sex, though? We're pretty noisy, and I really don't want to explain to a five-year-old why Daddy's spanking Mommy."

Justin laughed and pulled her into his arms. "I'm thinking the girls will spend mandatory nights out with their grandparents every other weekend. During those times, you will remain naked and possibly tied up."

Hope grew, a strong vine wrapping around her body to hold her upright. "I'd like that, Justin. I'd really, really like that."

He tipped her chin so that her gaze met his. "I won't brook disobedience, Trish. When you disobey me or mouth off, you will be punished. And when I want sex, you will give it to me. If I wake you up the same way I did this morning, then you will spread your legs and let me have what I want. If I turn you onto your stomach or order you on all fours because I want to fuck your ass, then you will obey without question."

Her thighs quivered, and cream soaked through the crotch of her sweats. Thankful Justin held her so close, she sagged against the solidity of his body. "Yes, Justin."

"If I tell you to suck my cock or if I want to lick your pussy, you can't say no. We'll use the safe word, of course, but you can't use it to control me. You can only use it if you need to use it. Do you understand?"

He promised to fulfill every one of her desires in a way that made it clear he desired the same things. Joy surged and swelled her heart. "Yes, Justin."

He caressed her lips in a kiss that said just how much he loved her. When he slid his tongue along the seam of her lips, she opened to him. The tenor of the kiss changed as he plundered her mouth, claiming his possession.

She surrendered.

~ * ~

BY MY SIDE

Oasis: Adult Fantasy Fulfillment

Think about what you want more than anything in the world. It isn't out of reach. Oasis is an adult fantasy fulfillment service that specializes in making your dreams come true. Anything from a weekend getaway with someone you love to an erotic encounter with a stranger—or strangers—can happen. Call us today and make your fantasy a reality.

*Oasis reserves the right to reject any application for any reason. Oasis is not an escort service. We match people on the basis of their fantasies and arrange for those fantasies to be fulfilled. Fantasies are fulfilled at the discretion of management.

Case 2

We've worked closely for over a year. Just for one night, I would like him to notice me, to want me the way I want him, to see that I can be the submissive he needs.

Chapter One

"Fuck." Sean Winquist slammed his cell phone on the hard surface of the mahogany desk in front of him. Though it technically belonged to him, the desk happened to be occupied by his assistant, Marcella Abbott. She jumped at the unexpected bit of violence from a man she'd never seen lose his temper, not once in the thirteen months she'd worked for him. "Two days. How the hell am I supposed to find a replacement in two fucking days?"

She smoothed her skirt and took a breath before she looked up from her keyboard. The heat in his hazel eyes had nudged them closer to brown. Marcella swallowed and squeezed her legs together. If he once directed that kind of heat in her direction, she would be naked and on her knees in no time. Who was she fooling? He had only to ask. Heat could be generated after the fact.

"I could do it."

His eyes widened in shock, and she dropped her gaze, afraid of a judgment she couldn't handle. She snaked out a hand, grabbed his phone, and examined it closely. If he'd broken it, she would need to make sure he had a new one.

"That was Gretchen."

He spoke softly, and she cringed at his tone. Day in and day out for over a year, she had been at his side. She traveled everywhere with him. She lived in a suite in his mansion. She planned his days and organized his house. At first he hadn't given her much to do. Within two months of her arrival, though, he had trusted every aspect of his life to her capable hands.

When she first began working for him, he would disappear for a weekend here and there. Marcella had arranged accommodations for a different woman each time. By the time six weeks had passed, he had divested himself of every one of his submissives except for Gretchen. Though he now only saw her sporadically, Marcella knew damn well when he spoke to Gretchen.

The tone in his voice conveyed a refusal. *Thank you, but no thank you.* He would gladly tie up Gretchen and whip her until she climaxed, but he wouldn't touch Marcella at all. Once, while traveling in New York City during the spring, she had slipped on a patch of ice. He'd caught her, pulling her so close to his body that she could feel the hardness of his chest against her arm and shoulder. And then his cheeks had reddened. He had let go and turned stiffly away, nodding vaguely at her expression of gratitude.

Why in the world did she lust after a man who hated the very thought of physical contact with her? She'd taken the chance only because of the wish she'd submitted to Oasis. Surely this development meant an opening for Marcella. They'd told her to expect fulfillment soon.

Outside of a new scratch it could have picked up anywhere, the phone hadn't suffered damage. She placed it back on the desk. Gathering her courage, she raised her gaze to lock with his. "I know."

He shook his head and turned away, but not before she caught the spark of interest that flared briefly in his eyes. "No, Marcella, you don't know. You have no experience with this kind of thing. Cancel the event. Refund the donations."

"No. Sean, you can't do that. We've spent four months planning this. People paid ten thousand dollars each to see you with a submissive." She didn't have to remind him that the money would benefit his favorite leukemia charity. His younger brother had lost that battle at the tender age of thirteen. Sean had been fifteen and completely helpless as he watched his brother's valiant fight.

He crossed the room and pressed his forehead against a windowpane. Tension radiated from his body. This meant so much to him. After achieving fame and fortune as a Hollywood producer by age thirty-five, Sean had turned his philanthropic efforts toward raising money for charities that funded research and provided assistance for families affected by leukemia.

Marcella's heart seized a bit as she watched him. Throwing caution to the wind, she rounded the desk and came to stand behind him. By moving away whenever she came too close, he'd trained her to keep distance between them. Now she ignored his unspoken rule. She reached out and rested her hands on his shoulders. A shudder ran through him, but she didn't let that bit of rejection dampen her mission.

"Sean, I know I'm not beautiful and sexy like Gretchen, but if you put me in one of those bustier tops and a mask, the lighting is low enough so that nobody will really know the difference."

Personally, Marcella found Gretchen's skeletal thinness unattractive. Women were meant to have curves. The augmented breasts that rounded out Gretchen's padded bras couldn't hope to compete with Marcella's natural endowment. Marcella didn't spend hours of time and thousands of dollars on her makeup or hair, but she did take time with her appearance. If

Gretchen was a ten, then Marcella considered herself a solid seven. Prettier than average, but not jaw-droppingly beautiful.

His shoulders moved as a desperate chuckle fell from his lips. "Fuck. Marcella, it's not about beauty. If it was just about beauty, I'd use you in a heartbeat."

The pulse in her throat picked up a little. He'd never before commented on her physical appearance one way or the other.

"Gretchen knows me. She knows what I want almost before I ask it."

Marcella barely refrained from gritting her teeth. The key to convincing Sean lay in her ability to keep her temper under control. He didn't respond well to outbursts. "I've worked for you for over a year. You've said several times that I always know what you want, and that I do it how you want it done."

He turned away from the window and regarded her somberly. "I need a submissive who doesn't question me. I need one who doesn't analyze my orders looking for a way to second-guess me. You're an excellent assistant, but you're not very submissive, Marcella. Look at how you responded to my order to cancel the benefit."

She waved away his concern. He might want a sub who didn't question him, but he sure as hell needed someone to keep him on his toes. "You don't want to cancel the benefit. This means too much to you."

His hands came up, and he grasped her upper arms lightly. Never before had he attempted such an intimate touch. "And you responded by refusing to cancel. You've spent the past five minutes arguing with me, trying to convince me to change my mind."

If she backed down now, her chance would evaporate. "Sean, I'm not second-guessing you. I know what this means to you. I'm trying to make sure you get what you want. I'm trying to please you. I spend every moment of every day trying to please you. I don't see much of a difference between being your assistant and being your submissive."

A muscle in his jaw ticked. "You're not my submissive, Marcella. If you were, you'd be facing a punishment right now."

Though she wasn't a whips-and-paddles kind of woman, any kind of punishment where he touched her body would be worth it. She shivered with anticipation. "When you interviewed me for this job, you asked me if I would have a problem working while you had a naked woman kneeling at your feet. I told you then that I was a submissive. You know as well as I do that you liked the idea of having a submissive for your assistant. You knew I would move heaven and earth to please you. Let me do this, Sean. Let me do this for you."

His hands dropped away. He straightened and took a decisive breath. When he moved around to stand behind her, Marcella didn't move. It might have been a little while since she'd been active on the scene, but she knew when to stay still.

"You'll be exposed in front of a hundred strangers who paid to see you that way."

She kept her eyes facing forward. "I know most of the people who will be there, because they're friends or acquaintances of yours. And I handled all the ticket purchases and background checks. Besides, I'll be under your protection. Nobody will touch me without your permission."

Nobody would dare. Sean might be quiet, but it was a strong kind of quiet, backed up by his physical strength and the innate power radiating from every pore in his body. He could have had a successful acting career full of leading roles. Instead he had remained behind the scenes, a carefully controlled powerhouse.

He stood close to her back. She felt the electricity of his chest as he hovered a maddening few inches away from physical contact. "Round one is teasing, a warm-up. You'd be bound to a bar above your head. A spreader bar would be placed between your ankles. I plan to use a heater, clamps, anal beads. One lucky person who donated an additional fifty thousand gets to choose another instrument of torture. Even I don't know what that is yet."

Having arranged for all the equipment to be there, Marcella knew exactly what would happen. She even knew what the donor had chosen as the instrument of torture—ice. If he used the heater the right way, the ice would both stimulate and soothe her hot skin. She even knew she wouldn't be allowed to climax in that round.

But he wasn't finished. "Round two is where I whip you until you come. The spreader bar will be moved to just above your knees. You'll only have the stimulation of the whip, Marcella. No physical contact and no dildos will be used."

Oh, but her panties were drenched just from the sound of his voice. She might have disclosed her submissiveness, but they'd never discussed the issue of masochism. With regard to that, she had a mild tolerance for pain. Too much and she wouldn't be able to orgasm. "That'll take a little practice," she said. "I can come that way. I've done it before, though not in a long time. I can do it for you."

Sounds of his uneven breathing drifted over her shoulder. She wanted him to press his body against hers so she could know whether this aroused him as much as it did her. "You're a very mouthy submissive, Cella."

She loved the way he shortened her name. He'd only ever done it those few times he'd indulged in spirits enough to make him relax his normally iron control. She liked to think it revealed the way he really thought about her, an unguarded moment when she could see the parts he kept hidden.

"You haven't agreed to use me, Sean. I thought we were still negotiating. You're laying out the conditions I have to accept before you'll agree to use me as your sub."

He chuckled, a distinctly unhappy sound. She wanted to turn, to take him in her arms, but she knew he would issue an automatic refusal if she pushed him too far. "And you're okay with the conditions so far?"

"Yes, Sean."

He inhaled softly, and she had the distinct impression that he was smelling her hair. He gathered her tresses and arranged them to fall over one of her shoulders, but he kept his hand tangled in her hair. "Round three fulfills a promise. You'll be bound to a table, spread out as an offering. After you're teased and denied, every person there will get to come close and see your naked body. Two donors will be allowed to touch you. You will be brought to orgasm twice, and not necessarily by my hand."

Shock robbed her brain of any coherent response. The original program, the one she had so carefully prepared according to Sean's specifications, didn't mention anyone else being allowed to participate. Marcella didn't know how comfortable she would be with a stranger touching her intimately.

"It's the ultimate gift a slave can give her master, Cella. Complete trust. You would have to trust that I won't let anyone harm you, that I won't let anyone violate your hard limits." Bitterness tinged his voice, making his words ring hollow.

They hadn't discussed hard limits. Marcella hadn't thought she would be allowed to have them. The progression of torture had been decided already. It should have been a matter of her agreeing to a specific order of activities.

She swallowed the lump in her throat. She trusted nobody more than Sean, but his tone didn't match his declaration. "It would please you to have another dom fuck your submissive while you and a roomful of people looked on?"

He made a strangled sound. "Please me? Do you really care about pleasing me, Cella? Or are you just volunteering to do this because it's for an important cause?"

Moisture evaporated from her lips. She licked them. "Both. We've been over this. Why can't you believe me, Sean? Why is this so difficult for you? You didn't hesitate for a second when Gretchen volunteered. Are you really so opposed to the idea of seeing me naked? Of having actual physical contact with me?"

He tightened his grip on her hair and turned her around. The ferocity of his expression made her knees weak. "I know Gretchen. I know what she likes and doesn't like. I know what turns her on. I know what makes her climax. I don't know any of your triggers, Marcella. I don't know your limits, and you don't know mine."

She searched his eyes, looking for the source of his irritation. It hadn't taken her long after she'd first begun working for him to determine that Sean's words rarely indicated the true cause of his upset. When she spoke, she kept her voice soft. "Including other doms wasn't part of the original agreement. I have no record of any extra donations. Is Gretchen making a power play? Is that why you're so angry?"

He jerked his head back, lifting his chin and pressing his lips together. Bingo. She'd found the true cause of his anger. Releasing his hold on her hair, he blinked away his surprise. Five steps put him near an expensive vase. She watched, uncertain where his temper might take him. This could derail their negotiation.

He flexed and relaxed his fist, repeating the motion several times as he brought his temper under control. "She went behind my back and solicited two more donors for this. When she told me about it yesterday, I let her have her way. She presented it as a gift. I honestly don't care if she wants to have multiple partners. We're not exclusive. I don't even see her that often."

"She's the one who framed it as an expression of ultimate trust." Marcella didn't need to know more to understand how Gretchen had manipulated both Sean and the situation. "That doesn't sound like something you'd come up with."

Now he turned back to face her. Marcella hadn't moved. "Thank you for volunteering, Marcella, but I can't do that to you. I know what it means for you to ask to do this for me, and I can't abuse your trust by allowing strangers to put their hands on you."

She crossed to her desk and lifted a program from the small box perched on the corner. "Nowhere on here does it mention additional donors or the inclusion of anyone else in your show. I have no record of additional donations. Who are they?"

Sean shrugged. "She didn't say."

Marcella fought the urge to laugh. "And you didn't ask?"

"I didn't care about that. I cared that she went behind my back. I cared that she was trying to play power games with me. I planned to stop seeing her after this."

His attitude exasperated Marcella. She perused the program as a way to keep him from seeing her annoyance.

A rueful laugh rumbled from his chest. "She accused me of seeing this as a business deal."

Marcella snapped her fingers. "A business deal. That's it. If Gretchen set this up and she's no longer participating, then the offer is void. Changing the submissive necessarily changes the parameters of the demonstration because the limits and preferences change. Everyone will understand the altered expectations."

They could change the progression of the rounds to better fit Marcella's preferences and limits. However, she didn't know how Sean would take a suggestion like that. After all, he had decided the original choreography. Part of Marcella wanted to ask if they could change the plan, but a larger part of her was afraid he would decide not to use her if she set limits that significantly altered things.

SEAN WATCHED, AMUSED, as the wheels in Marcella's brain powered full speed ahead. He loved the way her eyes sparkled when she had an idea. She snatched up her notebook and her laptop from her desk. The fact that she kept a notebook and a computer together made him smile. Marcella always took notes on paper. Once her ideas were fully formed, she digitized them. E-mails, schedules, and appointments would pour from her fingertips and appear on his phone and calendar.

She crossed the room and set the laptop on an ottoman. After kicking off her shoes, she settled onto the sofa and folded her feet under her luscious bottom. The blue cover of the notebook disappeared as she opened to a fresh page. Her pen flew over the paper. He had no clue what she could possibly be writing, but he knew better than to interrupt.

The first time he'd set eyes on her, it had taken him almost five minutes to form a coherent thought. Over a year later, he only managed to function around her if he didn't get too close.

She always smelled like cinnamon and vanilla. When he came really close, he sometimes caught a whiff of coconut. He wanted to bury his face in every part of her body to find out exactly where she used each scent.

He sat down on the chair across from her and raked his gaze over her body. The silk blouse she wore hugged the curves of her breasts and dipped down to show a bit of cleavage. He imagined licking her there. He would draw her shirt over her head and remove her delicate pink lacy bra. Though he hadn't seen it, he knew it would match the exact shade of soft pink in her shirt and in her lipstick. He would tweak and suck her nipples until they pebbled and she arched beneath him. Gasps and moans would fall from her lips.

Her hair, light brown with hints of ginger, fell over her shoulders. The ends curled. It had felt silky soft when he'd used it to turn her around before. He ached to feel it sliding through his fingers, tickling down his neck and chest. Brushing his thighs as she closed those kissable lips around his cock.

"Round one should feature several toys. The vendors all promised a percentage of profits from the event in donations. I've already cleaned up the selection they sent over and set them out in your dungeon." She lifted her gaze, meeting his briefly. Vendors would be on hand after the demonstration to sell sex toys and accessories to the titillated crowd. Sales of the implements he used in the scene would most likely be higher than those he bypassed. "I thought you would want to see which ones Gretchen liked best and use those. You mentioned using a heater and clamps. I think you should—"

He held up a hand to halt her flow of words. Round one would showcase his expertise with slow sexual teasing. She definitely had a way of reducing a sensual experience to items on a business agenda. "Marcella, as the submissive, you don't get to choose the toys. You can ask. You can beg. You can't choose or insist. That's not negotiable with me."

Color stained her cheeks. "I'm sorry, Sean. I just meant we'd raise more money if we showcased a variety of toys."

"I know what you meant. We'll try them out, but I'll be the one deciding which get used and which don't. Speak now if you want out of this. I won't force you to do anything you don't want to do." He held his breath and counted the long seconds that ticked past as she studied his face.

He wondered if his face pleased her. After he'd made his first million dollars, he had stopped accepting compliments from people. Most of them said what they thought he wanted to hear. Not Marcella. At her interview, she had straightened his tie without asking for permission, taking him to task when she found out he never untied the knot. He just loosened it to fit over his head. The sparks that flew from her hands through his chest had made him want to strip her naked and bend her over the back of the nearest couch. Later she'd told him to get rid of all his red ties. They didn't suit his coloring.

The way she sat, knees turned modestly to one side, turned him on more than if she'd knelt naked in front of him with her knees spread to reveal the soft folds of her pussy. Would it be light pink or dusky rose? How responsive would she be to his tongue and fingers exploring her wetness?

With her feet under her ass, the fabric of her skirt pulled snugly against her curves. He wanted to dig his fingertips into her hips as he sank his dick into her tightness.

"I wouldn't have suggested it if I wasn't willing." She dropped her gaze and stared at her notebook. "Round two features whips. That's the only one that worries me. I-I do okay with a flogger, but I didn't care for the cat or the single-tail at all."

Sean's attention jerked from carnal thoughts and landed on her embarrassed revelation. Earlier she'd mentioned needing to practice with a whip. "Everyone has different levels of pain they enjoy, Cella."

"I know." He had to strain to hear her. She drew a slow line in her notebook. "I'm just worried that I won't be able to endure enough. I've never been with anyone who used a cane or a tawse on me. I can't say I've ever wanted to try those things."

A fact filtered through Sean's consciousness. He'd kept his hands off her for more reasons than simply because he didn't want to chance driving her away.

"Marcella, shouldn't Eric be here? Shouldn't you ask him if he's okay with this first?"

Her brow furrowed, and her mouth puckered into a frown. "Eric?"

"Your boyfriend. Your master." He had to force the last word out. If he were her master, he wouldn't loan her out to anyone. He wouldn't allow anyone to put their hands on her. He wouldn't allow her to work insane hours for another man. Or woman. He would want all her attention focused on him, much as it was now.

She lifted her pretty brown eyes and brushed her bangs away from her thick, full lashes. "Eric and I broke up almost a year ago."

He felt like an ass, and not just because he welcomed the news. How had he not known? "Because you work for me?"

"That was the final nail in the coffin." She shrugged. "We wanted different things out of the relationship. It wasn't going to last, no matter what."

"What different things?" Though he knew damn well it wasn't his business, he couldn't stop himself from asking. She knew every detail of his personal life, but she'd engineered it so that he knew only select things about her. And he'd let her. Oh, he had rationalized it by telling himself he respected her privacy. Facing the truth meant admitting cowardice. He hadn't wanted to hear her talk about her boyfriend.

"He wanted a full-time sex slave, and that's just not me. I don't mind kneeling naked at my master's feet during a scene, but expecting me to cook and clean the house naked is too much. Hell, expecting me to do all the cooking and cleaning is too much. Plus he didn't seem to care about me, only my obedience. He punished me for the smallest infractions."

She trailed off and shrugged as if she hadn't said something that opened up a vast list of questions. Her pen flew over the lines in her notebook.

"Marcella, is Eric the reason you don't like the whip?"

Her momentum faltered. She tapped the pen against her teeth. "Maybe a little, but I've always had a low threshold for pain. He preferred to deny me attention and affection. I'd rather be whipped than be hurt emotionally."

Sean hated doms who disciplined their subs emotionally. The whole point of having a D/s relationship was for mutual pleasure and to deepen the emotional bond between the couple. Nothing good could result from insisting on emotional control over another person. Everyone had a right to feel what they felt. "That's abusive."

Her shoulders lifted and fell again. "I don't think he meant to be mean. He wanted me to beg for his time and attention, but I'm just not that kind of pushy, needy sub. I'm sure he'll find some woman with daddy issues and they'll get along just fine."

He let her have the evasion. She'd obviously moved on. Briefly, he wondered who she'd been dating if not Eric. He knew she'd spent several of her days off with a man, and he'd gone out of his way to not be around when her date had picked her up. He hadn't needed visual confirmation that he didn't stand a chance in hell with her. Before the demons of doubt could dig their talons in too deep, he ditched those thoughts. She was here with him now, and she had just promised to be his for the next three days.

"Round three." He stood and held out his hand to her—the first time he'd ever instigated contact. Now that she'd agreed to be his submissive, even if it was only temporary, he could let down his guard a bit. As soon as he had her in his dungeon, he'd be touching her all over. "I'll bring you to orgasm twice. You'll have no input into the choreography. Enough talk, Cella. We need to practice if I'm going to know your limits."

She looked at his hand and shook her head. "I'm not ready, Sean. Give me thirty minutes. I need to shave."

He blinked. "Shave?"

"Well, yes. I didn't anticipate being naked in front of anyone today, so I didn't shave."

He dropped his hand, a little stung by her efficient, businesslike rejection. However, the image of her naked body tied to his cross more than made up for it. He checked the time on his cell. "Thirty minutes. Come to the dungeon wearing only a robe."

Chapter Two

Marcella knew from paying the bills that Sean preferred his submissives to be hairless. Though she'd engaged in a few scenes with her dates in the time since she'd ended her relationship with Eric, she hadn't bothered to shave her pussy in a very long time. It hadn't mattered before. Now that Sean would be her master, albeit only for a few days, she wanted to groom herself in ways that would please him.

She arranged her hair in a sexy, sloppy upsweep. No matter how classy she made it look, it would end up a mess by the end of the scene. She preferred to enter a scene with some control over her personal disarray. Knowing Sean, it would be the only thing she would control.

The deep rose robe he'd given her as a birthday gift lay at the foot of her bed. Not a day passed that she didn't snuggle into the soft, silky feel of the fabric. As she donned it now, it slid over her skin, caressing her hips and the tips of her breasts. She tied the belt and headed down two flights of stairs to the dungeon.

She entered his domain, immediately feeling an electric charge at being there to do more than set up. Having worked so closely with Sean for over a year, she'd seen him at his best and at his worst. She trusted him completely.

A sound to her right drew her attention to that corner of the room. Sean leaned against a high table. He lifted a glass to his lips and sipped. Ice cubes clinked as they shifted, and she recognized the sound that had caught her attention.

He watched her silently. She dropped her gaze to the floor, fastening it demurely to a point halfway between them. If he wanted her to kneel, he would tell her to kneel. This moment, this starting point, was a test of her submissiveness. It would tell him so much about her level of responsiveness. She emptied her mind of everything except Sean.

The glass thudded against the wood. He closed the distance between them, coming to a halt inches in front of her. She focused on the thin line of hair that trailed from his navel and disappeared into his jeans. He had removed his shirt. Though she had seen him shirtless before, the sight sent a tremor up her spine.

He placed his fingers on her neck, spanning them just below her ear. Residual cold from the glass penetrated her skin, and a second tremor followed the first. "Choose a safe word."

"Oasis." She would forever revere the name of the wish-fulfillment service that had delivered Sean to her. She didn't know how they'd gotten rid of Gretchen, but they had, and she was thankful for that.

Sean slid his fingers forward to grip her chin. "Oasis. Your favorite band." A slight pressure tilted her face, and she peered into his eyes. "If you ask me to stop or you say no at any time, those words will also work. I don't play protest games. That's one of my limits."

She bit back her amazement over the fact that he knew her favorite band and nodded to acknowledge his limit. "What should I call you?"

"Master. For the next three days, I am your master."

She couldn't stop the pleased smile or the excitement unfurling in her chest. As usually happened, her profound sense of duty managed to take the lead. "Master, you should know that I'm on birth control and that my last tests came back clean."

His mouth twitched, the beginnings of a smile or a reprimand that never manifested. She hadn't asked for permission to speak. "And I'm sure you know all about my tests." At her nod—she handled all his mail and appointments—he continued. "Untie your robe."

An auditory response wasn't necessary. She complied with his order, loosening the sash and letting it dangle at her sides. The robe remained stuck to her body.

With one finger, Sean traced a path between her breasts and urged her robe apart. The warmth of the silk fell away. For the first time, Marcella stood exposed to his view. She held her breath and hoped he liked what he saw.

His gaze roamed every inch of her skin. Heat bloomed in the trails he left, though he no longer touched her. With agonizing slowness, he rounded her body. She felt his hands at her shoulders. The robe whispered a caress down her arms and pooled at her bare feet.

Sean's breath tickled behind her ear just below her hairline. He inhaled deeply, confirming that he had been enjoying her scent all along. Marcella's heart leaped and floated at this evidence of his interest.

His teeth grazed along the base of her neck. "Are you sure about this, my sweet slave? A hundred people will watch me tease and torture you. They'll watch your luscious body writhe and arch. They'll listen as you whimper with need. They'll watch your juices run down your thighs. You think I'm the draw, but you're wrong. They're coming to see you, Marcella. Are you really an exhibitionist?"

She wanted to shake her head, but she didn't want to move away from the teeth and lips that played over her shoulder and up her neck. "No, Master. I mean, yes, Master, I'm sure about this. No, Master, I'm not an exhibitionist."

His fingertips etched trails parallel to her spine. "I thought not. I will allow you a blindfold."

She exhaled, and tension drained from her shoulders. She hadn't realized how tightly her nerves were wound. "Thank you, Master."

He pressed his lips to her shoulder, a brief acknowledgment of her thanks. "I'm going to bind you several ways tonight. I might use the flogger, but I mostly want to see how you respond to different stimuli."

Light, feathery touches played up and down her arms. She wanted to sag backward to rest against his chest, but she knew that would not please him. Then his touch disappeared. She resisted the urge to turn her head and follow him with her eyes.

Darkness stole her vision. He adjusted the strap, securing it under where she'd piled her hair. Using only the soft pressure of his fingertips, he nudged the small of her back. "Walk forward until I tell you to stop."

With her vision compromised, her sense of balance wasn't the same. She took small steps, counting six when Sean told her to stop.

"Raise your arms above your head."

She felt her breasts rise as she lifted her arms. Wide leather cuffs encircled her wrists, and he tightened the buckles one at a time. Anticipation coiled just above her pussy. Bondage was definitely one of her triggers.

A motor whirred to life. The bar to which the cuffs were attached rose, forcing her almost to her toes. Cool leather closed around her ankles, and the tug and pull on the cuffs indicated a spreader bar held her legs apart.

Long silence filled the air, and her pussy grew moist because she knew he was looking at her, checking out every inch of her body. She waited patiently while her master looked his fill, which was his due.

"Beautiful. So fucking beautiful. I've never seen a sexier woman in my entire life." She felt the heat and smooth skin of his chest as he brushed against the pebbled tips of her breasts. She jumped in surprise. "And you're mine, Cella. All mine."

"Yes, Master. I'm yours." She understood the psychology of why he said the things he said. He had staked his claim and established the emotional atmosphere that permeated the dark of her blindfold. The vehemence underlying his tone lent a truth to his statement that couldn't be faked. She very badly wanted to be his.

Cupping her face, he urged her head back the tiniest bit. At five-eight, Marcella was only three inches shorter than her dream man. The way he'd stretched her most likely put them almost eye to eye. If he removed her blindfold, she would find herself gazing right into his golden eyes. Or might they be edged in green now?

He brushed his thumb over her lips. She parted them ever so slightly, offering but not demanding. The kiss, unexpected and completely welcomed, startled a gasp from her. She thought he would tease for a long, long time before he allowed her the taste of his kiss. Instead he devoured her lips and swept his tongue into her mouth. She quivered and melted under his onslaught, grateful for the cuffs and chains holding her upright.

He gripped her head and pushed his chest against hers. She had no leverage to balance his forcefulness, and his kiss literally knocked her off her feet. She ignored the increased stress on her shoulder and wrist joints, but he did not. He broke the kiss, leaving her breathless and wanting. She felt his hands on her hips as he moved her back into place so that her feet bore the brunt of her weight.

He massaged her shoulders. "How are you doing? Wrists okay?"

As he held her, his thumbs pressed just under her arms, where she was dangerously ticklish. She jumped at the sensation and swallowed an unwanted laugh. "They're fine, Master."

"Shoulders?"

She felt his frown. If she didn't know him better, she would have thought she had displeased him. His tight tone seemed to foretell the end of their game, but she knew his tone resulted from the depth of his concern. He had to trust her to tell him when he went too far. No master could read minds.

"My shoulders are fine, Master. I'm a little ticklish. That's all."

"I see. So torturing you with a feather would be counterproductive?"

She'd never once had a lover who engaged in light sensory play. So far they'd all liked bondage or they'd been on the prowl for a true painslut, which she was not. The prospect of Sean taking the time to learn her body in such a thorough and intimate way made her heart thump loudly. "It depends on what you wish to accomplish, Master. I'm not ticklish everywhere."

He didn't respond with words, and he didn't use a feather. He prowled her body with his fingertips, brushing them from her leather-clad wrists to her shoulders. He did this over and over, caressing every single inch of skin. He moved to stand behind her and lavished the same care over her back.

The pressure of the caresses changed. He used the flat of his hands. He traced trails with his fingertips. He rubbed the inside of his wrists over her hips. By the time he made it to her ass, he had added his lips and tongue. When he licked a path down her spine, Marcella felt as if her body would erupt in flames.

He worshipped her legs, down the back and up the front. She felt the puff of his breath against her bare pussy. She heard him inhale deeply. Normally she liked to be blindfolded, every sensation magnified a thousand times. Yet it robbed her of the sight of Sean's face as he looked at her, touched her. She desperately wanted the visual, especially because this was their first time together.

"Your cunt is one the most beautiful things I've ever seen, Marcella. It's the prettiest shade of pink, a little darker than what your cheeks turn when you blush. I think every time I see you blush from now on, I'll be picturing this." He brushed his fingertips over her mons and avoided her pulsing, weeping lips.

Cool air rushed across her slit as he blew, causing her to moan and thrust her hips forward.

"Your pussy is so wet and swollen, Cella, and the tip of your clit pokes out just a little." Heat seared her clit as he flicked his tongue over the sensitive nub. "It tastes musky and sweet. I think later I'll put you in the swing so

I can taste all of you. What do you think of that, my sweet slave?"

He licked just the tip of her clit again and again. Marcella struggled with an answer. She wanted him to put her in the swing right now and finish what he'd begun, but she knew he was practicing for the first round of the show, when she would not be allowed to climax. Her state of constantly heightened arousal would titillate the audience, keeping them on the edge.

"If it pleases you, Master." Really, it was the only reasonable response. Good submissives didn't demand, and she wasn't in the habit of topping from the bottom.

He rose to his feet. The scent of her arousal tickled her nose for a split second before he kissed her again. She tasted the barest trace of her juices on his tongue. He broke the kiss and patted her on the ass. "It pleases me."

He tickled over her ribs as he finished his exploration. He had yet to touch her breasts, but he hit a particularly sensitive spot, and she twitched and jumped.

"Ticklish?"

"Yes, Master."

He increased the pressure of his fingertips. "Now?"

Now she felt only the heat of his caress. "No, Master."

Abruptly, he stepped away from her body. The heat vanished, leaving quivering need in its wake. "We're going to play, Cella. I'm going to tease you a lot. You aren't allowed to come without permission. That will earn a punishment."

Marcella shivered. His threat had been vague. Punishment meant different things to different people. Just from what she'd overheard, she knew Sean had used a cane on Gretchen. Marcella had never experienced a cane, but she had seen it used on another submissive. The large man had cried like a baby and begged his mistress for forgiveness. By the time she'd finished with him, his back had been a series of striped welts. Marcella wanted to remind Sean she wasn't into that kind of pain.

"Punishment isn't meant to be pleasant." He continued as if he'd heard her internal monologue. "You won't enjoy it. If you enjoyed it, then it would be a reward." He stepped closer, coming up behind her when she thought he was still in front of her. He nipped at her earlobe. "Do you trust me, Cella?"

Her fears fell away as her iron will reasserted itself. She would not fail. Did she trust Sean? Absolutely. "Yes, Master. I trust you."

"Good. You'll need that trust because I'm going to test you."

Silence again. The sounds of drawers and the clink of ice. She waited, using years of practice to control her desire. The need pulsing between her thighs dissipated.

Wet heat closed around her nipple. Sean laved the tiny bud with his tongue and stretched it with his teeth. Marcella moaned and arched closer. He released her, but his fingers were there, pinching and pulling. She gasped and tried to move away, but the chains held her in place. When he finished, the sharpness of the remaining pinch indicated a nipple clamp. He did the same thing to her other breast.

Marcella loved wearing nipple clamps as long as they weren't tightened too much. Sean played with the tension, easing it back a little. She sighed when she got to the point where pleasure outweighed pain. "How's that, slave?"

"It's perfect, Master. Thank you."

The clamps moved and grew heavier. Cold metal slid along the skin of her breasts. An image of a delicate chain flashed in her memory. The chain had a series of larger hoops in the middle where weights could be attached. It also had a longer attachment with another clamp at the end that would connect her clit to her nipples. The tissues between her legs swelled, begging silently for attention.

He tugged on the chain and claimed her lips at the same time, swallowing her gasp. She melted into the firm softness of his lips, but that didn't stop her from noticing that he ran his fingertips lightly along her slit. Without warning, he plunged two fingers deep. He massaged her vaginal walls, exploring instead of stimulating, but the effect devastated her nonetheless. Orgasm threatened.

She moaned into his mouth, begging for a reprieve. Her body trembled. He withdrew his fingers. At odds with her mind, her pussy pulsed, chasing the feel of his fingers again.

"Mmmm." A slurp and a popping sound came from inches away. "I think we'll have to get to the licking part of the night sooner rather than later. Your flavor is distinctly addictive."

Marcella prayed he would remove her blindfold before that happened.

The air in front of her lost that electric feeling that came whenever he stood nearby. When she sensed him again, he stood behind her. He probed her anus with gel-covered fingers. She breathed into the sensation, relaxing the tight muscle because she knew the joys that awaited her.

The first small bead barely made an impact. The second stretched her a little wider, and the wand connecting them thickened. Each bead, successively larger, brought a little more pleasure than the one before. By the time he inserted the sixth, her body trembled and her pussy threatened to spontaneously orgasm. She inhaled deeply and let it out slowly. She tried to think about boring, nonsexual things, but her mind fixated on the things she felt and refused the distraction.

Her head fell back, and she lost control of her breathing. Sean cradled the back of her skull. He licked a line up the column of her throat and sucked on her lips.

"You're close, aren't you, my sweet slave?"

No sense in hiding anything from her master. "Yes, Master."

"I want to see you come, Cella. I'm going to finger you. I want you to hold off for as long as you can, honey. Ask first."

Any other master might have just fingered her until she begged. She liked the way he sometimes told her what he was going to do and sometimes didn't. When he penetrated her with three fingers—it had to be three, he stretched her so wide—all thoughts of gratitude fled.

He pumped his fingers into her, curving them to hit her G-spot every single time. Her hips tilted, both a reaction to his rhythm and a need to grind her clit against his palm. The chains didn't allow for much movement, but they gave a little.

"Beautiful. Fuck, Cella. I want to see your eyes."

She felt him yank the blindfold away, pulling her hair a bit in the process. Sean's face, a determined set to his jaw, greeted the return of her vision. A strand of sun-streaked brown hair fell over his forehead. His nostrils flared, and his lips parted. All at once, she came. The orgasm blinded her. She shouted, and he only thrust into her faster. Waves washed over her body, tingling up her arms and down her legs. She felt battered, completely at their mercy.

When she came down, she found her head resting on Sean's shoulder. He held her close with one hand on her waist, and he stroked her hair with his other hand. She wanted to hold him, but when she tried, her hand wouldn't move. The clink of chains reminded her that she was still bound in the center of the room.

"Thank you, Master."

He kissed her forehead. "Don't thank me yet, slave. You disobeyed a direct order. I told you to ask first."

She didn't think telling him the sight of his handsome face had sent her over the edge would lessen her punishment, so she kept her lips sealed. "I'm sorry, Master."

He released her from his embrace. She set her feet and readied her psyche for whatever whip or cane he chose to use. He knelt down and unbuckled her ankles. Then he stood and released her arms, massaging them from palm to shoulder.

"How are your arms, Cella?"

"A little sore, Master. They'll be fine in a few minutes."

He nodded, and a sense of satisfaction flashed behind his eyes. Green, she noted. Her thighs trembled, barely supporting her weight.

"Kneel." He pointed to a thick pillow on the floor a few feet away.

The foam inside cushioned her knees and saved her from those annoying little bruises that came from kneeling on hard surfaces. The chain connecting her nipples patted an uneven rhythm just below her sternum as she moved. She spread her knees shoulder-width apart and sat back on her heels. The beads in her ass shifted and rubbed, pressing against her still-throbbing pussy walls. She wanted to rub her clit, to prolong the pleasurable sensations.

Her hands automatically folded behind her back, preventing her from following through on her impulse. She waited in silence, staring at a snag in the rug under the spanking bench. Her mind wandered, caught on the imperfection. Would he want her to take care of that? She had never before entered his dungeon without his knowledge and approval. But now it seemed a little less "his" and a little more "theirs."

Denim-clad legs stopped in front of her. Marcella resisted her urge to follow them up, to see if a bulge in his jeans betrayed a desire for her. He squatted, flexing those magnificently powerful thighs. She wished desperately for permission to touch him, to run her hands over his body and worship him the way she had fantasized so many times.

Ice clinked. He held a glass of water out to her. "Drink, Marcella."

She unclasped her hands from behind her back and downed the water. The coldness slipped down her throat, bringing relief. She hadn't realized how dry she had become.

When she handed the glass back, only the few ice cubes remained. He accepted it with a smile. Her heartbeat sped up. "Good girl. Now spread your legs wider. Leave your hands on your thighs."

She did as he ordered. He reached forward too quickly for her to see, but she didn't worry too much since his aim would take him directly to her pussy. Something hard nudged the opening of her vagina. She looked down, but his arm and hand obscured her view.

"Relax, my little slave. This is just a mild punishment to help you cool down. I have lots of plans for this pretty little cunt. I can't have it overheating."

As he held the hard object to her opening and spoke, his play on words became clear. The glass dildo had been kept in the ice bucket. The temperature of the lubricant he'd slathered on took a moment to cool down. He angled the head and pushed the glass dildo into her pussy.

The unforgiving hardness took her first. Most dildos had some give to make them feel comfortable inside. Glass had no mercy. It stretched her wide, working with the beads in her ass, moving together ever so slightly with each breath she took.

Just when she began to grow used to this exquisite torture, the iciness of the glass penetrated her hot, swollen tissues. The temperature difference both shocked and soothed.

Sean watched her as she acclimated to this new sensation. "We didn't discuss cold play. Now is the time to tell me if it's one of your limits."

Marcella shook her head. "No, Master. I like cold play."

"You and your British bands." He grinned. "I'll have to take you to a concert the next time we're in England."

She started at the playfulness of his tone. Wasn't he about to punish her? Shouldn't he be a little more upset that she'd disobeyed him by coming without permission?

His knees crackled as he stood. "Kneel up, slave. Careful with that glass phallus. It's heavy. If you let it fall out, you'll earn another punishment."

A cold, hard dildo delivered punishment? Marcella wanted to laugh at his attempt. Obviously he took her admittance of disliking too much pain as reason to not use some of the harsher methods of punishment. She felt a little cheated. As a submissive, she craved knowing her place. She craved knowing the certainty of punishment as a response to disobeying.

Then she rose to her knees. Gravity took over, fighting her for possession of the heavy, slippery dildo. She clenched with all her might to keep it from sliding out and reveled in the level of Sean's insidiousness. Only the most creative doms administered punishments that were also challenges.

He'd moved behind her while she fought to obey his orders. Her fevered pussy quivered against the coolness and relaxed, making her fight that much harder not to lose the dildo.

A tug, and he removed two anal beads in quick succession. She gasped at the heady stimulation and the way it messed with her ability to control her vaginal muscles. Less than thirty seconds into her punishment and she wanted to scream at the impossibility of it all.

He pushed one bead back in. She whimpered a protest and received a stinging smack on her ass for it.

"I will not countenance a disobedient slave, Cella. Your body is mine to tease and torture, to please and pleasure as I see fit." He delivered a smack to the other cheek, and she struggled to keep any sounds muffled.

Wetness bloomed once again, fighting the cold in her pussy, but he didn't continue with his erotic spanking. He moved around to face her. She eyed the huge bulge in his jeans. Saliva pooled on her tongue.

"Hands behind your back, naughty Cella." She immediately complied, though her arms felt heavy and unfamiliar. "How beautiful you are. Pink cheeks everywhere. A nice, rosy blush staining your chest. That luscious pussy working so hard to please me."

With one finger, he flicked open the button on his fly. Next he drew down the zipper. If her pussy could whimper, it would have. As it was, it wept for what it wanted so badly. She knew he would deny her this reward for a while longer. Even if she hadn't disobeyed, he wouldn't have fucked her until he'd finished toying with her.

His open jeans only revealed a similar bulge in his black briefs. Once before, Marcella had happened upon him wearing only underwear. He had been standing in front of his closet door talking on his cell. A few minutes before, he had texted her with an order to hurry to his room with his itinerary. He had an important meeting and had awoken late, which meant they had to shuffle his other appointments. One sight of the hard muscles cording his legs and defining his ass, clearly visible through the tight briefs, had sent moisture pooling between her legs. She had been on the job for exactly one week.

The look of shock on her face must have recalled him to his state of undress. He had ended his call and hurriedly remedied the situation. Though she couldn't concentrate with him not dressed, she'd lamented the loss of such a sexy picture. She'd held on to the image and used it to fuel more than one masturbatory fantasy.

But now all professional courtesies had been suspended. He shoved his jeans and briefs down. His cock tangled in the fabric. Marcella envied the hand that reached in to free his erection, but that envy melted away once she came face-to-face with his cock. Though average in length, the thickness came as a surprise. Sean's lean build didn't lead her to imagine such girth.

She licked her lips.

He followed the path of her tongue, tracing his cockhead along her newly wet mouth. She longed to taste him, but she knew better than to open and take him inside. If she did that, he would deny her this pleasure on principle.

"Ask for it."

No hesitation on her part. "Master, please may I suck your cock?"

"Open your mouth, Cella. You'll take me inside; then we'll see whether or not you get to suck."

She read the subtext. Her mouth was merely a vessel. She couldn't take an active role until he gave permission. Obediently, eagerly, she opened her mouth and relaxed her jaw. He eased the tip inside and pulled back. She barely got a taste.

He pushed in again, stopping once the crown of his cock breached the welcoming heat of her mouth. She wanted to lick the rim around his head and dip her tongue into the small opening that leaked evidence of his desire. She wanted to suck him deeper. She struggled to keep her tongue still as he withdrew again.

No matter what the cost, she would pass this test. The glass dildo slipped an inch. Because of its smooth surface, she barely felt it move. Flexing her muscles, she urged it back inside, but gravity proved stronger. At least she stopped it from sliding completely out. She let a moan escape, the inevitable result of her struggle.

Sean worked his cock into her mouth slowly. Each time, he pushed in just a little farther than he had before. When he bumped the back of her throat, he paused while she fought her gag reflex. The phallus in her pussy slipped a little more, drawing her attention away from the cock in her mouth.

"Swallow me, my darling slave. Show me how much you want to please your master."

With perfect timing and rhythm, he thrust as she swallowed. "Fuck, Cella. You feel so fucking good. Put your hands on my hips so I don't knock you over. Hold still while I fuck your mouth." He gripped the sides of her head and growled the words in a voice that betrayed his lack of control.

His warning meant he wouldn't be gentle or considerate. She wanted neither. The thought of him using her mouth excited her like nothing else, except perhaps the thought of him using her pussy or her ass for the same purpose. She was proud to make her master lose control.

He thrust into her mouth without fooling around with a slow tempo or a long buildup. The muscles of his hips, so tense under her fingers, trembled as he pistoned. He tightened his hands on her head, and his seed coated the back of her throat. She swallowed her reward. He thrust twice more, and then he went still.

She took the opportunity to finally use her tongue on his softening cock. He pulled from her slowly, and she cleaned him as he went.

He released his hold on her head and pushed her hands from his hips. "Lie back, but keep your knees on the pillow. Can you bend like that?"

Once, her knees had been able to do that. To do so now would lead to tearing something important. Passing twenty-five had meant losing some of her flexibility. She shook her head. "I'm sorry, Master."

"That's okay. Lie on your back on the floor with your ass on the pillow. Put your legs in front of you, but keep them bent and out of the way. I want to see the dildo in your pussy and the beads in your ass."

Moving slowly, she managed to comply without losing the glass dildo. Though she didn't take the time to look, she knew it had slipped almost halfway out. Another millimeter and gravity would win the battle. She breathed her thanks at the change in position.

He stared down at her, and she saw that he had fastened his jeans. The flush spread across his chest and neck left the only evidence he'd recently found his release. "No clothes for the rest of the day. You'll spend the night chained to my bed."

Marcella started. She hadn't seen that coming. To her knowledge, he'd never chained a woman to his bed before. Questions whirled through her brain, but she shoved them away. He'd just ordered her to spend the night in his bed. That meant he didn't plan to end the scene any time soon. This, her dream, had come true. She would neither question nor argue.

Satisfied she had no protest to voice, he jerked his chin in the direction of her head. "Lace your fingers under your neck."

She complied, wincing as the clamps shifted and dug in a little differently due to the slight change in position. Now her entire body lay splayed and open. She looked to make sure Sean approved.

Possessiveness and desire flared in his eyes, two emotions she never thought he'd direct toward her. He turned and walked away, but Marcella didn't panic. She knew he wasn't going far. The position in which she lay alleviated any need for her to hold a certain form. She relaxed against the surprisingly comfortable wood floor and waited for her master.

He settled on the floor, his feet near her head and his ass next to her hip. He leaned over her body and set a tray of items on the other side. A tall glass filled with ice towered above the other things on the tray. She couldn't quite identify anything else without moving.

Fishing out one ice cube, he placed the small round piece in her navel. Marcella shivered and clenched her pussy tighter around the dildo, which no longer felt cold.

He ran his hand over her stomach and caressed the rounded globes of her breasts. "Don't move, Cella."

Before she could process the order, he removed one of the nipple clamps. Blood rushed back to the little tortured peak, stinging the starved capillaries with liquid heat. Marcella cried out and arched her back, instinctively trying to escape the sweet pleasure-pain. Sean closed his mouth around her nipple before she managed to relax her back.

The additional stimulation sent electricity zinging straight to her pussy. A glance down showed Sean's jaw working as he took more and more of her breast into his mouth. He grazed his teeth along her skin, and then he sucked hard. She watched, fascinated, as he released what he had been able to get into his mouth. It didn't immediately resume its original shape. Her nipple and areola remained squished to a stiff point.

He studied it with the same expression she'd seen him use when he perused art. Abruptly, he reached between her legs and removed the glass dildo. Her empty pussy ached for his hot, hard cock.

"Tell me about a time you enjoyed being whipped."

Before she could answer, he rocked two beads out of her anus and back in. She gasped at the sudden sensation.

He glanced back at her face. "Cella."

In all her fantasies, she hadn't thought he would try to carry on a conversation while in the dungeon. When they encountered one another during the course of a regular day, he conversed with her on a variety of subjects. However, when they worked, he did not fill the time with unnecessary chatter.

"It was a flogger. One with short falls. I barely felt it, but afterward my skin was so sensitive."

The rest of the beads stretched her as he rocked them back out. Each smaller than the last, the diminished pleasure gave her the feeling of things ending. She searched his face for signs he was finished with her.

His gaze heated a path along her splayed thigh. "I like the delicate areas of a woman." A small point of cold traced along the tender, sensitive skin of her inner thigh. He added his hot tongue, thrilling her with a contradictory sensation.

He moved the ice cube up her side, leaving a trail of cool water behind. He pressed the flat of his tongue to her skin and cleared away the water. Then he shifted his body, stretching it out next to her, and continued his exploration. She shivered when he made it to the underside of her arms. Lying on the floor with her hands tucked behind her exposed the most tender skin of her arms to him.

"Tell me about another time you enjoyed the flogger, my slave."

Marcella racked her brain. To her, the whip had always been a punishment. "I heard it can feel like a massage, but I've never experienced that. I'm sorry, Master. That's all."

He trailed ice and licked the track across her neck to her chin. He traced her lips, and then he seared them with his kiss. He thrust his cold tongue and the remnants of the ice into her mouth. She greeted him eagerly. Marcella wanted to feel him on top of her, inside her. She wanted him to claim her in all ways, and she'd never felt this way with another man before. Every other time she'd played a scene, she had always held back the most precious pieces of herself. With Sean, she didn't want to hide anything.

The kiss went on and on. It stoked tiny flames into larger ones. The length of his body pressed along her side, providing accelerant. Burning pain seared her breast as he removed the other clamp. She bucked, an involuntary reaction, but he held her down with the hand that cupped her breast and massaged her sore nipple.

Her body trembled under his onslaught. Nerve endings fired and short-circuited when they reached the juices flowing from her pussy, begging for attention.

He broke the kiss and raised his head. The hazel of his irises had darkened, and his taut muscles shimmered with repressed wildness. "Cella, get on the bed. Now."

In the far corner of his dungeon, a futon sat on a pedestal frame. In her mind, she called this his porn-star corner. Floodlights, pointed at the bed, illuminated every angle. Sean allowed no shadows in his play area.

Heeding the urgency in his tone, she scrambled to the bed as he headed for the light switch.

"Hands and knees."

She crawled to the center of the bed and lifted her head just in time to see the curtains on the walls part to reveal floor-to-ceiling mirrors. The reflected brightness of the lights caused her to wince. She blinked to get used to them.

He climbed onto the bed from the opposite end. Marcella nearly fell when she realized he had undressed completely. Pausing, he knelt up and let her look at him. Strong thighs led to his thick cock, which jutted from a nest of light brown curls. She followed the sprinkling of hair up his abdomen to his navel. Broad shoulders topped his magnificent chest.

Fever glittered from his eyes, and uncharacteristic desperation strangled his voice. "Say you want this, Marcella."

She rushed to assure him. "I want this, Master."

"No. Fuck the benefit. Say you want *this*."

More than anything in the world. Wordlessly, she nodded.

He growled and hauled her roughly against him. Her tender breasts flattened against the unyielding hardness of his chest. She thought he might kiss her. His hot, panting breaths heated her lips and fanned her chin.

Hooking a finger under the elastic holding her hair back from her face, he jerked it away. Tears pricked behind her eyes from the few places where it yanked a little too hard. She blinked them away, keeping her attention focused on Sean. She'd never seen him like this before.

He fisted his hand in her hair and pulled her down to the mattress. Anticipating Gretchen, Marcella had made it up with a fresh covering. A plastic pad below the sheet crackled under her weight. It crackled even more when he fell on top of her and ground his hips into hers. Finally he caught her mouth with his and swept his tongue inside.

Acting on instinct, she lifted her hands to his shoulders. She ran them over his skin, seeking to soothe his wildness with her submission. He nudged her knee with his own. She spread her legs wide and moaned as he settled his cock against her pussy.

He lifted slightly and slid his hand between them. The crown of his cock paused at her entrance. He captured her gaze and tightened the hand fisting her hair. "One last time, Marcella. Tell me you want this."

Finally she understood. He needed to know she yielded to him, not to the faceless specter of the audience that would be watching them. Reaching up, she caressed his cheek with a trembling hand. "I want this, Sean. I want you."

One thrust and he buried his shaft to the hilt. Marcella's mouth dropped open at the sudden fullness that had nothing in common with the glass dildo. Sean's warmth stretched and filled her pussy.

"Perfect. God, Cella you fit me so perfectly." He shifted to balance his weight on his elbows. "Wrap your legs around me, honey. I don't plan to go slow."

And he didn't. Marcella clung to him as he pumped his hips at an impossible pace. An inferno began low in her abdomen, fed by each of his frantic thrusts. Her arousal skyrocketed, and she felt the small pulses in her pussy that signaled an orgasm was near. "Sean, please let me come."

He neither paused nor slowed his actions. Sweat glistened on his shoulders and made it difficult for her to keep her legs clasped around him. "No."

She breathed. She thought about baseball. Images of tight asses in white pants came to mind, so that didn't help. Sean thrust harder and faster. His lips parted, and his eyelids fell to half-mast. This image of her master burned into her brain, and she realized her mistake. "Master, please let me come."

"No."

As much as she wanted to come, she wanted to please her master more. If he denied her, then she would stave it off. She gathered her determination and locked eyes with him. An unspoken challenge passed in the air. His eyes sparkled, and his lips stretched in a slow, sensual smile.

He slowed the pace of his thrusts.

Marcella's control faltered. A quick, hard fuck gave her a quick, hard orgasm. It was easier to gain and easier to keep at bay. This slow, measured style robbed her of any strategy for maintaining control.

The inferno altered and became a slow burn. It slipped under her defenses. Her insides melted, and her consciousness became fluid. She clutched frantically at his shoulders. Climax pressed urgently, a nonspecific feeling gathering force and searching for a focal point. Trying to escape it, she writhed. "Please, Master. Oh please let me come."

Leaning closer, he brushed a kiss across her lips. "Yes, my Cella. Come for me."

Chapter Three

Sean watched the woman beneath him undulate and arch. Her tight cunt contracted around his dick, pulsing hard and fast. The sight of the woman he'd wanted for so long climaxing in his arms sent him over the edge. He thrust twice more before he exploded.

He collapsed onto her chest and forced himself to roll to the side. Though he wanted to stay on top of her warm body, he didn't want to crush her. Marcella was proving to be an amazingly responsive submissive. Now that he'd figured out she couldn't resist finesse, it was only a matter of time before she would admit she couldn't live without belonging to him. After all, finesse was his strong suit.

She burrowed closer. He hooked his leg behind her knee to help her move as near as she could. He wanted her to say something, to let him know if he'd gone too far or not far enough. He'd certainly planned to play with her for a lot longer before he fucked her.

Before demons of self-doubt could haunt him too badly, her stomach grumbled.

"Sorry, Master." She mumbled the apology into his shoulder.

He'd tangled a hand in her hair earlier, and he didn't release his hold now. He pulled to tilt her face up. "Don't apologize for being hungry, my sweet slave. I'll arrange for lunch to be brought down here, and then I'll clean you up." Reluctantly, he released his hold on her and disentangled their limbs. "Don't move."

He used the house phone located next to the light switch to order lunch. The time on the tiny digital display showed it to be just past one. He had the rest of the day to spend with his new submissive.

He glanced toward the bed to check on Marcella. She lay where he'd left her and watched him with unasked questions in her eyes. A minute later, as he ran the water in the bathroom faucet, waiting for it to warm up, he told himself he hadn't fled to escape her questions.

Questions meant uncertainty. Uncertainty meant she played the game. This afternoon meant nothing more than practice to her. The bright lights pointed at the bed had always brought him joy. They allowed a slave to hide nothing. Pointed at Marcella, they allowed him to confirm what he already knew. Marcella revealed only what she wanted known. Even though he'd made her admit to wanting him, he couldn't be sure of anything until he called a halt to their activities and actually talked to her about it.

He didn't want to do that just yet, not if it meant finding out she only intended this as a temporary thing. Returning to the bed, he found that she'd drawn her knees up and wrapped her arms around them. Her eyelids fluttered open.

"Cold?"

"No, just—"

"Lie on your back."

She complied. He checked her nipples to see how they fared. Swollen and red with the sex flush that hadn't faded, they beckoned. He wanted to suck them into his mouth, but he refrained. She flinched when he brushed the pad of his finger over one.

He might have been worried that he'd hurt her too much, but her breath caught and her hips flexed. With a grin, he used the warm, wet cloth he'd brought from the bathroom to clean between her legs.

"I'm going to whip you after lunch. I'll give you this one choice. Would you like to be tied to my cross, or would you like to be tied to the spanking bench?" Personally Sean preferred the bench. It had a place for her torso to rest while her arms and legs were bound out of the way. It forced her to bend over the table, exposing her cunt and making it more accessible. He didn't care to whip a submissive for the sake of whipping.

The cross, while it kept her legs apart, didn't allow enough access. He wanted to find the rhythm and pressure she found arousing so he could make her come. She had already disclosed her dislike of pain. He had wanted to kiss her tenderly when she'd told him she could come for him. She didn't care to be whipped with a heavy hand, but she would try for him. Her dedication to pleasing him made him want to do anything to see her pampered and pleased.

"Master, you have a two o'clock appointment with Fuller, and I have to call the caterer."

He turned her over and smacked her ass three times, but not too hard. "Answer the question, slave."

When he released her to roll back, her brown eyes held a hint of smoke. "I wish to please you, Master. I would like to experience the spanking bench, but if it pleases you to use the cross, then I will submit there." A hint of defiance hid just beneath the surface of her statement. He and Fuller were planning their next big project. She wasn't going to let him miss his meeting.

Two sharp knocks at the door arrested the sarcastic retort that came to mind at her pretty speech. As he crossed the room to retrieve the cart his chef's assistant would have left in the hall, he silently breathed a sigh of thanks for the intervention. Accustomed to Marcella's sharp-tongued sense of humor, he didn't believe her submission. He would need to work on that.

With the changed circumstances, he needed to adjust his thinking. If he didn't trust her to be honest, how could he expect her to trust him? He returned to find her standing near the foot of the bed. Her demure posture and downcast gaze shimmered with grace. She had something to say. When Marcella had something to say, she didn't mince words, not with him.

He tensed. "What is it, slave?"

She glanced up, startled perhaps by his terse tone. "Master, may I have a few minutes alone in the bathroom?"

"Yes, of course." When she moved safely out of sight, he let his shoulders relax.

By the time she returned, he had arranged a chair next to the cart of food. Since he didn't usually eat in the dungeon, he didn't keep a dining table down there. They would improvise by using the cart.

He hadn't dressed. He sat in the chair naked. She came to kneel at his side. Head down, hands tucked demurely behind her back, knees spread, posture perfect. With his hungry gaze, he feasted on the beautiful sight in front of him.

Finally he patted his thigh. "Come sit on my lap, pretty slave. You'll feed us both."

Perhaps somewhere in the dom handbook, it stated he should be the one doing the feeding, controlling every bit of food that passed her lips, but Sean didn't operate that way. He'd actually masturbated to fantasies of Marcella feeding him. Her long, tapered fingers with that delicate French manicure would touch his lips and his tongue as she placed the food in his mouth.

"Use your fingers only."

She settled on his lap, her bare bottom pressing heat against his thigh. "Yes, Master."

He held her close with one arm circling her back. He crossed his other arm over her legs and rested it on her thigh. Her breasts swayed and jiggled as she cut the turkey sandwich into bite-size pieces. Next time he would have to request finger foods. The clamp had colored the deep rose of her nipple red. It called to him. He rubbed the pad of his thumb over the tip. She twitched.

"Does it hurt?"

"A little, Master. But it feels good too."

He palmed her breast as she shifted, turning to him with a small square of food between her fingers. "Feed yourself first. I love watching you eat."

She paused. Her eyes widened the tiniest bit, but hunger trumped surprise. The square disappeared into her mouth. She grabbed another and offered it to him. He made sure to catch her fingertips, sucking them lightly as he accepted the food. Her eyes widened even more, and the fresh scent of her musky arousal reached his nose.

They ate in silence, feeding more than their stomachs. By the time they'd cleared the plate of food, Sean's erection rested against Marcella's leg and her juices wet his thigh.

"Straddle me."

He took his cock in hand as she stood and arranged her legs on either side of the chair. She gripped his shoulders for balance, and he held her hips because if he didn't, he would go insane. Wordlessly she eased that velvet warmth down his cock.

"Ride, Cella. We don't have much time, and I want to see you come."

"Yes, Master."

She rose up and slammed down. Shocks of pleasure gathered at the base of his spine and tingled outward. He concentrated on the sensuous slide of her skin over his, reveling in all the ways her scent and touch intoxicated him. She gyrated and undulated, racing her way to orgasm and taking him with her. Her head fell back, and her eyes closed. Sean watched, fascinated by his beautiful slave, and he fell completely in love. Maybe he'd been in love with her all along, but this was the first time he allowed himself the freedom to bask in it. The stakes rose. Not only did he need her to admit she couldn't live without him, he needed to know she felt the same way about him.

Those thoughts shoved to the back burner when her sheath clamped around him. White edged his vision, and he fought the urge to climax. He pressed his palms into her breasts, flattening the tissue. Her body jerked, and she pushed against him, flattening them even more. He knew her sensitized, abused nipples had to ache, and he marveled at her enjoyment of this sweet pain. She might not like the whip, but he was learning what other kinds of pain she liked. He filed this knowledge away as her rhythm faltered.

"Come for me, Cella."

The impending orgasm drawing up his balls pressed him to do something, but he resisted helping her to regain the rhythm. He could have released her breasts to guide her hips, but he wanted to know how much control she wielded over her pleasure. She drew in a ragged breath and ground against him. The crude gyration pushed her over the edge. Her silky pussy pulsed, creating a vacuum that pulled at his own pleasure. She cried out, and he came with her.

She slumped against his shoulder, and he wrapped his arms around her body, holding her while they both shivered and convulsed with aftershocks. He drew his fingertips up and down her back until she settled into his embrace.

Things had changed between them, irrevocably shifted, and he didn't know the rules of their new relationship. The mild possessiveness he'd always felt toward her grew, crystallizing into something hard and unyielding. He hadn't wanted to use her in the benefit at all, and now he found it more difficult than ever to picture following through with their plan. The idea of sharing something so intimate with spectators left a sick and prickly feeling in his stomach.

However, he had promises to keep, and he could trust her to hold him to his word. Whether he wanted to do the benefit or not, she had committed herself, and she wasn't the kind of woman who went back on her promises. He had to honor that.

Didn't he?

Shaking away that thought, he kissed the top of her head. "Well done, my beautiful slave. Now go get dressed. I might like to see you naked, but I want it to be for my eyes only. Wear a skirt that stops above your knees. No underwear."

She started at his pronouncement, and he used a kiss to silence her before she could utter a word. If he tried to rationalize his declaration, she would realize the reasons for his reticence, and she would put an end to their blissful day. If he betrayed her trust by refusing to use her, he would lose her completely. Somehow he had to find the courage to push aside his desires and do the right thing.

Swiping the robe from where it had fallen on the floor, he grunted. He held the robe open. After she threaded her arms through the appropriate holes, he tied the sash.

"Fuller will likely stay for dinner. Whether he does or not, you will sit on my lap and feed me as you did this afternoon. Do you understand?"

Her eyes widened, and he knew visions of the way she had ridden him afterward occupied her thoughts. "Do you want me to call you 'Master' or 'Sean' while he's here?"

A grin split his face so wide it ached. The way she said his name had changed, subtly altered to reflect his new role in her life. "It doesn't matter which you use when we're not in this dungeon." He would use her choice of address to gauge her mood and her receptiveness. "Now go get cleaned up. I'll expect you to sit in on the meeting. I need my assistant with me."

Really he didn't. He just wanted her close to him.

She bowed her head, inclining it as a show of deference. "Yes, Sean. I'll be ready."

* * *

Marcella shivered as the lace on her pink bra brushed against her swollen nipples. He'd left the clamps on so long, they were going to be sore for at least a day. They'd heal just in time for the performance. A note of panic thumped deep in her chest. She didn't want to be put on display, but if that was the only way she could be with Sean, then she would do it. At least he'd promised to blindfold her. She hoped to God she didn't disappoint him.

She tugged a shirt over her head. The soft fibers of the fabric caressed her shoulders and chest as the shirt fell into place. After her session with Sean, every nerve in her body stood at attention, overreacting to the slightest stimulation. Glancing in the mirror, she smiled. Light pink suited her. The low-cut neckline plunged so far it nearly revealed the place between her breasts where her bra came together.

Would wearing a bra earn a punishment? She frowned. He hadn't said anything about it one way or the other. Beneath her skirt, which fell to midthigh, she wore nothing. Those had been his only instructions.

She ran a brush through her hair and slipped on a pair of sandals. Sean's reasons for wanting her at the meeting remained a mystery. He didn't need her there. Though the meeting had been a scheduled event, Fuller was Sean's best friend. The two of them were apt to spend far more time discussing matters not related to business than planning their new movie project.

Voices in the foyer drew her notice as soon as she came down the stairs. Fuller Dunne's deep baritone had always garnered attention. A man with a voice that deep was extremely rare. Marcella preferred the pitch of Sean's voice, which wasn't so deep that it reduced to a rumble when he lowered his volume.

Fuller had made a career out of his unique voice. In addition to acting, producing, and directing, he enjoyed the benefits of a lucrative contract as a paid spokesperson for a prominent insurance company.

The man towered over Sean by a few inches. He wore jeans and a startling pink button-down shirt.

Friendly blue eyes sparkled from beneath blond bangs that fell over his forehead, and a smile split his face when he caught sight of Marcella.

"Marcella! This is a treat. I almost never get to see you." He held out his hand as if he wanted to shake, but Marcella knew his game. Once he had her hand, he would pull her close for a hearty embrace.

She opened her arms and slipped into his welcoming hug. "It's good to see you, Fuller. How was New York?"

"Fabulous, but it's good to be home." He pressed a kiss to her cheek and released her.

The strange expression on his face as he stepped back made Marcella glance over her shoulder at Sean, who was frowning. She started, unsure of what had caused him to react that way. Fuller had hugged her in greeting from the first time they'd met. He often flirted with her as well. She didn't take it personally. Fuller flirted with everyone.

"Marcella, go make your phone calls and then meet us in the living room." Sean's tight voice matched the way he pressed his lips together. He turned and headed across the foyer. "And lose the shoes."

She glanced down at her strappy sandals and up at Fuller. He shrugged and spread his hands. "Has he been in a bad mood all day?"

Marcella shook her head. For a man who'd enjoyed three orgasms, he sure didn't seem to feel the calm relaxation that was supposed to follow.

"Well, we'll see if I can find out what crawled up his butt before you finish with your calls." He patted her on the shoulder and brushed past to follow Sean.

By the time she had confirmed the caterer, straightened out a problem with the menu, and put out fires with the florist and the cleaning service, nearly an hour had passed. She entered the living room on silent, bare feet.

The living room had been done by a decorator whose tastes ran opposite to Marcella's. White and cream furniture filled the room. Cream-colored, textured wallpaper coated the walls. The crown molding and all the wood furniture in the room had been painted white. Marcella thought it looked like an angel had exploded and left its mark all over the place, and not in a good way. This room did not suit Sean at all.

He sat on the center cushion of a large, deep sofa. When he saw Marcella, he scooted back and slung his arm over the top of the back cushion. She settled next to him in the place he'd so casually indicated.

She wanted to curl her feet under her bottom, but she sank down too deeply into the cushion to make that comfortable. Sean took her laptop and put it on the white, painted table in front of them. She opened her notebook and clicked her pen.

Glancing up, she spied Fuller sprawled in an oversize armchair. The damn thing nearly swallowed up the big man, yet he looked comfortable. He threw an amused grin in her direction. When Sean lifted her feet and turned her so that they lay in his lap, Fuller burst out laughing.

"Well, that explains a lot. It took you long enough."

Marcella fought a blush. She hadn't expected Sean to do anything that would indicate they had done a scene—not yet, anyway. "Sorry. There were a few issues with the benefit I had to see to."

"He didn't mean you." Sean rubbed his palm over the top of her foot. All tension left his shoulders. He lifted his gaze to meet hers. "Is there anything I need to do?"

She shook her head and flashed a smile. "You just show up and do your thing. I'll handle the rest. That's why you have me."

His eyes narrowed, but he didn't reply. She had made similar comments many times. Before, he had at least smiled in response. Now he looked away. "Fuller has an idea for spending more of my money. I want you to listen and take notes."

His cool response to her smile left her feeling a little uncertain. Under other circumstances, she might have said something about how Fuller always made Sean's money back tenfold, but now she said nothing.

At Sean's nod, Fuller explained the plot of his latest idea. Despite Marcella's reluctance to banter with either of them, she felt herself opening up in the face of Fuller's obvious passion. The relationship between the hero and heroine of the screenplay sounded like it would make for an entertaining, passionate, and sometimes funny action-romance. Soon she found herself commenting on his ideas and offering alternatives.

Conversation flowed and time flew. Sean's hands moved constantly over her feet and calves. He caressed up as high as her knee. Marcella liked the possessiveness of his actions. Fuller's eyes followed the movement every now and again, but he didn't say anything.

When the chef's assistant came in to announce dinner, Marcella's gaze flew to the white clock on the white mantelpiece. It chimed six as she looked at it.

Fuller pushed to his feet. He stretched and yawned. "I think it's time for me to hit the road."

Sean patted her ankle, a dismissive gesture. Marcella drew her legs back and put her feet on the ground. She tried to stand, but her muscles were too relaxed to respond immediately. Closing her notebook and stacking it on her laptop bought her some time.

"Actually, I'd like you to stay. If you haven't already figured it out, Marcella has agreed to be my sub for the benefit. Only she's never done anything in front of an audience."

Fuller's brow, two shades darker than his fair hair, rose. "You want me to watch?"

Marcella started. Good thing she hadn't forced herself onto her wobbly legs earlier. This request would have made her knees buckle. Not once had one of her fantasies involved Fuller. To be fair, he would be at the benefit, watching with the rest of them. But then he would be a face in the crowd, not the lone observer. She stared up at Sean. Her jaw dropped open, useless.

Fuller dropped his gaze to meet Marcella's. She always liked that he treated her as a person and not as a servant. He had an easy manner with everyone. It explained at least some of the reasons for his popularity among fans. "Marcella? Are you okay with this?"

If she couldn't perform in front of him in a private setting, how did she expect to not disappoint Sean in front of a hundred spectators? She swallowed her trepidation. "It's probably a good idea. I'd hate to get out in front of all those people and have a panic attack or have to use my safe word."

Fuller stared at her for the longest time. At last he turned his attention back to Sean. "You got pissy when I hugged her at the door, and you spent all the time she was working staring over your shoulder at the foyer, looking for her. Do you really think *you* can do this?"

Sean stiffened. "If you don't want to help, then just say you don't want to help."

"Help." Fuller played the word like a question or a heavy concept worthy of great consideration. He came around the table and held his hands out to Marcella. She placed her hands in his, and he tugged her to standing. True to form, once she stood, he kept hold of her hands. "Are you asking me to watch or to help? Those are two very different requests."

Sean didn't answer, and Marcella bit her lip. She knew what he was thinking. "In the second round, I have to orgasm from being whipped. I haven't done that in a long time. I think Sean might need your assistance, even if you're only there to give advice."

He massaged his jaw with one hand and looked at Sean. When he dropped her other hand, Marcella felt her confidence fade. Perhaps Sean found her attractive, but Fuller had his pick of beautiful women. His flirting had always been harmless and innocent. It wasn't like either of them expected Fuller to have sex with her. Perhaps this request crossed the boundaries of their friendship.

Finally he broke the tense silence. "What's your safe word?"

"Oasis."

Fuller's hand dropped from his chin, and both brows disappeared under his floppy bangs. His surprised expression morphed into an easy smile. "Oasis? Then by all means, let me help out."

Did Fuller know about Oasis? Would he tell Sean about her subterfuge, tell him he was the fulfillment of her fantasy? Marcella glanced at Sean, a quick movement to check out his reaction to Fuller's abrupt commitment to helping. His brows knit in momentary confusion, but then they straightened out. He slipped his arm around Marcella's waist and guided her toward the door on the far side of the room that led to the dining room.

"Let's eat first. I can't have my slave passing out too early in the game."

Once inside the dining room, Sean pulled a chair out for Marcella. This wasn't something new. He always opened doors and seated her first, even when they ate in informal settings. She glanced up at him, an unasked question in her eyes.

He leaned close. His breath tickled her cheek. "Don't worry, slave. You'll make it to my lap by the dessert course."

The way his tongue lingered over the word *dessert* caused a shiver to run from Marcella's breasts to her pussy. She sat where he indicated and spread her cloth napkin over her lap.

Sean took the seat next to her, and Fuller settled in across the table. The long table could easily accommodate twelve, yet they managed an intimate arrangement. The door to the kitchen opened, and Gabriella, the chef's assistant, brought steaming plates to them. Sean wasn't big on soups or salads, except for lunch, so they generally only ate two-course meals. This suited Marcella just fine. Although Sean's personal chef had a habit of making meals saturated with butter and fat, over the course of the past year, Marcella had advocated for healthier meal choices.

The savory smell of peanuts assaulted her nose as Gabriella, a woman in her sixties who enjoyed bossing Sean around, set the plate on the table. Marcella's shoulders slumped at the chicken satay with a spicy peanut sauce. There were a handful of dishes she couldn't resist, and this was one of them. Living with Sean meant she would never have that chic, thin body every other woman around him seemed to have. Visions of how Gretchen would look naked danced in front of her eyes, taunting her with a Hollywood ideal she could never achieve.

Gabriella winked at Marcella. "We used reduced-fat peanut butter and light coconut milk. Three hundred calories, tops."

Sean wrinkled his nose at her. "You lose any more weight, I'm going to tie you to that chair and force you to eat a healthy amount of food."

Heat crept up her neck. She hadn't known he'd noticed her recent diet. "I have five pounds left to lose."

Gabriella rolled her eyes and left the room. Fuller regarded her with an amused quirk to his lips.

Sean growled and slung his arm over the back of her chair, leaning so close the electricity of his body jumped the gap to set excitement racing along her nerve endings. "I've seen you naked. You can't spare five pounds."

The blush deepened. She focused on the grains of rice and resisted the urge to fan her face. Her personal weight goals were really none of his business. "Sean, don't—"

"Slave."

One word, a warning and a reminder. She couldn't argue with him today, tomorrow, or the day after. "Yes, Master?"

"Eat all the food on your plate, or you will be punished."

Gabriella had given her a reasonable portion. Marcella nodded. "Yes, Master."

Fuller chuckled as he loaded another bite onto his fork. "Dessert should be fun."

Sean dropped his overbearing pose, and they settled into the easy rhythm of conversation they had enjoyed all afternoon. A little later, Gabriella cleared away their empty plates and brought German chocolate cake for dessert.

"Thanks, Gabby." Sean sank his fork into the soft, moist cake. "Are you guys taking off for the evening?"

"Yep." Gabriella shot a sly smile in Marcella's direction, making her wonder how much the chef's assistant knew about what had happened in the dungeon earlier. "Make sure those plates get to the sink, or there will be hell to pay in the morning."

Marcella twisted her napkin in her hands, trying to resist the pull of the cake. It wasn't a large slice, but she had been doing so well following the plan her nutritionist had recommended. She was proud of the progress she'd made so far, and her stomach was pleasantly full. At last she pushed her plate aside.

"Eat."

"I ate dinner, Sean. I'm full."

He narrowed his eyes at her, but he didn't pursue the topic.

Fuller leaned across the table and took her plate. German chocolate cake was his favorite dish. "You know, Sean, it occurs to me that you're asking Marcella to do two things she's never done before at the same time. That's not exactly playing fair. Don't get me wrong; sometimes subs need for things to not be fair. I'm just urging you to consider the scope of what you're asking."

Sean sat back, his mouth puckered in a frown. Marcella worried that Fuller's point would make Sean decide he couldn't use her at the benefit. The idea of someone—anyone—taking her place as Sean's submissive made the satay churn in her stomach.

He pushed his chair back, sliding it smoothly across the wood floor. Pointing to the place on the floor between him and the table, he snapped his fingers. "Cella, stand here and face me."

The tone of the order commanded a place deep inside her soul. It amazed her how quickly she could transition from thinking of him as Sean to thinking of him as her master. "Yes, Master."

He fingered the delicate lace edging the hem of her light pink shirt. A small smile played around the corners of his mouth. "Remove your shirt."

Shocked, she failed to react. She had assumed he wouldn't ask her to undress until they were in the dungeon. He had promised her a blindfold. She hazarded a quick glance back at Fuller. He'd seen her in a string bikini. Her bra covered more of her flesh than her bikini top did.

And within the hour, he would see her completely naked. He would see her splayed out. He would watch her being whipped, and he would witness her orgasm if she managed to have one under those conditions.

Sean didn't hurry her, and he didn't seem to grow impatient with her hesitancy. He watched her silently, with a steady gaze that held an expectation and a promise. As her master, he would keep her physically and emotionally safe. He would push her boundaries. He had asked for her trust. She couldn't take that back now, not when he'd been every bit the master she'd wanted.

Gripping the lace between her fingers, she lifted the shirt over her head.

"Fold it and put it on your chair."

When she had done that, she stood before him wearing only a bra and a short skirt that would flare out to show everything if she twirled in a fast circle.

His gaze roamed her body, an electric caress that prickled every inch of her skin. Desire flared green in his eyes, and the juices between her legs thickened in anticipation.

"Take off your bra and put it with your shirt."

Reaching behind her, she unhooked the bra. As it dropped away from her breasts, it took the body heat trapped there with it. Her nipples tightened and pebbled. They tingled as if he'd actually touched her.

A ball of tension pinged through her body and left trails of unfulfilled expectation behind. She waited an impossibly long time for him to do anything other than study her nakedness.

Finally he pointed to her skirt. "Slide it down your legs slowly. Bend at your waist, and don't let it drop from your control."

The dining room table came up to a height just below the bottom of her ass cheeks. Fuller would get an eyeful of not only her ass, but of her slit as she bent over. The day after tomorrow, a hundred people would see the same thing. Her juices flowed a little faster, and she knew without looking that her bare pussy glistened with moisture.

She hooked her thumbs under the elastic waist and pushed the skirt down over her hips. By sheer dint of will, she didn't hesitate when it came to the point where Fuller would see her ass. She concentrated on watching Sean lick his lips as he caught sight of her slit. Bending as he'd dictated meant Sean's view would be obstructed while Fuller still enjoyed a show. She told herself that the heat flaming her face had everything to do with the reverse flow of blood as she bent over and nothing to do with the shyness she felt.

At last she folded her skirt and placed it on top of her bra. With her hands at her sides, she stood in front of Sean, once again waiting for his next order.

He didn't make her wait long. Rising to his feet, he snaked one hand around her waist and used the other to grip the back of her neck. His lips pressed hard, demanding entrance. The soft steel of his insistence made her knees quake as the need to submit to this man she loved spread through her core. She opened, and he swept his tongue into her mouth. She wanted to grab his arms or wrap her arms around his neck, but she knew better than to move without permission.

She moaned and melted against him, tilting her head to help him achieve a better angle. He deepened the kiss. Fireworks, warm and tingly, exploded near her heart. When he ended the kiss and stepped away, she fought the urge to grab him back.

With his hands holding her firmly on her waist, he lifted her onto the tabletop.

"Lie back, my slave."

Marcella eased herself back until she lay across the table. The cool wood sent a slight chill through her body. She chanced a quick peek at Fuller, to find him grinning down at her. He sat in his chair, less than a foot from the top of her head, enjoying the last few bites of her cake.

"Blindfold her."

Fuller set his cake out of the way and folded his cloth napkin carefully. She lifted her head so he could ease it underneath. The world went dark as the soft linen molded to her contours.

He tied it on the side of her head so the knot wouldn't cause discomfort. His breath sounded near her ear. "Don't worry. I didn't use it at dinner. A fortuitous circumstance."

"Thank you." Marcella wanted to ask if they'd planned this. Even though it looked like a spur-of-the-moment thing, Fuller was an excellent actor. This could have been staged, but she couldn't think of a reason why they would feel it necessary.

"Fold your hands behind your neck, Cella."

Sean's warm hands caressed her thighs, a small weight of promise that made her swelling nether lips throb with remembered heat. She placed her hands under her neck and made a mental note about how much he seemed to enjoy this position. Perhaps when this fantasy ended, she could use this position in a casual manner to remind him of the incredible sex they'd shared.

He eased her thighs apart and slid her toward him to hang a little off the edge of the table. "Good girl. Remind Fuller and me of your safe word."

"Oasis."

She couldn't hear the sound of snickering, but she swore the word made Fuller laugh. The future definitely held a private conversation with his name on it. She wondered about his association with the wish-fulfillment service. Had he used it? She hoped to God this wasn't his fantasy. While she liked Fuller, she wasn't comfortable with the idea of teasing him or turning him on, not in an intimate setting like this. As a one-man woman, she wanted Sean and nobody else.

Hot lips seared a path along her inner thigh. She shivered at the juxtaposition of the cool wood below her and the heat Sean generated.

He lifted his lips, but he retained his grip just above her knees. "Are you okay, Marcella? Too cold?"

Her nipples, still sore from the extended use of clamps earlier, had shriveled to such tight peaks that they throbbed painfully. While her skin might be a little chilled, she enjoyed the sensation because she knew once he whipped her, the heat would make her long for this coolness. "I'm fine, Master."

Sean eased her legs farther apart, opening her to him completely. Wet fire seared her slit. He licked long trails and short flicks, unhurried strokes that casually explored every fold of her pussy. His tongue teased around her clit and pressed it flat. The light touches triggered an avalanche of heat as cream rushed to her pussy.

She moaned, a low sound that broke the silence to plead for something more. Teeth, lips, and fingers would all be welcome. This slow foray would drive her insane before long. If he increased his pace or his pressure, she could counteract the urgency with breathing and reminders to please her master.

But this seduction by degrees would drive her over the edge whether or not she wanted to go. It would rob her of every ounce of control. She didn't have the skills to survive this kind of onslaught. She breathed deeply and cautioned herself to be patient. No man could or would keep this up for very long. Even men who professed to love oral sex never spent too much time worshipping a woman's pussy. Sean might be an exceptional man, but he was still a man.

Minutes passed. Heat built, a measured inferno that lacked friction and violence. Her thighs shook, and the tremors spread through her body. He seemed singularly focused on enjoying her texture and flavor. The soft moans vibrating from him every now and again attested to exactly how lost he had become between her legs. She wanted to thrust against his mouth, but she knew it would only prolong the torture. Had she earned a punishment she'd forgotten about? He'd been very clear about administering her punishment earlier.

Behind her neck, she dug her fingers into her skin as she struggled to stay still. Oh, why hadn't he tied her down?

A whimper escaped, and a moan followed. She lost the battle and thrust against his face. "Master, please."

He bit her clit. Her pelvis tilted, jerking away from his mouth, but he held her down with a firm grip on each thigh. She went nowhere, and he didn't ease the pressure of his bite.

"I'm sorry, Master. Please, oh please. I'm so sorry."

The pressure eased, indicating he'd accepted her apology. He closed his lips around her tender clit and sucked away the pain. He eased two fingers into her waiting pussy and finger fucked her cunt as gently as he sucked her clit.

Tears escaped the corners of her eyes and were swallowed by the blindfold. How dare he be so gentle with her? She'd craved this kind of treatment from a dom, but she'd never thought it would happen. For some reason, dominant behavior and sadism seemed to go hand in hand with every dom she'd ever met. Though she'd fantasized about Sean and how perfect they seemed for one another, she had never thought he would turn out to be everything she wanted in a man.

Suddenly the solidity of her emotional foundation fell away, and she faced the edge of the cliff far sooner than she thought possible. Her panted breaths took on more and more volume as she struggled to stave off her orgasm. "Oh fuck. Master, please let me come."

He didn't answer. Her body shook with effort and emotion. The pleas falling from her lips came faster and louder, each cry more desperate than the last.

At last, at long last, he lifted his mouth away, releasing her for a brief second, but he didn't stop the slow thrust of his fingers. "Come, my slave. Scream it out for me."

Deep pulses began in her pussy the moment he gave the order. When he resumed sucking her clit, the mad rush of pleasure only increased. The world shook and screamed down around her taut body. She arched from the table, and the blindfold no longer mattered. Nothing mattered except Sean and the way he mastered her body and soul. Reality splintered as she ceded control of her pleasure to her master.

When she came down, she found herself enclosed in Sean's arms. He had tucked a blanket around her back. It curved around her hips and fell over her legs. Her cheek rested on his shoulder, and his hand traced reassuring paths up and down her arm.

She opened her eyes. Someone had removed the blindfold, but she had no idea when that had happened. Sean smiled down at her.

"Thank you, Master."

He pressed a kiss to her forehead. "You performed beautifully, Marcella."

She hazarded a glance around the dining room. Fuller and all the dessert plates were gone. "Did Fuller leave?" Heat crept up her neck as she asked the question. Really she wanted to know whether or not she would be able to face him now that he had seen something she had shared with very few people.

"He's giving us some time for aftercare. He's waiting downstairs."

The last vestiges of her orgasmic fog lifted. Though she had aced this part of the test, she knew she wasn't out of the woods. Even if things weren't weird now when she saw Fuller again, submitting to her master in front of one person wasn't the same as submitting in front of a room full of people.

And the whip still awaited her.

Chapter Four

The darkness brought by the blindfold sharpened her awareness of sounds and smells. The faded scent of peanut sauce vanished by degrees the farther she moved away from the kitchen and dining areas. The leather of the restraints Sean had used to bind her wrists behind her back creaked as she tried to adjust the position of her hands.

Sweat and musk colored Sean's normally clean scent. The familiar aroma quieted the butterflies in her stomach. Whether freshly showered or slick from time spent doing physical activity, his unique scent never failed to make her feel safe and comfortable.

The density of the air increased as she descended the stairs that led to the dungeon. She didn't know if her perception was colored by trepidation or if the air conditioning just didn't circulate efficiently on the lower level. Being naked, she didn't mind the slight increase in temperature brought by the higher humidity.

Through it all, Sean never left her side. He maintained his position behind her and a little to the left, his hand always somewhere on her body, his presence and innate strength lending support and courage. He wrapped his hand around her arm on the stairs to keep her from stumbling. His fingers tickled the small of her back as he guided her down various hallways.

Now he rested a hand on her shoulder. "Stop here."

Strands of her bangs slid from beneath the blindfold. Sean pulled them out so they lay against her forehead. He fiddled with her hair, smoothing caresses along its thick length. Though he seemed to like the sloppy style she'd affected before, he didn't ask her to put it up again. At last he slipped the blindfold, an overlarge sleeping mask, up to her forehead. Immediately she dropped her gaze.

With the curve of his finger, he urged her chin up. "Marcella, look at me."

Apprehension made her need to swallow a few times as she obeyed his order.

"You don't have to do this."

Oh, yes she did. If she didn't, he would find some other submissive to bring to a climax under the power of his whip. No matter what the cost, she would be what he needed. She didn't want to do this, and lying outright to Sean was not acceptable, so she phrased her response carefully. "I want to please you, Master."

His lips pursed, and she sensed a refusal lying just behind them.

"Please let me do this."

Finally his head bobbed in a curt nod. "All right. Let's use the stoplight system. You're familiar with it?"

Bless him, but this wasn't about control. Marcella had no problem ceding complete control to Sean. He had repeatedly earned her trust, and she craved his domination. Giving her this additional level of control made her fall for him even harder. "Yes, Master. Red means stop. Yellow means slow down. Green means everything is okay and keep going. It's also consent."

He smiled, his lips curling with satisfaction while firmness glittered from his hazel eyes. "Give me your color."

She liked how he phrased it as an order. These details meant so much, and they went a long way toward soothing her nerves. "Green, Master." With him, her color would always be green.

"Once we're inside, I won't touch you except to put the restraints on you. Fuller won't touch you either. Nothing but the whip will be allowed to give you any pleasure."

She noted that he didn't sound pleased with that rule. When he'd talked about it before, he had always sounded like he looked forward to the challenge. Now he sounded a little miffed that he had to keep his hands off. She didn't mind if he broke the rules, but she wasn't exactly in a position to tell him that without sounding like she was topping from the bottom. She had too much respect for Sean to do something like that.

"Yes, Master. I understand."

He eased the blindfold back into place and rearranged her bangs to fall over it. A soft breeze followed the soft *click* announcing he'd opened the door to the dungeon. Her nerves tingled with anticipation. Though she didn't exactly look forward to the whipping, she looked forward to being bound and to the sex play that would happen afterward.

With a hand on her back, he guided her to the spanking bench. He moved his hand up her back to grasp her neck, and he pushed her down, bending her over the padded bench. A long bar no wider than a two-by-four supported her torso. The soft pad pressed between her breasts, which dangled down each side to hang free. This modified bench would let her master have access to her breasts and nipples.

A longer, wider beam supported her hips. The padding on the edge was a little thicker than anywhere else, and for that Marcella was grateful. Her hip bones could jab annoying bruises into her skin and rub it raw. The additional padding would prevent that from happening so quickly.

Sean adjusted something near her head before he pressed her face down. Divine softness cushioned the periphery of her face. She hadn't known the table had the same kind of arm as a massage table. Bless him. Now she could breathe, and this would alleviate any tension on her neck. Other tables forced her to turn her head to the side, which stretched her muscles oddly and affected the sting of the whip.

The leather strips binding her wrists slackened and fell away. Sean's strong, warm hands caressed a path up her back and down her arm, moving it into place. Cool leather cuffs encircled her upper arm and her wrist as her master belted her in place. He did the same thing with her other arm, and then he secured cuffs around her thighs just above the knees.

A thicker belt covered her lower back. It would keep her from squirming away from the whip. This was both a safety measure—if she moved and he struck an area he hadn't intended to strike, it could cause internal damage—and another instrument to strip away control.

Being tightly bound called to Marcella's soul in a way nothing else quite could. This, more than anything else, would help her get through this stage of the game. Her pussy already wept, begging for his touch. She took a deep breath and let it out slowly, welcoming the beginnings of subspace.

His breath tickled her ear, and she thought he might kiss her, but then she remembered his rules. No touching.

"You are so fucking beautiful like this, Cella. My Cella. My slave, bound with her legs spread, her ass and her pussy open and waiting to take anything I want to dish out. I could leave you like this and do nothing but stroke your skin. I could clamp your clit and your nipples. I could play with your ass, stretch out your pretty little anus in a hundred different ways. I could lay ice cubes all over your body and watch them melt."

Cream gushed from her pussy at the pictures he painted. Her breaths came harder and faster. Yes, that's what she wanted. She wanted him to use her body, to play with her until she begged him to fuck her. And then she wanted him to take her any way he chose.

He moved away, and soft strips of leather brushed across her shoulders. She couldn't count them, but she suspected he used a cat-o'-nine-tails. A tremor ran through her system. The last time someone had used a cat on her, things had not gone well. While no permanent damage had been done and her lover hadn't been at all abusive, she hadn't been able to orgasm that night.

Concentrating, she tried to figure out what kind of falls the cat had. She detected no beads or flat pieces, and that made her immeasurably relieved. The falls explored her back. They trailed over her ass and down her thighs. After some time passed, she felt her muscles relaxing under this tender torture.

Then the cat disappeared. Before long, the sensation of leather caressing her skin returned, but the number of falls seemed to have multiplied by a hundred. He'd exchanged the cat for a heater. The falls were shorter and more numerous, and the sting it delivered tended to be minimal.

"I'm going to warm you up, slave. I'll tell you when it's going to hurt."

Marcella appreciated the warning. She didn't fear pain or the whip; she just didn't find it erotic.

The first few smacks felt nice. He peppered her back with the softest sensations. The steady staccato beat a rhythm into her muscles that relaxed them. Her entire body turned to liquid.

Fog enshrouded her mind. Just when she thought she might fall asleep, Sean spoke again. "You're warmed up, my Cella. These next ones will sting. Give me your color."

She didn't hesitate to answer, and her speech slurred when it came out. "Green, Master."

Not a second passed before white heat seared a path near her left shoulder blade. That harsh sting had come from the cat. Tears pricked behind her eyelids, and she sucked in her breath.

"Breathe, Marcella."

She almost jumped at the sound of Fuller's voice. She had completely forgotten he was there to witness this torment.

"Breathe, Cella." Sean's command echoed Fuller's recommendation.

She inhaled and exhaled, taking slow, controlled breaths that the next sting of the cat ruined. The tears broke free and fell, but she held back the sobs so he wouldn't know she didn't love this. He rained more blows across her back. She tried to give herself over to the pain, but she couldn't seem to find that place where it turned enjoyable.

The blows halted abruptly. "What color?"

She inhaled deeply and dug even deeper for her resolve. "Green, Master."

Leather sang through the air and smacked sharply on the fleshy part of her ass. This stimulated her a little more, but it didn't do for her what she knew it did for other submissives. Sean expected for this to not only arouse her, but to bring her to orgasm. If she were able to respond to this the way Gretchen did, she would have climaxed by now.

Marcella's imagination had always been active. Perhaps she could arouse herself with sexual thoughts—mental pictures of Sean naked, the remembrance of what it felt like to have him thrusting into her body, claiming it the way only he could. Every time she felt her body responding, though, the sharpness of the falls cut through and jerked her back to the present.

This wasn't working. Sean alternated sides of her body, never striking the same location twice in a row. Her tears returned, this time as much from frustration as from the pain throbbing through her system.

A soft caress whispered across her temple, and fingers dragged light paths through her hair. "This is what you want. This was your wish, wasn't it?" Fuller's voice rumbled almost too low for her to hear. Sean wouldn't be able to make out his words.

She panted to get her breathing under control. The fire blazing across her back and over her ass didn't allow her to speak. She was too afraid her safe word would tumble out.

"You want to be his. You want him to be your master, to control your pleasure. You want to submit to him with every fiber of your being, don't you? He's everything to you. He's your friend, and now he's your lover. He's the other half of your soul. You were made for him, Marcella, and he's waited a long, long time for you. Give this to him, honey. I know you want to."

Fuller, bless his soul, whispered her deepest desires, marking them with an undeniable truth possessed only by the spoken word. Yes, she wanted to give this to Sean. From the bottom of her heart, she wanted to please him, but she was failing miserably. Her tears came faster, and she couldn't stop the loud sobs that racked her body so hard they shook the bench.

The steady *whistle-smack* of the whip halted. A dull *thud* sounded, and the door to the room opened and closed. Chilly air rushed across her flaming back, turning her sobs to shivers. The buckles loosened and fell away, freeing her arms and legs. Strong hands lifted her and wrapped a blanket around her body. They weren't Sean's, and this man carried the scent of Fuller's spicy aftershave, not Sean's comforting aroma.

Marcella lifted the blindfold away to find Fuller's arms around her. She pushed at his chest, but he held fast.

"If I let go, you won't stay standing for long. Let me take you to the bed and set you down."

She nodded and glanced around the room. Through the fog of her misery, she noted Sean's absence. She let Fuller help her sit on the edge of the futon in the porn corner. "He's gone. I failed."

Hot tears tracked down her cheeks. The pain knifing through her chest doused the fire on her skin.

"You didn't fail, Marcella." He urged her closer, and she rested her head on his shoulder. "He failed. He doesn't like to fail at anything. You know this."

She knew. She knew all too well how he reacted to failure. Throw out the entire project and start fresh. Since she was nothing more than a project, she knew he was finished with her. It didn't matter who failed or who was at fault. Their affair was over before it had really begun.

She eased out of Fuller's comforting embrace. She needed to process this, think it through, and grieve for her missed opportunity. "I'd like to be alone, Fuller."

He studied her for a moment, and then he nodded and left the room. The door slammed shut behind him.

* * *

With his back sliding along the cold wall, Sean sank to the floor and scrubbed his hands over his face. He didn't know exactly where he'd gone wrong. The warm-up had definitely relaxed her muscles. He'd almost gone overboard and put her to sleep. He filed the effectiveness of that away for when she was stressed and needed to relax.

When he'd switched to a flogger with longer and fewer falls, he knew it would have more of a sting. The people who would be watching at the benefit would expect the flogging to have a bite to it. Every time it whistled through the air, the tension in the room would rise a little more. While his main job was to bring Marcella to orgasm, the side effect would be the titillation of the audience. He hoped to titillate a little more cash from them in the form of donations to the leukemia research foundation he favored.

But Marcella hadn't responded the way he'd expected. When she'd told him she'd only climaxed once under the sting of a whip, he'd taken that to mean she'd been with doms who lacked finesse. He knew how well she responded to finesse. He had been confident in his ability to show her the wonders of a good flogging.

"What the hell are you doing?"

The door slammed so hard it shook the wall behind Sean's back. He lifted his head to find Fuller standing over him, hands fisted on his hips. Sean dropped his gaze to where his arms rested on his knees.

"Are you just going to sit out here and pout while your sub is bound to a bench in there?" Fuller kicked the toe of his shoe into Sean's bare foot. "You're being a shitty dom right now."

Sean picked at his cuticle. "I've been a shitty dom for the past half hour. She's not even wet. I brought her down here wet."

"She submitted to you."

His answering laugh redefined pathetic. Yes, she had submitted to him. She'd done it on the basis of an affection and respect he'd spent the last year earning. "This wasn't supposed to be a punishment." But that's all it had ended up being. She hadn't enjoyed it at all. She'd tried her hardest. He recognized her effort, and he loved the iron will backing it up. She had done her part, but he'd failed to give her what she needed.

"No, but you did learn how to punish her, didn't you?"

Something Fuller had said penetrated his brain. Sean shot to his feet. "You left her tied up in there?"

Fuller's nose wrinkled with disgust. "No. You left her tied up in there. I untied her, covered her up, and tried to give her some aftercare. She refused me, man. She wants you. She needs you to let her know this isn't the end."

The end. How could this be anything other than the end? He'd never failed with a sub before, and now he'd failed with the one who could destroy him if she left. This morning had gone so well. Later, in the dining room, she had responded to him beautifully. She had warned him that she had trouble climaxing under a whip, but he'd been so confident in his skills that he'd dismissed her worries.

She had responded to both bondage and gentleness before, but she seemed to be immune to them both when he added the whip. This couldn't be anything but a punishment, and she had done nothing to deserve punishment. Quite the opposite. She had done everything she could to please him, including not faking her response to the whip.

Fuller slammed both palms into Sean's shoulders, pushing him back against the wall. "Damn it, Sean. I've watched you pussyfoot around her for a year. She loves you, and you're throwing it all away right now. Get in there and hold her. You have a responsibility to see to her aftercare. Tell her you're proud of her. Apologize for fucking up. Tell her she means something to you, because right now she thinks she doesn't mean shit to you."

As always, his best friend had a point. Marcella hadn't used her safe word, and she hadn't signaled yellow or red. Stopping had been his decision alone. He needed to fortify his courage, get back in there, and find out how badly he'd fucked things up between them.

He nodded at Fuller with finality. Fuller grinned, his smile conveying an encouraging smugness. Sean turned away, knowing his friend would understand if he didn't show him out tonight.

THE DUNGEON'S PADDED walls muted all sounds, but the extreme silence of the room felt unnatural. Marcella sat on the futon, hugging her knees. She rocked back and forth with tiny, unconscious movements. A soft, cream-colored blanket enshrouded her body and helped her curtain of hair hide her face. He swallowed his gut from where it seemed to have lodged in his throat.

She shouldn't have to comfort herself. That's my job.

Wordlessly, he sat next to her and pulled her into his embrace. She stiffened, but she didn't pull away.

"I'm sorry." She sniffled a bit, evidence of tears he couldn't see because her face remained buried.

He smoothed his hand over her hair. "None of that, Cella. I'm sorry. This is my fault. I shouldn't have let it go on for as long as I did. You told me in several ways that flogging didn't do it for you."

"I tried. I wanted—" She broke off in a sob, and her tears came faster.

This situation required firmness and compassion, a combination difficult to achieve. With both hands, he guided her face up until her gaze met his. Because she meant the world to him, he dropped his guard and spoke from the heart. "No, Cella. Don't do this. I'm so proud of you for trying, for doing this to please me. You have no idea how much I cherish the gifts you've given me. Your trust and submission mean the world to me. We're learning each other in a completely new way. Flogging just isn't your thing."

Uncertainty wavered in her eyes and deepened the frown lines marring her trembling chin. "I know I'm not the most desirable type of submissive. I should have been more explicit this morning. I'm sorry, Sean. You deserve better than this."

"Stop." His patience dried up the moment he realized she was giving him an out. "You are the submissive I desire, and that's all I care about."

He silenced anything more she might say with the soft press of his lips. She opened to him, melting into the sweetest kiss he'd ever given. It didn't stir passion, but it soothed them both. She sighed against his lips, and her trembling subsided.

She didn't protest when he unwrapped the blanket, cleaned her up, and tended to the pink skin of her back. Truthfully, he'd barely scratched the surface of what he could do with a whip. He'd spent the time trying to make it look harsher than it felt. In an hour, no evidence of the whipping would be detectable on her back and ass. She wouldn't even have a lingering soreness to remind her of this evening.

When he was satisfied with her physical health, he rewrapped her in the blanket and scooped her up in his arms.

Her eyes, wide with surprise, lifted to his. "Sean, you shouldn't be picking me up like this."

Marcella's height nearly equaled his, and her curvy build lent her an earthy beauty absent from so many of the plastic women with whom he had played in the past. He thought back to her concerns at dinner and threw her a crooked grin.

"Honey, you're not nearly as heavy as you seem to think. Now shut up and call me Master. We're not quite finished with that." He still needed to assure her that he had no intention of giving her up.

She curled closer to him, resting her head on his shoulder. "Yes, Master."

Two flights of stairs later, he proudly dumped her on his bed. The blanket parted and fell away, revealing her luscious curves. "If you need some privacy, now is the time to ask."

She shook her head and swept her gaze down his body. Her lust-filled stare gave him permission to proceed. Some doms liked to demand and take from their submissives, but Sean only liked to take what was offered. It didn't have to be an overt offer, but he did prefer gifts of self to the spoils of conquest. He liked that this new dynamic meant he caught those little looks that revealed the depth of her attraction.

As he turned down the bedcovers, she lifted her body to help. With the sheet and quilt at the foot of the bed, he turned his attention back to situating her according to his desires. Too many nights, he had fallen asleep with the fantasy of her lying next to him. He meant to make the most of every moment of this reality.

She had said earlier that she and her last boyfriend had parted ways because he wanted a full-time sub and she didn't want to be one. Sean needed to know if she meant that, because he wanted her full-time. He needed her full-time. He wanted to know she was at his beck and call. He wanted to wake up every morning and know she belonged to him.

When he'd bought this bed, he had done so with the expectation that his eventual wife would be sharing it. The headboard, made from thick, sturdy wood, featured hidden eyelets to which he could hook bondage gear. Of all the aspects of the D/s lifestyle, the idea of bondage appealed to him far more than any other. Marcella seemed to share the same predilection.

This day had given him so many reasons to hope.

He left her for a moment to get the restraints he wanted. Put away in a nearby chest, they had never been used. This was the first time in over a year that he'd let a woman stay the night in his bed.

As he threaded the nylon straps through the headboard, he hazarded a glance at her face. He had to know she wanted this. Her brown eyes watched him expectantly. Desire clouded her irises a bit, and her chest rose and fell with increasing rapidity.

He wound the straps around her wrists, securing them tight enough so that she had no doubt he restrained her, yet loose enough to let her move. Her hands rested on the pillow next to her head.

"Move around." He wanted her to explore her range of movement so she would know exactly what he had done.

She pulled both arms down, demonstrating a full range of motion. The bindings weren't meant to restrict her movements, especially not while she slept. If a situation arose where she would need to remove the restraints herself, she could take them off and put them back on easily.

Once she finished, he reached back up to the headboard and pulled the slack in the lines until her arms were secured above her head. She tested this arrangement too and found no give.

Her heated gaze found his, and he couldn't resist claiming her mouth in a brief kiss. Then he pulled the covers over her body. "Are you comfortable, Marcella?"

She nodded slowly, legions of unasked questions swimming in her eyes. If they had been down in her office, they would have poured from her mouth. He liked knowing she trusted him to answer everything in his own time and in his own way.

She watched silently while he moved about the room getting ready for bed. He turned off all the lights except one reading lamp. Under the heat of her steady gaze, he stripped away his clothes and climbed into bed. He rolled until his body covered hers.

He could have pushed her legs apart and claimed her with one thrust and no kisses, but he didn't want her that way this time. He needed to show her what she meant to him.

Her soft skin beckoned, and he heeded the call with his hands and his lips. Taking his time, he explored every inch of her body. He caressed her arms and kissed the tender skin on the underside of them. He worshipped her neck and drew soft circles around her breasts until she panted and arched to beg for more.

Sean loved the way she responded to his touch. She had wonderful breasts, just enough to fill his hand. He kneaded them both at the same time. Her nipples swelled to points under his palms. Flattening one hand, he ran it over the stiff peak.

Beneath his body, she shifted and sighed. He caught the musky scent of her arousal, but he resisted easy temptation. She would learn that he liked foreplay almost more than the main event. He could spend hours touching her body, playing with the sensual responses he seemed to effortlessly elicit.

When he finally closed his mouth around her nipple, she arched and moaned. He sucked lightly at first, running his tongue over the taut peak just as he had done with his hand. She whimpered, and he kept up the onslaught. When his own passion pressed too hard, he sucked her flesh into his mouth. The slow buildup and the sharpness of pain made her body jerk and arch.

He smiled at her physical reaction and at the increasingly loud moans that rumbled from deep in her throat. By the time he made it to the juncture where her thighs met her pelvis, she wiggled uncontrollably. He loved that she gave herself over to passion so completely. Bondage was meant to do that, to free her to surrender completely to her passion and to her master.

He didn't give her what she wanted. Instead he continued experimenting with the way she responded to different pressures and sensations. Tomorrow night he would turn her over and worship her back the same way he was worshipping her front tonight.

At last he spread her wide and tasted the sweet cream coating the precious lips between her legs. Her hips thrust forward, begging for a firmer stimulant, but the restraints around her wrists prevented her from going too far. He lapped at her, savoring the power of lavishing this pleasure on the woman he loved. Trailing his fingers and tongue along her pussy, he memorized her textures and folds.

Bringing her to orgasm this way wasn't his intention. Before too long, she writhed, trying to escape him and to stay put. "Master, please. Oh please."

Sean lifted his head and gazed up her body. Soft light reflected from the sweat glistening on her skin. The slight curve of her stomach called to him, as did the twin round globes rising and falling with the rhythm of her panted breaths. Her pillow lifted her neck and head so that she had a clear view of everything he did.

"Please what?"

He blew a stream of cool air over her mons. She quivered, her body trembling with need. "Please let me come, Master."

With the tip of his tongue, he flicked her clit and tasted her passion. Her entire body lifted, strung with the same tension as a bow, and her mouth fell open. Her fingers dug into the top of her pillow. Reveling in the power he had over her, the power she'd gifted to him, trusted him with, he watched her struggle to hold off her orgasm.

At last he spoke the words. "Come for me."

He locked his lips around her clit and sucked hard. She screamed, and her juices exploded. He lapped at them eagerly, smearing her essence all over his mouth. Rocketing up her body, he entered her pussy before it stopped pulsing.

Boneless and liquid, she offered no resistance. Her eyes widened the tiniest bit, and her pussy clenched him harder.

"Clean my face, slave. Use your tongue."

She lifted her head to angle her mouth, and he felt the delicate flutter of her tongue against his skin. He thrust into her, establishing a slow rhythm that he could keep up for hours. The pulsing of her tight channel changed to match his pace, and he claimed her lips in a tender kiss.

"You have permission to climax as many times as you want, Marcella." She had already submitted to him completely, and she had endured an unearned punishment just to please him. He needed to show her that her sacrifices would always be appreciated and rewarded.

He gritted his teeth when she convulsed around him only seconds later. Her already tight channel clamped down and nearly succeeded in milking him. Only his strong desire to give her more kept him from climaxing.

With unerring precision, he pumped his cock into her welcoming pussy. She whimpered and moaned. She begged, mindlessly calling his name and melding her soul with his. The next time she came, she screamed and thrashed and carried him over with her.

He collapsed on top of her, burying his face in her hair, too spent to move. After some time, he jerked awake. The light cast by the reading lamp showed that she had fallen asleep as well. With a supreme effort, he loosened her bindings so that she could move and rolled his body so that he wasn't crushing her. He drifted to sleep with one arm around her waist.

Chapter Five

Marcella woke to the feeling of Sean pushing his cock inside her pussy. In the darkness of the room, she could only make out his shape. She lifted her arms to draw him closer, and the nylon bindings whispered across the silk of the pillow above her head. She realized he had loosened the lead, but he hadn't freed her from the cuffs. Immediately hot juices flowed to her pussy, and she involuntarily clenched around him.

In all the years she'd been active in the lifestyle, she'd never once wanted to wake up bound. Yet the idea of sleeping in restraints next to Sean just made her feel safe, secure, and loved. And it turned her on a lot.

The restraints he used would be easy to undo. She could get up in the morning and take them off by herself. She could release herself right now if she wanted. The restraints didn't keep her bound to this bed. Sean did. His presence, his approval, his affection, and his authority kept her here. The cuffs were only a symbol of his power.

He lifted her legs and hooked her knees over his shoulders, and he pounded into her harder and harder. This quick fuck marked her as his. He had been generous earlier, and now he took what he wanted. She wondered if his permission to come as many times as she wanted still stood.

Heat and pressure built in her core. She gripped his biceps and held on for the ride. "Master, please may I come?"

"Yes." His voice had that growly, half-asleep sound.

He slammed into her one last time. His body went stiff, and his hot semen shot into her pussy, setting off a new round of convulsions. She uttered a pleased sigh and loosened her tight hold on his arms as he released her legs.

Shifting to the side, he collapsed half on the bed and half on top of her body. In moments his even breathing told her he had fallen back asleep. She smiled in the dark, pleased that she was able to be here like this for him. Her mind wandered as she wondered what it would be like to be here with him like this every night.

She thought back over the past year, remembering that he'd never had a woman spend the night. Surely it meant something that she was here in his bed. The way he'd looked at her and the way he'd touched her all hinted at strong feelings. Perhaps Oasis would deliver more than she'd asked for. Maybe they could deliver what she really wanted from Sean.

* * *

When she woke again, the darkness of the room didn't hide the stillness that marked waking up alone. She groped for the bedside light and hoped she didn't knock anything over with the lines of the restraints leading to the headboard. If this were her room, she wouldn't bother with light. She knew the topography well enough to stumble around in the dark.

A notebook lay open on the table under the lamp. She rubbed the bleariness from her eyes and read his note.

Release yourself from the cuffs. I left a robe on the divan for you. Go about your morning as you usually do. I'll drop by your office after my run.

The idea of a typical morning left her a little deflated, especially after the events of the past twenty-four hours. She returned to her suite, showered, and dressed. He hadn't left instructions about what she should wear, but she didn't really expect that. Sean let her manage his life; he had never once tried to manage hers.

She chose pale pink dress pants and a white, low-cut blouse with a pink flower-print design on the lower half. He seemed to prefer her in delicate, overtly feminine outfits. The white pumps she usually wore with it remained in her shoe rack. She went downstairs for breakfast, her feet bare.

He wasn't there.

She checked e-mail while she munched on a bagel and sipped her coffee. If things kept up the pattern of a typical morning, he would breeze into her office in about an hour with his hair still wet from his shower.

After she confirmed everything for the next day, she checked her phone for the string of "to-do" texts Sean always sent during his run. For a physical exercise he did to clear his head, he sure thought up a lot of things that needed to be done during that time. Today was no exception.

Call and see if my dry cleaning is ready. Set up meeting with Fuller for next Monday re: investors. Cancel the benefit. Refund donations.

Marcella struggled to breathe. She felt as if someone had punched her in the stomach or knocked her off a really high wall, and she'd landed flat on her back.

She blinked back useless tears and reminded herself how she had failed the night before. Of course he couldn't use her for the benefit. While maybe she was the right kind of submissive for him, she still wasn't right for the kind of show the audience would demand.

Swallowing her pride, she opened the file with his lists of contacts. Fuller picked up on the third ring.

"Please tell me Sean didn't do anything stupid."

Marcella didn't have it in her to laugh at his greeting. "He wants me to cancel the benefit."

Fuller's deep chuckle came through. "Looks like your plan worked."

She gasped. Not much in her plan had come out as she'd intended. "I don't know what you're talking about."

"Come now. You wouldn't go through all the hassle of using Oasis just to play for a day or two." He didn't sound angry or upset about the benefit, and she knew he understood full well what this meant to Sean.

"I never planned for him to cancel the benefit." And she wouldn't cancel it. She would call Gretchen and make amends. The show had to go on.

"He's a possessive bastard, and you mean too much to him. He did not enjoy having me there last night. No way he's going to let a hundred people share what's between you." Fuller would defend Sean until the end. While she wanted to believe what he said, Sean's behavior hadn't led her to believe he thought there was more between them. Neither had it indicated the opposite—he'd actually been quite difficult to read.

This was going nowhere fast. She changed the subject. "Fuller, how do you know what Oasis is?"

The crackle of static hissing through the phone emphasized the silence. Then his sigh came through loud and clear. "I got a call yesterday morning on my private line. Very few people have this number. They offered me a fantasy. I set the terms, fill out a mountain of paperwork. They find a woman whose fantasy fits mine. I thought they were an escort service. Then I saw you with Sean, and I realized they were who they said they were."

Marcella had prohibited Oasis from contacting Sean directly. A refusal would have been too humiliating. They had managed to engineer events so that she could offer herself in such a way that a refusal wouldn't shatter her fragile ego or her working relationship with Sean. "They won't tell you who requested you?"

He chuckled again. "Maybe I'll steal a strategy from you and request her by name."

Marcella worked her teeth against her lower lip as a seed of hope grew in her heart. She hoped her guess proved correct. "Fuller? I'm not canceling the benefit. I'm going to call Gretchen and beg her to reconsider."

She could feel the tension radiating through the phone in Fuller's silence. At last he cleared his throat. "Sean won't do it."

"Well, I don't know that until I tell him she's back on board. You know what this benefit means to him."

"It doesn't matter. You mean more." His assurance came out as a growl, confirming Marcella's suspicion.

"So maybe you'd be okay with stepping in and taking his place if he refuses?" This time she held her breath and waited.

At last Fuller exhaled, and she heard the relief in his voice. "I'm always willing to help my best friend."

BY THE TIME Sean sauntered into her office with a cloth shopping bag and a tall cup of coffee an hour later, she had finished making calls.

He dropped the bag on one of the comfortable chairs facing her desk and sank into the other. He set his steaming cup next to her keyboard and leaned forward.

"Good morning, Marcella. Did you get my text?"

She nodded, her stiff response broadcasting her displeasure.

He locked gazes with her, holding her in his spell. "Did you do what I asked you to do?"

"I called Fuller. Your dry cleaning is ready, so I sent Gabriella to pick it up." She set her mouth in a stubborn line. "But I didn't cancel the benefit. I called Gretchen instead. She's agreed to come by today so you two can negotiate exactly what will happen."

His fingers curled into fists, his eyes narrowed, and his lips compressed until they turned white. Marcella had seen him this angry before, but his ire had always been directed elsewhere. Other people quaked at the air of danger he affected, but she wasn't impressed. Okay, maybe she was a little afraid.

"I told you to cancel it."

She rose to her feet because there was no way she could sit still under the force of his glare. Breaking eye contact, she paced to the window so she could focus on the pretty summer flowers blooming outside. "This means too much to you. And Gretchen would never have canceled in the first place if I hadn't interfered. I'm sorry. I never meant to mess this up for you."

The silence behind her pulled at her conscience, and she turned back to find his glare had morphed into bafflement. "How exactly did you interfere?"

"Oasis," she said. At his incredulous expression, she held up a hand. She hadn't meant it as a safe word. A sub calling out a safe word could cut a dom to the quick. "They're a wish-fulfillment service. I wished for a night with you. I didn't mean for it to mess up your benefit. I really thought I would be able to do what you needed me to do."

He rubbed his clean-shaven jaw, but the signs of his anger had disappeared. She didn't know if it scared her more to see he wasn't angry. Perhaps he had been looking for a way out, and now she'd handed it to him. At least she could give him back his freedom.

Finally he leaned back in the chair. His hands dropped to rest on his thighs, and he didn't look at her. "You paid a wish-fulfillment service for a night with me?"

Butterflies in her stomach churned her bagel and coffee unpleasantly. She never thought she would have to tell him her dirty little secret, but she owed him an explanation if she had any hope of convincing him to use Gretchen at the benefit.

"Yes." And she didn't regret it, but she hated that he could hide his thoughts and emotions from her so completely. "I think they convinced Gretchen to cancel on you. She wouldn't have done that without their interference."

He pushed to his feet and closed half the distance between them. He trapped her in the crosshairs of his steady gaze, and she couldn't move from her position in front of the window. "Cancel the benefit. I'll make the donation from my private account. The foundation will receive money either way. I always planned to match the amount raised."

She knew that too. Regret stabbed at her gut, releasing ten kinds of toxic poison. She swallowed tears back. This was no time to cry. She needed to lift her chin and take responsibility for the fallout. "No, Sean. Please don't punish me like this. I know I messed up. I've learned my lesson. I won't interfere ever again, and I will go quietly if you want to fire me."

"Punish you? How does this punish you?" He took a step closer. "I don't want to do a scene with Gretchen or any other woman, Cella. Your arrangement punishes me, and I refuse to accept it." Two steps and he closed the distance. "I can't do the benefit with another sub, and I refuse to do it with you. Call me a possessive or a jealous bastard, but I don't want to dress you in skimpy outfits or parade you naked in front of anyone. I don't want to share the gift of your submission. It's mine, Cella. You gave it to me, and unless you take it back, it belongs to me alone."

Marcella's heart soared, but guilt tainted his declaration and turned her joy bitter.

He leaned over her, bracing his hands on either side of the window. The oak molding turned his eyes mostly brown, but that didn't dull the danger glittering from them and emanating from the taut lines of his body. "Are you taking it back?"

She shook her head, the only part of her that could manage to move. "No. I'm not taking it back."

"Good. Cancel the benefit. You might have wished for a night with me, but you're getting a whole lot more, my Cella. I'm in love with you." One hand dropped to grip her hip. "I have been for a long, long time, but I've been wary of messing up our relationship by suggesting something you didn't want. You belong by my side, and I was willing to take you any way I could get you."

His other hand came down to run a caress along her collarbone. "Now that you've contrived to change the nature of our relationship, I'm not letting you go. I'll take you to the dungeon and help you deal with your guilt later, but you will cancel that benefit and you will stop arguing with me about it."

No argument came to mind, especially since she'd barely processed anything after he'd declared his love. Her gaze flickered to his lips and back to his eyes. "I love you too, Sean."

He swooped in and claimed her lips, establishing his ownership and his domination. Then he broke the kiss and backed away. She endeavored to catch her breath while he seemed to return to business mode.

"Before I let you carry out my orders, we have two things to discuss." He motioned to the sofa on the far side of her office. She snatched her laptop and notebook from her desk, but he took them from her and put them back. "You don't need these."

Marcella sat gingerly on the edge of the center cushion. Normally her mind would be whirling to organize the million phone calls she needed to make, but just now she couldn't seem to form a coherent thought.

Sean settled in next to her and turned her to face him. "Cella, you said you ended your last relationship because he wanted a full-time submissive. I have to be honest with you and tell you that I want that from you. I'm not saying you can't continue to work or that I want you to walk around naked or sit at my feet, but things will change from the way they have been."

That made sense. Things couldn't stay the same, not with the added element of their sexual relationship. She nodded. "Like last night." He had demanded her presence at his side, and his hands had been in constant contact with her skin.

He sandwiched her hand between his larger, stronger ones. "Like yesterday. I've wanted to get you in my dungeon for a long time. You can expect to spend time there several days a week. I want you by my side unless you have a specific reason not to be. And I want you tied to my bed every night."

A shiver ran up her spine as she remembered the way he had claimed her last night and the way being cuffed to his bed had made her feel whole and alive.

His caress spread. He rubbed his thumb over the underside of her wrist. "I will love you and cherish you. I will spoil you and pamper you. I'll reward you when you've earned it and punish you when you need it, but I will demand a lot from you in return, Cella. I want your heart and soul."

She blinked, a little shocked and a lot under the influence of his brand of magic. He wanted her heart and soul? He already had those things. Marcella licked her lips and took a deep breath. She'd never wanted to be a full-time submissive because she didn't want to give someone else complete control over her life. In her previous relationships, that extra spark and deeper connection always seemed to be missing. It didn't inspire her to want to do anything other than scenes.

But she knew Sean, and she knew he wasn't overly controlling or unreasonable. He might be demanding and dominant, but he also possessed a great amount of empathy and flexibility. The terms of their relationship would always be negotiable. He needed the perspective she brought to his life. In return, he made her feel emotionally safe and secure. She knew he meant it when he declared his love for her, and she knew she was the most important person in his life.

Her voice trembled, but her hands stayed steady. "Being a full-time submissive requires an enormous amount of trust. I've never trusted anyone the way I trust you. I've never had the sense that you want me to be something I'm not. I don't have the feeling you expect me to let you walk all over me, or that you want me to accept everything you say without argument. You respect me, and I gave you my heart and soul a long time ago."

He reached into the shopping bag he'd put on the floor. She hadn't noticed him pick it up from the chair by her desk and bring it over. He extracted a long black velvet box, out of which he pulled a delicate necklace. An odd-shaped heart dangled from the lowest point. Marcella peered closer and read the inscription. *Sean's.*

"I want you to wear my collar." He inserted a tiny key into the back and the heart split in half, revealing that it was actually a lock.

The heart symbolized that she belonged to Sean and that he had given her his heart. A tear fell from the corner of her eye. Fuller had once told her that Sean had never offered his collar to anyone. Unable to form words, she nodded.

He placed the collar around her neck, locked it, and put the key in his pocket. The depth of emotion simmering in his hazel eyes slammed into her gut, and her need to make sure he got everything he wanted reasserted itself.

She'd forgotten to tell him about Fuller's offer. "Sean, what if Fuller took your place at the benefit? He's played with Gretchen before." She held her breath and hoped he didn't repeat his insistence that she cancel the event.

Sean sighed. "He's not exactly dominant enough for her. I'm not sure he's comfortable assuming that kind of role."

Fuller's whispered encouragement made her think he knew exactly what it felt like to be in her position. Or he desperately wanted to make someone feel that way about him. Marcella leaned forward and brushed a kiss across Sean's lips, testing the change in their working relationship. "I already talked to him. We can't let four months of work go to waste. You can still be the host, and I'll be by your side for moral support."

Chuckling, Sean lifted her onto his lap. "By my side. Exactly where I want you. I like that."

~ * ~

OUT OF MY LEAGUE

Oasis: Adult Fantasy Fulfillment

Advertisement

Think about what you want more than anything in the world. It isn't out of reach. Oasis is an adult fantasy fulfillment service that specializes in making your dreams come true.* Anything from a weekend getaway with someone you love to an erotic encounter with a stranger—or strangers—can happen. Call us today and make your fantasy a reality.

*Oasis reserves the right to reject any application for any reason. Oasis is not an escort service. We match people on the basis of their fantasies and arrange for those fantasies to be fulfilled. Fantasies are fulfilled at the discretion of management.

Case 3a

I have to get him out of my system. One day, please. Just give me one day where someone who looks a lot like him tosses me over my desk, spanks me, and gives me what I need. Then I want to spend a nice, relaxing day on a beach with a spectacular view of the Caribbean. I know the second part isn't quite what you guys do, so I'm happy if you can swing the first part.

Case 3b

She drives me crazy. That little package of hotness wrapped in baggy clothes. I want to strip her naked and show her another side of me. Well, I know that'll never happen. I'll settle for someone who looks exactly like her. And then I'll need to get my head back together before I have to face her for real. Someplace warm. With a beach.

Chapter One

The Wednesday before Thanksgiving was the worst day in the school year. Most students at Sault Ste. Marie State University would be heading home for break, and many had already begun the trek from Sault Ste. Marie to the Lower Peninsula. Canada was closer than home for most students. Some took the entire week off. Brave souls.

Mia sighed and wished she had enough courage to blow off even a half day of school. Working as a teaching assistant got her a discount on tuition and helped defray the cost of room and board, but it also meant that she didn't have the option of ducking out early. Her boss was an anal-retentive professor who liked to pontificate and who insisted on marking down papers a third of a grade for every mistake in grammar or punctuation. That meant Mia got to spend hours poring over papers, assessing them for correct content and looking for the tiniest error. Even the best papers had two or three proofing errors.

She hoped and prayed to be assigned to another professor next semester, but Dr. Brindley had taken a shine to her as an undergrad, and so he had requested her for the last three semesters. Soon, though, she'd have her master's degree in sociology. Then she could pursue her doctorate at a school with no Dr. Brindley. Two of the programs to which she'd applied were located in warmer climes. While she loved the Upper Peninsula, after seven years, the six months of winter had lost its charm.

The sharp squeak of the door opening interrupted her musings. Though she shared the common area connecting the sociology professors' private offices with all the other TAs, the other professors had let their student slaves leave early. Some had even canceled class. Not Dr. Brindley. He was holding office hours until the very last minute, which, thankfully, was fast approaching.

That left Mia as the only person in the reception area. A divider halfway across the room conspired with her diminutive height to block her view of the door. Based on the heavy footfalls shaking the floor and heading in her direction, it could only be Kaelen. Well, that and the fact she hadn't checked off his name as one of the students who attended class this morning and turned in his paper. She tapped her pen on the paper on her desk and glanced at the clock. Office hours officially ended in thirty seconds. He was cutting it close.

She saw the top of his head over the divider a second before he came into full view, but the extra second didn't give her the time she needed to steel herself against what was coming.

Light brown hair, straight as a board, flopped over his right eye. Smooth skin covered his high, sharp cheekbones, underlining the intensity of his slate gray eyes. A day or two of beard growth darkened his cheeks, and she wondered if it would be scratchy or soft. He covered his broad shoulders and lean body with a black fleece jacket, jeans, and heavy work boots.

If anyone fit the perfect model image of a sexy lumberjack, Kaelen Sebastian did. Only he wasn't a lumberjack. He was a student in Dr. Brindley's Advanced

Methods class, and he had a nasty habit of coming late to class. Dr. Brindley absolutely hated Kaelen. He railed against the man's cockiness, his lackadaisical approach to life, and any other perceived flaws.

This marked the second semester in a row that Mia had to deal with Kaelen. It also marked the second semester in a row that she tossed and turned at night whenever Dr. Brindley had a paper due. Without fail, Kaelen always appeared for office hours and asked for help with his paper. And without fail, she became a bumbling idiot who couldn't think straight around a drop-dead-sexy man.

Kaelen was nothing if not consistent. He flashed a crooked smile that showed one dimple. Charm oozed from his pores. He shoved one hand into the pocket on his jeans, lifting that fleece enough to give her an unobstructed, eye-level view of how well his package filled that denim. "Hi, Mia. Why aren't you already on the road?"

She could roll her eyes and incline her head to Dr. Brindley's office, blaming him without saying a word, but she didn't believe in blaming other people for her actions. Sitting up straighter and squaring her shoulders, she gave him a tight-lipped smile. "I'm scheduled to work until five."

Those smoky eyes glanced at the clock above her head and back down. "It's five o'clock."

On cue, the door to Dr. Brindley's office opened, then closed. He locked it and slid the keys into his jacket pocket. The polite smile on his face turned into a mild sneer when he spied Kaelen.

He froze for a second, and then he dismissed Kaelen completely. Tipping his hat at Mia, he bowed his head.

"Have a nice holiday, Ms. Calloway. I'll see you Monday at one."

Kaelen didn't seem to notice Dr. Brindley's terse dismissal of him. He turned all the power of his brilliant smile on the self-aggrandizing professor. "Hey, Doc. I hope you have a great Thanksgiving."

"Thank you." His tone didn't match the meaning of the phrase. Without further exchange of pleasantries, Dr. Brindley left.

Mia gathered the papers she hadn't yet graded and threw them into her bag. She only had a handful left to read. If she didn't have to check them so closely for errors, she would have finished by now, but it was better to take the time with them now than have Dr. Brindley notice something and make her redo the entire stack.

And tell the class their papers were late because his TA lacked the ability to pay attention to details. She had been mortified the first time he had done that, and she went out of her way to make sure it would never happen again.

Kaelen came around and leaned against the side of her desk. He had unzipped his jacket when she wasn't looking. Underneath he wore a blue plaid flannel shirt. The top three buttons were undone. A white cotton shirt crossed the span where she should have been able to see his chest. She'd seen him in a short-sleeved shirt that molded to his frame before. The sight had made her tingle in ways her vibrator couldn't seem to cure.

She spied the yellow plastic binding of a report cover peeking out from under his arm. Shaking her head, she grabbed her jacket from the back of her chair. "No. Don't even ask."

He leaned closer, and the spicy, clean scent of his aftershave tickled from her nose to her pussy. That crooked smile sent pangs to her chest, and she wanted to drown in his dimple. "Mia."

She loved the way her name rolled from his tongue. The two syllables had never sounded so sexy. His voice made her mind take flight and imagine a hundred sensual possibilities, all of them ending with the two of them naked, sweaty, and exhausted.

She dropped her gaze and focused on her serviceable, comfortable black shoes. That led her to take in the thick tights that sucked in a few of her extra pounds and kept her legs warm. And then she looked at the shapeless gray dress. Gray looked so much better in his eyes than it did on her body.

Drawing attention to herself had never been a high priority for Mia. She was smart, not pretty or artistic. Looking down provided a reality check. A man as handsome as Kaelen Sebastian didn't flirt with someone as unremarkable as Mia because he was interested in conversation or kissing. Nope, he wanted special treatment that would save his grade. Shoving an arm into her jacket, she shook her head. "No. Dr. Brindley was just here. You should have talked to him."

He lifted the other half of her jacket to help her put it on. His fingers brushed against her shoulder, sending shock waves crashing through her system. "Office hours are over. He wouldn't have talked to me."

She folded the flap to close her bag. Kaelen put his hand over hers. Electricity shot in all directions, but she was sure she was the only one who felt it. She jerked her hand away. "You could have walked out with him."

"I'd rather walk out with you." He flashed that dimple again. Damn if it didn't make her resolve waver a little.

She stiffened and tried not to show how much he affected her.

"Please? I had to work last night. The paper is finished, and it's damn good too. I think you'd like it."

Students had used those excuses with Dr. Brindley before. She knew how he would respond. "School is a priority. You should have organized your time better."

"Paying my rent and eating are priorities too. I got called in. I have to work. You work. You know how it is."

Mia had never turned in a late paper in her life. She normally finished early, sometimes with a week or two to spare. She bristled at what had been said and what was implied. If she accepted the paper, he would let her pretend she wasn't a nerd with no social life. If she turned him down, she would only confirm what they both knew to be true.

He flashed that smile again. Her knees grew weak, but fear of losing her job kept her focused. "If you slip it into your bag, he'll never know. He'll think I turned it in early and you just didn't mention it."

There it was. Professors gave nerdy students preferential treatment, cut them some slack when they messed up because they were better students than everyone else. Mia fit the mold. She knew the score. Professors had overlooked her mistakes a few times, though she had never abused the privilege.

And now Kaelen had maligned her character, and she could only think about what it would feel like to have him hold her down, shove her legs apart, and grind his hardness against her willing body.

WHEN SHE SHOVED her glasses up the bridge of her nose and pressed those lips in that prim line that had him fighting a serious urge to leap across the desk and kiss the vinegar right off her face, Kaelen knew he was fucked. His job as a Sault Ste. Marie firefighter sometimes meant he had trouble making it to class on time or finding time to work on a paper. Fires didn't care about deadlines.

But he refused to use that as an excuse. The paper had been close to completion when he was called in. People burning to death always took precedence over a paper. By the time he got home this morning, he had been too bleary-eyed to think, so he'd crashed for a few hours. He had finished the paper when he got up that afternoon.

He knew she wouldn't have them graded by the end of the day. She zipped her jacket in one smooth motion. Tugging at the strap to her bag, she tipped it from the chair to thump on the floor. He winced as she lifted the strap over her head to settle on her opposite shoulder. Poor woman was going to be grading papers when she should be spending time with her family. Or her boyfriend. Someone as beautiful and intelligent as Mia had to be taken. That was why he'd asked Oasis for a look-alike. Even if she was single, there was no way in hell Mia was interested in him. He wasn't close to being her type. That didn't stop him from dreaming about the possibilities.

She flipped her head back, jutting out her chin and setting her ponytail in motion. "I didn't make a mistake." Spots of anger stained her cheeks.

Kaelen leaned forward to hide the growing problem in his pants. He caught a whiff of spring freshness mixed with feminine heat, and he had to fight the urge to bury his face in her neck and inhale. "I didn't say you did."

"No, but you want me to take the heat so you can get away with turning in a late paper. He knows you weren't in class. I could lose my job for that."

He wanted to lay her across the desk, lift her dress, and paddle her until she begged for release. It had absolutely nothing to do with the paper or the don't-fuck-with-me-attitude he found infinitely attractive and everything to do with the fantasies he had about her almost every night. In thirty-six hours, he would have approximately what he wanted. That gift certificate for Oasis had seemed like a joke at first.

Now, looking forward to paddling the ass of a woman who was supposed to look a lot like Mia kept him from acting on that impulse. Standing this close, he realized how short she was. He had nearly a foot on her. If he pulled her close, she could rest her cheek against his chest, and he could rest his chin on the top of her head. He could push her back a little and kiss her forehead. He could push her back a little more, tip up her chin, and taste those rosy lips.

Shaking the fanciful thoughts away, he forced himself to look in her eyes. She inhaled sharply, her eyes widened, and she seemed somehow softer. "You won't lose your job for this. He won't even know."

The shock fell away, and that glazed look, a bit of passion unleashed, faded. He longed to grip her tightly and force her to stay where he wanted while he finally sampled her kiss. Would she respond by letting loose that passion, or would she kick him in the nuts?

"I'll know." She looked him up and down, not quite hiding the shades of hurt he hadn't intended to make her feel.

Damn. He'd never get it right when it came to Mia. If she looked at him with longing and vulnerability just once, he would be putty in her hands. He'd completely forget about the damn paper as he drowned in her bliss.

The door slammed shut behind her. He leaned against her desk and clenched his fists around nothingness.

Chapter Two

Mia sat in the used Malibu she had managed to buy her sophomore year of college and stared at the cabin in front of her. The vinyl siding made it look a little more modern. She hoped it would be warm inside.

The cabin wasn't in the UP, but it was less than an hour from the airport near school. Though she hadn't expected it, the package from Oasis had included a plane ticket and two nights at a time-share in the Bahamas. When she returned late Sunday night, she wouldn't be far from home.

For the bargain-basement price she paid to make this fantasy happen, she would be surprised if the inside had modern plumbing. This was not one of their more expensive packages.

The shiver that ran up her spine when she climbed out of her car had nothing to do with the near-freezing temperatures and everything to do with nerves and anticipation. In her entire life, she'd never done anything remotely risky, and now she was about to let a stranger spank and fuck her. And then there was some secretary-slut fantasy of his that would round out their time in the cabin. She'd agreed to be his sex slave for most of the day. Eight hours. Just another day at the office, and then she would be off to enjoy a relaxing day and a half in the sun.

Since she would only be at the cabin until five, and it was barely eight now, she elected to leave her suitcase in the car. Oasis had sent an outfit with the welcome package that reiterated all the rules and guidelines to which she'd agreed.

As if that weren't enough, another set of the rules was laminated and taped to the front door. No names were there, as both she and her mystery man had elected to be anonymous. His fantasy included spanking an administrative assistant. Hers was to be spanked. She didn't care about the secretary part. It worked out.

She wondered how much he'd look like Kaelen, and how disappointed he would be when he found plain old Mia sitting at the desk, waiting for him. The chances of them finding someone exactly six-two who had the same build and coloring as Kaelen were slim. She'd take shorter, but he had to have those smoking-hot eyes and that heart-stopping smile.

His outline had specified she wear her dark hair in a ponytail. The instructions actually called for dark brown hair, which was good because Mia wasn't willing to dye it or wear a wig. It allowed for very little makeup. Mascara and lip gloss, but only if she insisted. No powders, no eyeliner, no lipstick. He didn't want to see earrings, piercings, or a necklace, but a bracelet or an anklet was okay.

That was fine. Mia occasionally wore bracelets and anklets, and she only trotted out necklaces for special events. Her ears weren't pierced, and neither was any other part of her body.

SHE PUSHED OPEN the door and looked around curiously. There were four rooms. The main room, which could have been a living room, contained the bare bones of an office set. One desk sat in the middle of the room. Armoires were arranged against one wall. Two windows faced a small clearing in the back. Looking out, she couldn't see how it was different from the front. A line of trees blocked her view past the clearing. Since it was late autumn, most of the leaves had already fallen to the ground. They would be brown and soggy from the rain they'd been having.

She wandered through the doorway to the left and found a kitchen. The cupboards were full of cookware, plates, glasses, and flatware, but no food. It didn't matter. They wouldn't be there for long. She had eaten a good breakfast, and she could grab a quick dinner on her way to the airport.

Two closed doors greeted her on the other side of the room. One had to be a bathroom. The other was probably a bedroom.

She'd waited until she got there to open the box containing the outfit she was supposed to wear. It wasn't very different from what she normally wore. She would have worn her own clothes, but this outfit had weak seams that would allow him to rip it off. She'd fantasized about Kaelen ripping off her dresses. In this fantasy, he had agreed to be Kaelen for her. Maybe he didn't know the name of her secret crush, but he knew he was playing a role, just as she knew she was playing a role for him.

It made her feel better to know he was using her the same way she was using him. And she didn't feel all that weird about the fact she'd have sex with a stranger in an hour or less. It appealed to a decadent side she'd kept hidden, a part of her that wanted to throw off society's constraints and her parents' expectations and live on the wild side for just a little while.

Of course, given the background checks and the sex safety classes Oasis had made her attend for the past six weeks, she had complete faith in their selection process.

Their advertisement said they reserved the right to reject anyone's fantasy for any reason. They'd chosen to accept her fantasy, and they'd even worked with her to come up with something she could afford.

She wondered why there wasn't at least a sofa in the "office." She guessed they'd have to make do with the desk and chair for her part the day's fantasies. She honestly hadn't thought through what would happen beyond the spanking and fucking. That might only take a half hour. She didn't know how quickly her fantasy partner would deliver the details.

With a sigh, she headed for the bathroom with the unopened box. She had about fifteen or twenty minutes before he was supposed to arrive, plenty of time to get ready.

The bathroom was huge. It had a walk-in shower that could fit several people and a large jetted bathtub. The massage table gave her pause, being in the bathroom and all, but she could appreciate that it might go with a fantasy about being pampered.

She closed the door and examined the steel hooks screwed into the back and the bar across the top. Restraints dangled from it. Because she didn't know the man she was meeting, she hadn't consented to bondage. If she had, this door would definitely have been in her fantasy.

Ripping open the box, she peeked inside. The black polyester mass was a shapeless dress that would cover from her chest to the middle of her calves. The straps over the shoulders fastened like a jumpsuit.

Reaching back inside, she pulled out a knit sweater to wear over the top of the dress. Patent leather shoes, the utilitarian kind, and crew socks were the only items left inside. She dumped the box upside down just to make sure there wasn't anything extra. She hadn't asked for the shoes or the socks, but they were a nice touch.

A scrap of paper fell out. It looked like the fortune found in a Chinese cookie. *Do not wear underclothing.* She squinted at the note, puzzled at the command. But then she shrugged. It made sense to forgo a bra and panties.

Five minutes later, Mia surveyed her costumed appearance in the bathroom mirror. It only showed her top half, but she didn't need to see the rest. She had a couple dresses like this in her closet at home, and the sweater looked like one she wore frequently because the office tended to be a little cold.

Her hair was already in the requested ponytail. She headed to her desk, which had some papers stacked on it, waiting for her to grade them. Nothing felt different. Even the lack of panties and bra didn't make her feel naughty or decadent. She picked up the contract to read it one last time.

* * *

Kaelen followed the long, winding drive to a little cabin that didn't look at all like what he had specified in his fantasy. An older-model Malibu was parked outside. He started, a little surprised at that level of detail. He hoped the woman inside had those same simmering chocolate eyes and the same rich chestnut hair as Mia. His fingers itched to free those long tresses and comb through them. That kind of detail mattered to him more than her driving the same make and model of car that Mia drove.

He wondered what she would think about the outfit he'd chosen for her to wear, and he wondered what she expected from him, exactly. Oasis had been very open about the fact they were fulfilling one another's fantasies.

Spanking a woman turned him on like nothing else, except maybe watching her climax. Lingerie and cleavage were nice, but a pink ass made his cock stand up and take notice. He wanted to hear those kittenish moans of pleasure from Mia, but this woman who had agreed to be her stand-in would have to suffice.

If anyone asked him to describe the perfect woman, he would describe Mia. He suspected she hid a sexy body behind those shapeless sack dresses and baggy shirts she always seemed to be wearing. The little blushes that darkened her cheeks whenever he asked for a favor made his jeans become uncomfortably tight.

The first time he'd seen her, she'd stood in when Brindley had to leave campus unexpectedly. She'd talked about the importance of independent variables, and she'd cited successful and flawed studies in her examples. When he'd read about the topic before class, it hadn't seemed all that interesting. But Mia brought a passion to her lecture that infected every single person in that room.

Her eyes had sparkled, and her hands had moved expressively. She had walked around the room, sitting in the back when she showed charts and diagrams through the data projector.

She'd settled into the empty seat next to him as she talked through the data. Her cinnamon and vanilla scent had tickled his senses, but the excitement she didn't attempt to hide had captivated him. That day, he had sought her out at Brindley's office, inventing some long-forgotten excuse just to see her.

That passionate woman had vanished, replaced with someone professional and cordial. He'd tried talking with her about variables, but her reception had been cool at best. Then he'd tried to move the conversation forward, guiding it toward topics that would spark that passion he'd so loved about her. He'd been about to ask after her course of study, but Brindley had poked his head out of his office and told her to get back to work. Her gaze had fallen to the pile of papers on her desk, and she'd told him to see Dr. Brindley if he had any questions about the content of the class.

He had recognized her humiliation. She was the kind of woman who went out of her way to please people. She didn't handle harshness or being reprimanded very well. He wanted to punch Brindley for making her feel that way.

After that, she had quickly withdrawn from any attempt he made at interaction. Women usually fell over themselves to clamor for his attention. He had never developed the skills to break through this wallflower's defenses.

He made it up the steps, but he paused with his hand on the door. Going in, he knew it wouldn't be enough. Playacting with a stranger couldn't sate his longing to feel Mia's lips moving under his, her soft moans growing louder as he held her down and ripped off her clothes.

With a groan, he adjusted his cock, which had automatically hardened at the thought of seeing Mia. At least this woman had asked him to wear something he found comfortable. Jeans, work boots, and a flannel shirt under his fleece jacket. It was his standard fare, and it did nothing to further the fantasy element or feed his sense of anticipation. It was too familiar to be sexy. Oasis had offered to send him the outfit, but he'd declined, preferring to wear his own clothes.

He exhaled, gathering courage, and pushed the door open.

* * *

The door didn't squeak as it opened, another way in which this place was different from the real thing. The clear sounds of the wind rustling through the crisp fall leaves and the distant calls of birds came into focus and faded as the door closed them out again.

She stared at the rules she had read and reread, swallowing convulsively to ready herself for however he might begin the scene. Perhaps he would come in angry, spank her first and ask questions later. Maybe he would want to banter a bit, ease into the role of disgruntled student.

His heavy footfalls didn't shake the floor, but they echoed through the quiet room. When she looked up, her heart stopped. Those smoky gray eyes stared at her, and his full, sensual lips parted in surprise. He stared at her long enough for her to realize that he hadn't expected to see her there. Then his broad shoulders sagged the slightest amount, and that was all the confirmation she needed.

This joke was too cruel.

Yanking open the drawer, she struggled to maintain her composure. She grabbed her keys and headed to the door, brushing past him as she rounded the corner. He watched her go, his mouth opened, but she didn't stay to hear what he had to say. Screw her clothes. Good thing she'd left her suitcase in the car. She unlocked her door, using the key because her Malibu predated keyless entry. Just as she reached for the handle to open it up, he lodged his hand against the frame, holding the door closed. She jerked as hard as she could, but it was useless.

"Move, damn it."

"No. Mia, talk to me."

A harsh wind whipped against them, battering her with the scent of fabric softener and aftershave mixed with Kaelen's distinct maleness. She didn't want to talk to him. She wanted to kiss him. She wanted to climb up his solid frame, wrap her legs around his narrow hips, and grind her mound against his cock.

"I did. I told you to move. Damn it."

His other arm came down on her other side, caging her between his hot body and the coolness of her car. Not one for cold, she gravitated to the heat. When she bumped into his chest, she yelped and whirled around.

"That's not talking. That's ordering. You're not here to give orders. You're here to take them." His soft tone didn't hide the firmness of his authority.

So much heat crept up her neck and suffused her face that she knew she'd passed pink and gone straight to red. Of course he knew the details of her fantasy. How utterly embarrassing. How completely pathetic.

She ducked under his arm and went around to the passenger side. Sliding across the console would get her to the driver's seat just as well. Except for the fact Kaelen followed her to the other side, it was a solid escape plan.

Wasting no time, he put his hands on the door, caging her once again. "There's nothing to be embarrassed about. We must both have the same fantasy."

She closed her eyes and let the sound of his voice wash through her system. Way deep down, she wanted to give in, but her better sense took over. "If you think I'm going to go back in there with you so you can take out all your anger on me, you're mistaken. I'm not stupid."

And she desperately didn't want anyone to find out about this. Not only was he likely mad about his paper, he now had this debacle to lay at her feet. She didn't think he was the vindictive type, but this was the kind of story that inevitably made the rounds, if only because it was so improbable.

His body trembled. "I'm not angry with you. I'd never do anything to you that you didn't want. You set down very specific guidelines that I agreed to before Oasis would let me come here."

Leaning forward, she shrank against the car. "Like hell you're not mad. I refused to take your paper. You'll fail the class without it."

"My desire to turn your little ass pink has nothing to do with your refusal to take my paper. Yeah, it sucks, but it's between me and Brindley. It doesn't involve you at all." He moved closer, tightening her cage. Power and strength vibrated from him, and he hadn't touched her yet. "Please don't walk away. It's one day where we both get to live out our deepest fantasy."

The images and feelings generated by her fantasies paled in comparison to coming this close to being with him. But this fantasy was supposed to include a look-alike she would never have to see again. Though she really didn't think he had it in him to hurt her, she held fast to her decision. "You can't have expected to find me here. It's going to be awkward enough when we get back to school. We don't have to add fuel to the fire."

He nestled his forehead against her shoulder. "For fuck's sake, Mia. When I described the woman I wanted to see here today, I modeled her after you. I did everything but request you by name. You must have done the same thing with me. I thought it was odd how closely your parameters matched me, but now I see why. You want me as much as I want you. God, I'm so glad I won that gift certificate at work and not someone else. It's like it was meant to be."

Her mind reeled as she processed his declaration. Men like Kaelen didn't bother with shy, unprepossessing women like her. He commanded attention wherever he went, and she did her damnedest to fade into the background.

She turned around, dislodging his head from her shoulder, and pushed at his chest to move him back. He gave her space, but he held her there with his smoldering gaze.

"You can have any woman you want."

"I want you." He didn't blink, and his steady expression didn't change.

She bit her lip and shook her head at the implausibility of his statement. "Why? Do you have some kind of weird fantasy about being with an unattractive woman?"

His brow furrowed briefly, the affectation gone before she could figure out what puzzled him. "No. I have a fantasy about bending you over that desk and spanking you until you come. I have a fantasy about ripping off your clothes and hearing you scream my name. I have a fantasy about doing those things with *you*. According to all the paperwork you filled out, you have the same fantasy."

Mia swallowed. There was no denying the similarities. "How do I know this isn't about revenge?"

He sighed and ran a hand through his hair. It fanned through his fingers, sticking up in light brown spikes that settled back more or less the way they'd been before. "I set this up more than three months ago, way before you refused to slip my paper in with all the others. There was nothing to avenge."

As his argument penetrated, she grasped at any excuse to deny herself what she wanted. Her dreams had never come true before, not when they involved relying on another person, and the fact she might get one day with Kaelen scared her as much as it thrilled her. She didn't know if she had the courage for this. "Now there is."

"What do you want me to say?" He shoved a hand in his pocket, lifting the fleece to expose the flannel underneath. "Am I pissed that you wouldn't take my paper? Not really. I would have been shocked if you had. You're not exactly a rule-breaker. I can respect that. But I didn't come here to talk about that or think about it. I came here because every time I see you, I have to go home and take a cold shower. I'm here because I need to get you out of my system. Don't walk away from something you want because you're afraid of what might happen down the line. I think we can both agree that what happens here stays here."

Well, she couldn't argue with his logic. She picked at her nails, clicking one against the other in a sound that annoyed everyone sooner or later. "You promise this stays between us? It could complicate things for both of us back at school."

Kaelen's curt nod almost had her reconsidering her decision, but the way he pressed his lips together made her think he was more nervous than anything else.

"I'll stay."

Tension drained from his shoulders. "Then get your ass inside, Calloway. This is going to be a lot of fun."

Chapter Three

Mia rearranged the piles of paper on her desk. She glanced toward the door, but nothing happened. Tapping her fingers on the desk, she figured that she'd only been seated for thirty seconds. Any reasonably thoughtful man would give her a couple minutes to prepare. Frowning, she wondered if Kaelen was a reasonably thoughtful man. She didn't know all that much about him.

He'd dropped a few hints, but they had been in the context of charming banter. Wanting to rationalize the way he focused on her and nothing else, she had groped for a sociological explanation for his behavior. The things he'd said were likely based in truth, but they could have been embellished or facts omitted to present him in a positive light. After all, most of the time he talked to her, he wanted her to do something for him. Dig through the stack of papers because he'd forgotten to include the last page. Read over a draft to find out if it would pass muster with Brindley. Verify information he could have looked up on the Internet. E-mail a copy of the syllabus.

Exhaling a shaky breath, she picked up the stack of papers again and began sorting through them. Things that looked like e-mails in one pile. Photocopied articles in a second pile. Another list of their agreed-upon rules in a third pile.

The air pressure in the room changed. Vaguely she noted the sharpened sounds of the outdoors. They muted as a sequence of thumps and a click indicated the door was closed and locked.

She willed herself to not look up. It didn't work. Her gaze rose to meet his, and all the breath left her body. He smiled as he stopped in front of her desk, half of his mouth lifting in a way that sent tingles fluttering to her stomach. "Hey, Mia. How come you're still here so late?"

Dropping her gaze to the stack of papers still in her hands, she studied the top one. E-mail pile. She put it where it belonged. Her hand shook a little. "I have some things to finish before I leave."

"Always the good little assistant."

She lifted her chin, setting her jaw at the jibe. "And what's wrong with being a good assistant? Some people actually take pride in their work, no matter now menial or unimportant others consider it to be."

He bent forward and rested his hands on the top of her desk. "That's a whole lot of attitude for such a cute little thing."

On a normal day, she would be able to come up with five snappy comebacks to put him in his place. Of course, on a normal day, he would never comment on her attitude or call her a cute little thing.

Pressing her lips together, she decided to change the subject. "I'll be closing up in a minute, and everybody has left. If you have business with someone, I suggest you leave a note." She pointed to the other side of the room. "The boxes for each professor are over there."

Standing tall, he squared his shoulders and unzipped his black fleece jacket. The blue and gray flannel just made his eyes look darker, hotter. Her breath caught. If things kept going this way, she might pass out from lack of oxygen.

He withdrew something from an inner pocket and threw it on the desk. It took only a second for her to recognize the yellow binding on the plastic report cover. She glanced up at Kaelen, but he wasn't looking at her. He shrugged out of his jacket and hung it on the knob of an armoire.

She took a closer look at the report. The clear cover let her read the first sentence, but Kaelen's nearness and the imminence of the scene prevented her from concentrating on the meaning of the words.

"Attitude." His tone had changed to soft and firm. All the times she'd spoken with him, he had been friendly and charming, flirty, even when he wasn't pleased with her response. "You need to be taught a lesson."

Surprised at his tone, she lifted her gaze. Her eyes felt impossibly wide, but she couldn't do anything about it. Her breath came in short pants, and heat flooded between her thighs. She thought about running, but her leaden legs wouldn't cooperate. "A lesson?"

His dimple showed when he flashed a cocky smile. He leaned over her desk, pausing with his face inches from hers. "Babe, remind me what your safe word is."

Shock pulled her from the scene. Blood once again flowed through her arteries, bringing a fresh supply of energy to her cells. "Oasis. Didn't they tell you?"

"Safety. I want you to remember that you have the power to stop this at any time." His low, confidential tone soothed her senses. She didn't know how to tell him how much it meant that he took the time to show he cared, that he knew what he was doing.

"Thank you."

In one powerful motion, he swept everything onto the floor. Her carefully arranged piles ended up in a heap. The lone pencil bounced and rolled, the *ting* echoing in the silent room. "Time for your lesson."

Her stomach dropped, and her legs worked when her brain told them to kick into action. Leaping up, she turned around and grabbed the handle to the door that was probably the bedroom. It was the only room she hadn't yet seen.

An arm banded around her waist and lifted her from the ground. Kaelen hauled her back against his hard body. She wiggled and fought, but she got nowhere. She felt like an empty sack in his arms, something easily hoisted and held. Helpless.

As someone who was always in control, Mia struggled with the feeling of helplessness. On one hand, she liked to be in control. On the other hand, she craved having it taken away. She craved being able to trust someone else enough to cede complete authority over her body.

She trusted Kaelen today.

He placed her on the desk, facedown, her breasts flattened against the surface and her hips dangling from the side. Angling her toes down, she barely managed to touch the floor.

Kaelen reached under her sweater and hooked his fingers into the collar of her dress. With one mighty tug, he ripped the loosened seams and pulled the back of her dress away from her body. Stunned, exposed everywhere below her sweater, she failed to move.

"Beautiful. I knew you were hiding something spectacular under all those baggy clothes." His hand burned hot against her cool flesh. He caressed her thigh and hip, his hand traveling a narrow path. "Curves this luscious are dangerous."

Mia didn't consider herself thin or fat. She was unremarkably average. She carried a little extra flesh on her hips and around the middle, enough to encourage her to wear a bathing suit that covered her stomach, but not enough that she felt self-conscious about it. She had other things to feed her insecurities.

"Why do you wear such baggy clothes?"

She didn't feel the need to dignify that with an answer. This was a scene, not a date. His jeans weren't tight, and those flannel shirts didn't advertise the iron muscles she felt when he held her to him. She threw the question back. "Why do *you* wear baggy clothes?"

A loud *crack* rent the room. Mia started more at the sound than the feel of his hand smacking her ass. He rubbed his palm over the spot where he'd struck, spreading heat like body butter. "Don't worry. I'll help adjust this attitude of yours."

Planting her hands on the desktop, she pushed up. He countered with the heel of his hand pressing between her shoulder blades. Another smack landed on her bare bottom.

"Stay down, babe. If you're good, I'll make you come. If you're not, I'll tie you to this desk and keep you on the edge until I feel you've begged enough. Your choice."

Mia didn't want to fight. The small part of her that wanted to resist only protested on the grounds that it might be difficult to face Kaelen afterward. But he'd promised that what happened in this cabin stayed in this cabin. She relaxed, turning her head to rest her cheek against the coolness of the wood beneath. "I'll be good."

"That's what I thought."

He smacked each cheek once. A pleasant heat began to bloom. This wasn't Mia's first spanking, not by any stretch of the imagination. She'd dated a man who liked to give erotic spankings. It was the only time she experienced a climax with him, and she'd lingered in the relationship far longer than she should have. He had stayed in it for the same reason. They had nothing in common except for their love of spanking.

Just like her and Kaelen.

Another sharp slap brought her back to the present. "I know that look on your face. Focus. Keep your attention on me and what I'm doing, otherwise I'll have to teach you manners as I adjust your attitude."

His hand landed on her ass again and again, forcing her to pay attention to the exquisite heat barreling through her system. Of its own volition, her ass lifted after each blow, seeking the return of the sting radiating across her skin.

She moaned.

"You like that?"

"Oh, yes."

Kaelen stroked his fingertips over her hot, quivering flesh. She whimpered in response. He didn't hurry his foray. If anything, he slowed his strokes, drawing them out along a longer path. One by one, her muscles relaxed. Tension drained from her shoulders. She sank against the desk, no longer straining to touch the ground with her toes.

His finger slid along her slit, teasing the edges of her labia. The tip of her clit, enlarged and throbbing, peeked out. He brushed against it lightly, lingering long enough that she knew he was bent on tantalizing her. "So wet. You're dripping. Would you like me to touch your clit?"

As if it could hear his offer, her clit swelled even more. "Yes."

The heat of his hand withdrew, but it came back quickly. He centered the blow over her swollen lips. She yelped, but she didn't protest. Heat bloomed.

"Attitude, babe. That's no way to ask for a favor." He delivered another series of slaps, all of them falling on her ass and upper thighs.

Her pussy dripped, silently pleading for attention. She couldn't help but beg for relief. "Please touch my clit."

Those lethal fingertips returned to caress paths over her burning ass. "Do you need it?"

"Yes. Oh please. I need you to touch my clit." Need made her entire body tremble. She'd beg any way he wanted.

His finger grazed the tip of her clit too lightly to do more than tease. "Like this?"

"Harder. Please. Oh, please touch it harder."

He pressed, squishing it at such a leisurely rate that she felt every single way the sensitive nub changed shape. She moaned and struggled to keep her hips from thrusting against his hand.

"You're trembling." He rotated the pressure of his finger, widening the circles until he traced a path around the little nub. "I think you need to come."

"Yes." Breathless permission fell from her lips, a plea she hoped he'd heed.

"You were wearing a dress like this the first time I saw you, teaching that class for Brindley. Everyone said you were a better instructor. You are, but I had a hell of a time concentrating on what you were saying. I was too busy thinking about tearing off your clothes, bending you over my lap, turning your ass pink, and fucking you. Slow. Fast. Hard. Gentle. Change it up until you lost your mind and screamed my name."

"Kaelen," she whispered, a sound halfway between a whimper and a plea. "Please make me come."

"Tell me you want my fingers inside you."

"Yes, please, anything."

He thrust two fingers into her opening. Her cream eased the way, making the motion smooth. He took his time, exploring her walls, mapping them with his fingertips. "Soft. You're so soft and hot and tight. God, you're going to feel like heaven around my cock."

The walls of her vagina flexed at the promise of being stretched by his cock. Pyroclastic showers of heat shot through her system. Tears pricked behind her eyes, evidence she wouldn't be able to hold off the strong orgasm building low in her belly.

He added a third finger, stretching her wider as he thrust them in and pulled them out. With his other hand, he smacked her ass to a different, faster rhythm. "Come for me. Don't hold it in."

She screamed. The conflicting sensations and rhythms blasted her so far over the edge she lost sight of everything. The world flashed behind a white light.

By the time her senses returned, Kaelen had stopped smacking her ass. He'd slowed the rate of the fingers he thrust inside, drawing out the orgasm as it faded. Her pussy throbbed and her body quivered.

He lifted her and sat down in her chair. The front of her dress fell away, but the bulky sweater still covered her breasts. She curled up on his lap, letting her head fall against his strong shoulder. Unable to move, she watched as he raised his fingers, glistening with her juices, to his mouth and licked them clean.

"I knew you'd taste like heaven."

Chapter Four

Kaelen looked down at the woman in his arms. She watched him with a wide, wondering gaze. Her brown eyes were three shades lighter than he'd ever seen them, and he couldn't stop the satisfied smile that stretched his lips. He'd done that to her. He'd changed her from a ferocious mountain lion to a purring cat.

And he wasn't finished yet.

The swell of her hip fit perfectly in the palm of his hand. For that matter, she fit on his lap and in his arms as if she had been made for him.

He traced a slow path up her thigh and over her hip. He followed the slight curve of her stomach, pushing her sweater up and out of the way. She stirred, protesting his attempt to strip away the rest of her clothes.

"You don't mind me seeing your bottom half naked, but you have a problem showing me your tits?"

She narrowed her eyes and tried to push away, but he held her tight and laughed. "I fail to see what is so amusing."

He laughed harder. "You. You're amusing. Such a little firecracker."

She struggled harder, her ire matching his amusement. "I think we're done here."

All laughter fled, and he lasered her with his sudden sobriety. "Oh, no, babe. We're just getting started. You still have quite the attitude. I can see I have my work cut out for me."

Her struggles ceased. She sat up in his lap, her spine ramrod straight, and he loosened his grip enough to allow it.

She still had to tilt her chin up to look him in the eyes. "This is just weird. You're a little too good at this."

He shrugged, uncertain what she meant. Since he didn't quite know how to react, he aimed for cocky. She seemed to respond when he behaved like that. "You can't tell me you don't appreciate good. I made you scream my name."

A blush made its way up her neck to stain her cheeks and the tips of her ears. "This is true." Her lips parted, as if she had more to say, but she pressed them together instead of speaking. Finally she walked her fingers up his arm and paused at his shoulder. "Will I be doing any more screaming?"

He removed the band binding her hair. Using both hands, he ran his fingers through her deep brown tresses, spreading her hair around her shoulders where it fell in soft waves. "Screaming. Begging. If you're a very good girl, some sobbing."

Her eyes flared wider. He recognized her struggle to reconcile her need to be perceived as a capable, independent woman with her need to surrender. Kaelen played with her hair, loving the silky feel as it slid through his fingers, and he gave her the time to wage her war. He wanted her. He yearned to let loose his inner alpha male, but he needed her to want that from him.

At last she lowered her gaze. "What happens here stays here."

If that was what it took, he'd agree. Of course, he'd use all the insights he gained today when he began his quest to win her heart. That would have to wait until they got back to school, though, because he wasn't going to do anything to interrupt their fantasy day. "Yep."

She gripped the hem of her sweater and lifted it over her head. It was a swift movement, not slow enough to tease or so fast that he suspected nerves. The stony look on her face hid her exact emotions, but it clued him in to her discomfort.

For the longest time, he just looked. She was as beautiful as he imagined. Her legs were short but pleasing. Heart-shaped hips curved up, dipping in at her waist. Her perky breasts were small. They fit her size perfectly. If he spanned his hand across her chest, he would be able to just barely grip them both. She was a handful in more ways than one.

Thin, pale scars circled both nipples where the pink areola met creamy skin, barely visible at all. He estimated that in a year or two, they would disappear completely. He longed to ask about them, but he knew this wasn't the time. At least he understood her stony expression.

He slid his fingers along her cheek until he cupped it in his palm. Because she was so much shorter than he, he didn't have to do more than lean forward to brush his lips against hers. He wanted to kiss her slowly, tell her without words that he could handle whatever secrets she hid.

But he was unprepared for the electricity that jumped between them, singeing him to the core. A loud moan rumbled from deep in his chest, filling the room.

Her hand shot out and tangled in his hair, and her lips parted to let him deeper.

He drowned in that first kiss, chasing wave after wave of sweet bliss until he forgot how to breathe. She broke away and collapsed against him. Short bursts of her hot breath fanned his skin, and her breasts heaved, brushing against his chest.

"Damn. You're good at that too."

She sounded too disappointed for his ego to stand many more of her compliments. He stood, dumping her to the floor. She scrambled to her feet and turned her fiery glare on him.

"Take your shoes off and bend over the desk. You definitely didn't learn your lesson." If he knew his little firecracker as well as he thought he did, she wouldn't want him to treat her any differently just because he'd seen a few puzzling scars.

Her eyes flashed, but he read the relief behind them. She lifted her chin, jutting it at him as she kicked off her shoes. "You're not man enough to teach me a lesson."

He couldn't stop half of his mouth from forming a smile. Yes, he definitely preferred this undiluted attitude. Without a word, he gripped her by the back of the neck and forced her to bend over the desk. Her luscious ass bore no traces of the spanking he had so recently delivered. Obviously he had gone too easy on her.

He needed something that would deliver more bite than his hand. Being more into role-playing than BDSM, he hadn't asked to have paddles or other implements meant to please a masochist, and he never wore a belt. The desk had been equipped with a phone, papers, and a stapler. What other authentic items might he find in a drawer? As a last-ditch effort, he yanked open a drawer.

The first drawer revealed a box of condoms, pads of paper, pens, and pencils. The second contained files. Another had folded clothes in it. He recognized the outfit he'd requested for her to wear when she played the part of his secretary. Had she hidden it there or had Oasis placed it there? Either way, it was a good thing he'd stumbled upon it.

On the other side, the top drawer yielded staples, pushpins, and other office supplies. In the back, he found a wooden ruler. It would have to do.

In the course of his search, he had slid his hand from her neck to the center of her back. He put a little more force behind the hold because he knew she was going to protest with more than a scream.

He tested the implement against the tender skin of his forearm. It smarted and left behind a sting, but it didn't actually hurt.

Turning back to Mia, he ran a hand over the smooth skin of her ass and suppressed the urge to caress it with his lips. "This is going to hurt you more than it hurts me, babe. Feel free to scream as loud as you want. Let all that attitude out."

Knowing better than to wait for her to figure out what he'd been doing in the drawers, he brought the ruler down sharply on her ass. She bucked and screeched, but he had a firm hold on her. He waited a second, giving her a chance to use the safe word. When she said nothing, he lifted the ruler. It had left a bright pink, rectangular streak on her skin.

He traced his fingertip over it. She hissed, but the scent of her arousal betrayed her true reaction.

Mia had some issues with body image, and those scars on her breasts held the key to why she hid her body behind baggy clothes and prim manners. He didn't mind that she always pulled her hair into a ponytail or that she almost never wore makeup. He preferred natural beauty, which she had in spades.

If it took a day of spanking her to get her to let go of whatever ailed her, then he would gladly spank her until he had no feeling left in his arm. Then he would switch sides. He wasn't as good with his left hand, but he would manage.

Lifting the ruler a little higher, he concentrated the next blow over her other cheek. He rained smacks over her ass until she stopped fighting and her angry screeches turned to quiet sobs.

Her ass glowed with bright red streaks. He fought with the urge to take her into his arms. That wasn't what she wanted today.

"How are you doing?"

She sniffled. "I'm okay."

He ran his fingertips over her hot skin. She trembled and moaned. Oh yeah, she was okay. He snatched his jacket from where he'd hung it and folded it on the terrazzo floor. "Kneel on the jacket. Keep your legs apart."

She pushed her body away from the desk. He watched her face as she knelt, checking to make sure she was as okay as she claimed. She bore tear-stained cheeks, but her eyes were clear, and she exuded a calmness he'd never before seen. Pride puffed his chest. He'd given her that.

Running his hand down the front of his shirt, he quickly unbuttoned it. He threw it, the rags from her dress, and her sweater to the floor. A line furrowed between her brows for all of two seconds before she looked up at him with serene expectation that changed to undisguised lust.

"I want you on your elbows and knees. I'm going to fuck you, and this is all the padding available." He knelt behind her, watching as she bunched the clothes in a way that cradled her elbows, forearms, and head. Her pussy glistened, and her juices dripped down the insides of her thighs.

Fumbling in the drawer for a condom with one hand, he ripped open his jeans with his other. He shook a little as he rolled it onto his cock. How many times in the past year had he dreamed of having her this way?

He lined up his cockhead with her opening. A sigh issued from between her lips. "Ready?"

"More than ready."

She was tight. He sank in slowly, stretching her walls to fit around his girth. She braced herself against the floor, providing a counterbalance so she wouldn't slide away. He gripped her hips and pushed until the heat from her pink ass singed his skin.

So small and hot, she sheathed him in a vise he never wanted to escape. If he wasn't careful, he wouldn't last long, and he wanted this to last. He was going to rock her world.

She pushed back against him, grinding her pussy in a circle and whimpering. Her prickly attitude had completely disappeared. She was a docile kitten, her claws temporarily sheathed.

"None of that." He swatted her ass lightly. It was enough to send a tremor that left her with an arched back. He ran his hand up her spine and tangled his fingers in her hair. He pulled a little. She purred. He pulled harder. She moaned, and her pussy quivered. "Are you close?"

"Mmmm-hmmm." She convulsed again, a precursor to a climax.

"Let's see how many times I can make you scream my name."

He withdrew and thrust back into her slowly, savoring every sweet inch. It didn't take long for him to realize the sedate pace drove her crazy. She reached between her legs. He felt the increased pressure on his cock as she touched her clit, and he was glad he couldn't see what she was doing. Watching her masturbate would be enough to send him over the edge.

Her squeaks and moans came to a crescendo, and her pussy pulsed around his cock. He gritted his teeth and continued with his slow pace, riding out the sweet seduction of her orgasm and knowing he also prolonged it.

When it diminished to occasional twinges, he renewed his grip on her hair, pulled harder, and increased his pace. Her ass lifted to meet his thrusts.

"Oh God, oh, Kaelen. Please, please, Kaelen, please."

Drunk on the heady pleasure of being inside her, he didn't understand what she wanted. "Please what?" His question came out slurred, but he didn't care.

"This. What you're doing. Please don't stop."

"Not a chance. You haven't screamed my name enough."

Three more thrusts and she did scream his name, inserting way more than the two syllables it usually had. He held on to her hip and pounded into her tight heat.

She stopped fingering her clit, bringing her hand forward to support her weight. Her entire body, softer and more pliant after two orgasms, trembled and shook beneath him. She whimpered when he released her hair, but her body bucked again when he used that free hand to press and rotate against her clit. Her walls shook with a series of powerful convulsions that pulled him deeper and milked a climax that stole his vision. He shouted something loud and incoherent.

Kaelen barely controlled his fall, managing to land half on her right side and half on the floor. He pulled her into his arms and held her close. It seemed like she was part of him, an extension of his body and soul. This new feeling caught him off guard. He'd felt close to a woman before, especially after sex, but not like this. Nothing he experienced with Mia was quite comparable to anything he'd encountered before.

She slid her hands up his chest and locked her arms around his neck. Her small, firm breasts pressed against him. "You're trembling."

He felt her lips against his shoulder. He wanted to touch her everywhere, explore and memorize the perfection of the woman who had captured his heart.

Holding her even tighter in his arms, he kissed her forehead. "So are you, babe. Don't worry. I've got you."

Chapter Five

The hardwood floor pressed against her hip uncomfortably, but Kaelen's firm body cradled the rest of her with a warmth and security that made her reluctant to shift. She'd never been one to cuddle after sex. Usually she dived for her shirt, even if she planned to stay the night.

Kaelen had stared at her scars, but to her relief, he hadn't asked.

And that kiss had knocked her socks off. He certainly knew how to use those lips. The man had lethal skill, and it bothered her. It was just another indication of his perfection, and she had never been comfortable around perfect people. Seeing faults and imperfections in others brought her no small measure of comfort. The more flaws people had, the more she felt a connection with them.

She didn't understand why she felt so connected to Kaelen. The afterglow usually faded by this point. He'd been holding her for at least twenty minutes.

At last he relaxed his hold, easing her away and capturing her with a searing kiss. The tip of his tongue slid along the seam of her lips. She surrendered to his demand, parting to let his tongue sweep inside and claim temporary dominion.

His fingertips traced a path up and down her spine as he settled back, letting his head fall to the floor. "How are you doing, babe?"

She sighed and pushed away. "I wish you wouldn't call me that."

He sat up, and his jeans brushed against her thigh. She turned away from the way they gaped open to show his semihard cock. "Babe?"

"That."

The hand on her back dropped away. "Why?"

"It's demeaning." She tried to put some distance between them as she reached back for her sweater, but he snaked his arm around her waist and held her close.

"How so?"

Having located her sweater, she snagged it, but it didn't move much. Kaelen was sitting on it. "You're on my sweater."

He shrugged. "You're going to be putting something else on for the next scene. You won't need it. Are you going to answer me?"

She didn't have a good answer, other than that the level of familiarity irritated her. "It implies I'm incompetent and inexperienced or that I'm lesser than you."

He laughed, a real, honest sound originating deep in his belly. When he finally quieted down, he wrapped his arm around her shoulder, pulled her closer despite her best effort to resist, and kissed her forehead. "It implies I find you incredibly hot and desirable, and it's familiar and intimate, but it doesn't say anything about your competence and experience or anything else."

Having spent enough of her life being the object of laughter and ridicule, she didn't take kindly to his amusement at her expense. She rolled her eyes at his declaration and wiggled away.

"Where are you going?"

"Bathroom." She tried to flounce away, but he grabbed her hand.

"Your next outfit is in there." He pointed to the bottom left drawer of her desk.

Crouching down, she yanked the handle. Metal rolled over metal. The two scraps of cloth looked like they could be the white blouse and plaid skirt she'd anticipated earlier. She gathered the clothes in the crook of her arm and fled to the safety and privacy of the bathroom.

The next part of the script called for her to be his administrative assistant. Secretary. He'd be her boss. When she'd read the scenario, she couldn't help but notice the blatant sexual harassment of the scene. At the time, she'd figured if he was willing to play the role of Kaelen in her fantasy, she would return the favor by playing the role of secretary/slut for his fantasy.

Having Kaelen show up changed everything. She had expected to bend over in a short skirt and file papers, play at being chased around a desk, and be groped when she leaned over to give him a file. But she hadn't expected Kaelen to be that man. She wondered why he'd cast her in such a demeaning role.

But she had found the scenario exciting when she first read it. If she pushed the idea of Kaelen out of her head and focused on the facts, she could do this and have fun with it. The man with whom she'd spent the last two hours had melted her with his kisses and fucked like a champion. She could do worse. She might not be able to walk tomorrow, but she'd be relaxing on a lounge chair on a beach in the Caribbean. She wouldn't need to walk.

Already the pleasant ache and burn on her ass had faded to little more than a memory. The effects of a spanking rarely lasted longer than an hour. She'd never been spanked with a ruler before, but she'd found it to have less bite than a leather paddle. She wasn't a true masochist who wanted something drastic like a wooden paddle or a riding crop.

Mia shivered at the prospect. She liked the lighter slap-and-tickle aspects, and she liked the upcoming scenario because she sometimes fantasized about having a man tell her what to do and treat her like a sexual object. However, she'd walk out on any man who tried to do that at other times. Role-playing like this was completely new to her.

She frowned at the naked woman with wild hair in the mirror. Kaelen had never treated her badly or talked down to her. He flirted incessantly, and he used his charm way too much, but he'd never been rude or crude. Perhaps she should give him the benefit of the doubt. This scenario presented a safe, consensual way for both of them to explore a dynamic neither of them wanted to put into permanent practice.

Fantasy and role-play provided for healthy expression and exploration of alternate ideas and frowned-upon social norms. She ran her hands through her unruly tresses. Her hairbrush was in the bag she'd left in her car. She wondered if Kaelen would run out and get it.

A knock on the door startled her from her thoughts. "Yes?"

"I have a bottle of water. You have to be thirsty after all that."

She cracked the door the slightest bit and reached her hand out for the bottle. "Thanks."

He'd fastened his jeans, but he hadn't put a shirt back on. "Hey, do you know how long you might be in there? It's the only bathroom in this place." He handed the water over.

"Let me throw on some clothes and you can go first. I have to get a few things from my car."

When she emerged a few minutes later, she was wearing the same baggy jeans and shapeless sweater in which she'd arrived.

He looked her up and down, a frown marring his brow. "That's not the outfit I picked out for you."

She smoothed a hand over her hair, hoping to tame some of the mess. "I'll get dressed after I run to my car."

The frown didn't go away, and Mia found that she didn't like seeing it. In all their interactions, he'd rarely frowned like that, even when he didn't get his way. "It's a little chilly outside. Do you want me to get it for you?"

"Thanks, but I got it. You go ahead and do what you need to do. I'll be right back."

He grabbed her wrist as she went by. "Are you okay with this? You don't have to do this if you don't want to."

She couldn't look away from the concern shining from his gray eyes. He'd fulfilled her fantasy. She would take this part with the playful grain of salt in which it was intended. "I'm okay with this. Just don't expect me to behave like an airhead."

The line between his brows disappeared, and the brilliant smile that melted her bones reappeared. "That'll work. I like smart chicks." He released her wrist, but he slapped her on the ass before she was out of reach. At her expression of mild disapproval, he shrugged. That smile never faded from his face. In fact, it grew. His dimple put in an appearance. "Practice."

She couldn't stop herself from returning his smile. "You've practiced enough on my ass."

He shook his head and started toward the bathroom. "I'll never get enough of your ass."

The door closed, ending her chance to say anything in response. It was no use anyway. She was out of her league when it came to his level of flirting. Since she would be on the receiving end of his flirtation, charm, and sexual advances for the next few hours, perhaps she should just relax and enjoy it. After all, that was kind of the role he'd asked her to play, and it did appeal to a soft part of her she'd buried in order to nurture her pragmatic side.

When she returned to the cabin, the bathroom door hung open. A file folder waited on the desk, though the papers and other office paraphernalia were still on the floor where he'd flung them when he'd cleared the desktop.

She glanced at the closed door behind the desk. It was a bedroom. It had to be. There was nothing else left. How would that play into his boss-secretary fantasy?

What a puzzling man. Outside the confines of school, there seemed to be a lot more to him. Perhaps she'd underestimated him when she'd stereotyped and dismissed him from everything but her sexual fantasies.

Ten minutes later, she had tamed her hair back into a ponytail and shimmied into the outfit he'd selected. It reminded her of something from a porno or a rock video.

The green plaid skirt was almost long enough to cover her ass. From Kaelen's height, he wouldn't be able to see anything, but if she bent at all, he would have an unobstructed view of everything. Underwear and hose weren't allowed, but he'd left a pair of low-heeled, strappy sandals for her feet.

The white button-down shirt had a little pleat in front that made the shirt cup her breasts. It barely covered her midriff, and it was so thin that the white lace demi-bra was easily visible through it. In the subdued bathroom lighting, she could make out the rosy color of her nipples.

Mia spent more than a few minutes staring at the stranger in the mirror. She never wore tight clothes, and she avoided looking into a mirror for longer than necessary. So many years of hiding her figure had spawned a habit not easily broken. Somewhere along the way, though, she had turned into a curvy woman with more than a little hint of sex appeal.

On a whim, she released her hair from the band holding it together. Soft chestnut locks floated over her shoulders. Her eyes appeared larger, and she looked feminine and a little wanton.

Still not the kind of tall, cool beauty she pictured at Kaelen's side.

She shrugged at the image staring back, turned off the light, and headed to her desk. Having to do actual secretarial work seemed unlikely. This was a sexual fantasy, not an answer to a disorganized person's prayers. She knocked on the door to let him know she was in position, and then she spread the discarded sweater over the seat to have a barrier between her skin and the leather chair.

Time ticked by as she sat there. For the first time, she became aware of the black-and-white clock hanging over the door and the *schick-schick* sound it made to mark every second.

With nothing else to do, she gathered the papers from the floor and set them on the desk. The yellow binding of the report holder Kaelen had thrown down earlier caught her attention. She opened the cover and attempted to read the first sentence, but the door flew open.

Turning, she found Kaelen transformed. The jeans and flannel were conspicuously absent. In their place he wore dress pants, a shirt, and a plaid tie that matched her skirt. The man had a thing for plaid.

"Calloway, get your pad and pen, and get your cute little ass in here."

Mia lifted her brow at his 1970s tone. "My cute little ass? Isn't that going a bit far?"

He matched her expression. "You knew the conditions of employment when you accepted this job. You're my assistant, here to assist me in any and every way I need assisting."

There was no pad of paper in sight, so she grabbed some of the papers on the desk. If he was serious about her having to write stuff down, she would make notes on the back. A quick glance around the floor helped locate the pencil that had been there earlier. Standing, she beamed a tolerant smile at him. "Well, then I guess I better do what you say, or I'll find myself out of a job."

She breezed by him, sailing into the room with her head held high. She glanced around, surprised it wasn't the bedroom she thought she'd find. It was definitely an office.

The door closed behind her, rattling in its frame to protest the force Kaelen had used. "No, but I would have to tie you to the desk to teach you a lesson. That's a fun way to start the day. If you feel you need a lesson right now, let me know."

Mia shook her head. Bondage was on her list of things that weren't going to happen. She just couldn't see letting a stranger tie her up. Kaelen wasn't a stranger, but she still wasn't ready to push her boundaries that far. "I'm good."

The office appeared pretty generic. A large desk dominated the room. A chair, a mass of black leather, sat behind it, and a set of matching chairs were situated in front. Two file cabinets, several bookshelves, a hope chest, and two armoires lined the room. Windows let in light on two walls.

Kaelen settled into the larger chair behind the desk and pushed a stack of files across. Momentum took the top three to the floor. "Oops. You'll need to pick those up before you file them."

She couldn't stop the are-you-serious look from taking over her face. The sardonic part of her wanted to critique his porno choreography. She reined that part in long enough to kneel down and gather the papers.

Since they were all blank, she shoved them into folders randomly. Glancing up, she found him peering over the desk, supervising her progress by looking down her shirt. "Enjoying the view?"

He winked. "Yep. Ms. Calloway, you have great tits. It's a shame you hide them behind shirts."

She wondered if he referred to the bulky clothing she usually wore or if he wanted her to remove the scrap of shirt currently preserving her modesty. She stood up and set the files on the edge of his desk. "Where would you like these filed, Mr. Sebastian?"

He settled back into his seat and pointed at a filing cabinet on his side of the desk, all of five feet away. "Bottom drawer."

Having spent the past couple of hours naked around Kaelen had made her a little less self-conscious, but the ribbon of a skirt left nothing to the imagination. She crouched down and opened the filing drawer.

"Now, Ms. Calloway, we've talked about this before. Bend at the waist. It's better for company morale."

A glance back at him revealed the distinct absence of his cocky grin. Heat smoldered behind his eyes, and suddenly she wanted to see how long she could tease him before he grabbed her and went wild.

She tried for a coy smile that must have been effective, because his breath hitched. "We can't risk company morale, Mr. Sebastian." She stood and tried again, this time bending at the waist. She kept her feet apart for balance, also assuring him a better view. "Is this better?"

"Yes. File slowly. I wouldn't want you to pull a muscle."

Sliding the folders into random spots took almost zero brainpower. The heat of Kaelen's stare manifested as a physical force that caressed her exposed folds, leaving her wet and craving real contact.

When she finished, she faced him and his tented pants. Now she sported the cocky grin. "Did you enjoy the view, Mr. Sebastian? Is there anything else you want filed?"

His gaze raked over her body, repeating the trip a few times. He stroked his hand over the bulge in his pants. Mia had never before seen a man take such pleasure in his desire. "Yeah, file my cock in your mouth."

The sauciness she had felt moments ago at flashing her pussy for his pleasure faded. She hesitated. Oral sex had been on her list of things she wouldn't do, not with a stranger. However, she didn't necessarily want to hold Kaelen to the same restrictions. Maybe. She'd never gone down on a man before. She hadn't thought her inexperience in this matter would be an issue. Now, faced with the prospect of disappointing Kaelen, she faltered.

"Is there a problem?" He halted the hand stroking his erection.

Gingerly she knelt between his knees and reached for his fly.

He caught her hands and her gaze. "Ms. Calloway, do you have a problem with fulfilling the responsibilities of your job?"

She understood his look to mean he wouldn't force the issue. This was her choice. "I just... Your order surprised me. That's all."

Realization dawned. He blinked hard and squeezed her hands. "No oral. That was one of your limits. I'm sorry. I forgot."

"That's okay. I didn't want to do this with a stranger. I'm okay doing this with you." She shook off his hold and unfastened his pants. Ample evidence of his arousal sprang forth. Kaelen hadn't bothered with underwear either. "I'm just not sure what you like."

He stared at her for so long that she found the courage to meet his gaze. Though his expression was unreadable, she didn't see any kind of censure. "Touch me with your hands first. I like when you start slow and take your time. Cup my balls. If you're going to squeeze or roll them around, be gentle. They're very sensitive. When you add your mouth, start with your tongue. Do that, and you'll figure out what I like."

Grasping her cheeks gently, he tilted her face up and brushed the pads of his thumbs against her mouth. He explored her lips slowly and thoroughly, taking his time. When she took a ragged breath, he bent his head and replaced his thumbs with his lips. By the time his tongue entered her mouth, he'd coaxed forth a blaze that spread heat from her chest to her toes.

When the kiss ended and he pulled back, they both took a moment to catch their breath. "Plus, I like to watch you touching me. I might not last too long."

Emboldened by his kiss and by his detailed encouragement, Mia took his cock in hand. She trailed her fingertips over the shaft, enjoying the smooth hardness and listening for his smallest reactions. His breath hitched when she caressed the cleft at the head and right under the ridge around the crown.

She didn't spend all her time on those spots, however, reasoning that she had a few that gave her a little more of a jolt, but it was nicer to spread the attention. It ramped up the anticipation factor.

He gripped the arms of the chair. From the corners of her eyes, she saw his nails turn white.

Reaching underneath, she cupped his sac. A casual exploration revealed that he preferred a few kinds of movements, such as when she rolled his balls gently in her palm, more than he liked any particular place caressed. She liked hearing the hisses escape his lips and the way his knees shifted, bobbing against her sides, as he struggled to stay still. Touching him like this, causing these reactions, gave her a heady rush of power that sent heat to her core. She shifted, squeezing her legs together to concentrate the feeling.

When she added her tongue, he groaned. "Fuck, Mia. You're lethal, babe."

She didn't mind the moniker so much anymore, but she was reluctant to call it a term of endearment.

She licked the smooth skin of his shaft and circled her tongue around his purpled head. The glistening drop at the tip tasted salty and tart. Getting into the spirit of things, she made her way down to his sac. On a whim, she sucked one of his balls into her mouth.

She heard a *thump* and looked up to make sure he was okay. He'd thrown his head back. The sound had been the back of his head hitting the frame on top of the chair. His lips worked, forming letters and oaths, but the only thing that made sense was her name.

Wrapping her hand around his shaft, she pumped once. His entire body twitched, so she did it again. She switched her lips to his other testicle, mouthing it gently as she stroked his cock.

A light sheen of sweat glistened on his chest and stomach. He was close. Hesitantly she released his balls and closed her mouth around the darkened head of his cock. She sucked hard, taking it as deep into her mouth as she could. She wrapped her hand around the base to pick up the slack there.

He tangled a hand in her hair, but he didn't try to guide her action or control the pace she set. When he tightened his grip in warning, she sucked harder. He shouted, and his ass shot off the chair. She lifted with him, giving his balls a little twist, and swallowed in time to the pulsing evidence of his orgasm.

When he came down, she released his cock and laid her head on his thigh. In the silence that followed, she heard his rapid breathing keep time with the pounding of her heart. She knew he had enjoyed the experience, but shades of doubt were creeping into her brain. He had a great sense of humor. He was intelligent, fun, and thoughtful. The more time she spent with him, the more she talked with him and got to know him and had sex with him, the less she could deny how deep her feelings for him ran.

Chapter Six

If he stopped looking down at the woman whose head rested on his thigh, his heart rate might return to normal. The manic beating wasn't caused by the clear view of her cleavage or the image of her lovely lips sliding up and down his shaft and everything to do with the sure knowledge that things could never go back to being the way they had been.

The prospect of seeing her three times a week in class and not being able to wink at her based on the foundation of a permanent relationship tasted metallic in his mouth. Fear. Receiving a blowjob had never before left him in a state of mind-numbing fear.

To be fair, the sex act itself had nothing to do with the deep ache starting in his chest. The way she bit her lip and hesitated when he told her what he wanted betrayed her lack of experience. The possessive part of him smiled in satisfaction, reveling in the fact he was her first. If the rest of him had any say about it, he would be her only.

Despite her inexperience, or perhaps because of it, she had taken the time to figure out what he liked. She had lingered over the details of pleasuring him instead of rushing through the task in an effort to get him off and get it over with. He fast-forwarded to the care she would take picking out plates while they were registering for their wedding.

Christ. Never before had getting sucked off made him look forward to shopping.

Leaning down, he slid his hands under her arms. "Babe, I want you on my lap."

She lifted her gaze, and he saw the fire simmering behind her light brown eyes. Sliding her knees on either side of his, she flashed a tentative smile. "Well, this padded leather is a lot easier on the knees than the wood floor."

He laughed. "Next time I'll include a couch or a bed in my fantasy."

She giggled, a devious sound he'd never expected. "I guess we both have desk fetishes."

In Kaelen's mind, the only fetishes he had involved Mia. He'd take her anywhere he could get her. Instead of answering, he cupped his hand around the back of her neck and drew her close. Slanting his lips over hers, he feathered a soft kiss that did little more than tease.

Mia gripped his shoulders, digging in harder the longer he kept the kiss light. The perfume of her arousal saturated his senses, and her hot wetness hovered inches from his cock, which showed no sign of rising to the challenge.

But he took his cue from Mia and didn't rush anything. They had hours yet, and he was determined to make them count. Show her how good being with him could be.

A bell chimed through the building. Mia jerked her mouth away from his and looked toward the door. Her eyes took a moment to focus. "Doorbell?"

He nodded. "Lunch is here, babe. Be a good little secretary and go get it."

She backed away and stood up, smoothing down her skirt and wearing an uncertain expression. "You're wearing a lot more than I am."

"Yep." He tucked his cock into his pants and fastened them. "Go get lunch or you'll find out how I discipline a sucky assistant."

She rolled her eyes at his unintentional pun. "Let me guess. You'll tie me up and spank me?"

He chuckled. "Nope. Spanking was your fantasy. While I'm not opposed to it at all, it doesn't figure into my fantasy of having you as my beautiful and slutty administrative assistant, tempting you with my potent masculinity, and then making good on my promises."

She glanced around the room, her keen eyes searching for something. "Where is your jacket?"

Though he knew the person from Oasis who had delivered the food would be long gone—they had a strict policy of not intruding—he wasn't willing to humiliate Mia, and it was cold outside. He pointed to the top drawer of the filing cabinet.

She snagged his black fleece and left the room. He hoped it smelled like her when he got it back. She wasn't gone long, but when she returned, she looked puzzled.

"What's wrong?"

"Nobody was there. I mean, I couldn't even hear a car driving away. That's a little spooky." She set a white paper bag on the desk and unrolled the top to open it up. "Oh, goody. I love subs."

He watched with a grin on his face, enjoying the simple act of seeing her unpack food from a paper bag. She divided the chips and soft drinks, and then she sniffed at the paper wrapped around each sub to determine what was inside.

"You like Philly cheesesteak too?" she asked.

"Yeah. Is that what you got?"

She nodded. "This explains why they asked what kinds of food I like. I thought some of the questions were a bit much, didn't you?"

Kaelen laughed. The questionnaire had asked everything from his shoe size to what color nail polish he preferred to see on his partner's toes. And those were just the foot-themed questions. "Yeah, but they got it perfect, so I'm not about to complain."

PERFECT. KAELEN'S ADJECTIVE took Mia by surprise, and she didn't know why. Her first impulse was to interpret it to mean he found her to be the perfect person to fulfill his sexual fantasies. But that was a little too difficult to swallow. Men as tall, handsome, and charming as Kaelen inevitably ended up with women who matched. Mia had always pictured herself with a man who was about five-seven, a little round in the middle, a little bald on the head, and a little boring in the bedroom. Her last serious boyfriend had been most of those things. His lackluster brown hair hadn't begun to thin yet, but given that even his mother's hair was thin, it was just a matter of time.

Mia didn't have a problem with any of that. Acting out this fantasy through Oasis was her way of sowing her wild oats before she settled down with the man who would tolerate her body and love her brains. He'd want to get married, get their careers firmly launched, and then have a couple of kids. He might not be the kind of man who coached T-ball, but he'd attend all the practices and put his heart and soul into cheering for their son or daughter.

Kaelen likely only meant that things were going well so far. Mia was approaching this assistant fantasy with a sense of humor, and she was committed to the role. He probably appreciated her effort. She definitely appreciated the effort he put into fulfilling her spanking fantasy. Going all out for this part of it was the least she could do.

The unnatural silence in the room brought her mind back to the present. She glanced up at Kaelen. He bit into his sub sandwich without taking his eyes from her.

She sank into one of the two chairs in front of the desk and unwrapped her sub. "So, is this a break, or are we still in our roles while we have lunch?"

Kaelen grinned. "I guess we should take a break. Otherwise I'd have to ask you to take off my flannel, and then the sight of your cleavage and your snatch would mean I couldn't finish lunch. And I think we both need to refuel for this afternoon. In addition to harassing you some more, I have to do some product testing. You know, actual work."

Mia had read the scenario script so often she'd committed it to memory. It contained no references to actual work. She swallowed and sipped her drink. "It turns you on to watch someone do secretarial work? Does the tapping of fingers on a keyboard bring back fond cybersex memories?"

His rich laugh filled the room, infecting her with a smile she couldn't wipe from her face. Several moments passed before he settled down enough to shake his head at her humor. "I bet you'd be good at sexting."

"I'm taking off my bra. Oh, my nipples are so hard for you." She approximated mechanical speech the best she could, but sarcasm remained the dominant part of the tone.

Kaelen got into the spirit of things. "I'm hard, babe. Stroking fast. Faster. Fastest. Touch your clit. Come for me." His dimple manifested, and her thighs trembled despite the deliberate lack of passion in his speech.

She looked him up and down, licking her lips as licentiously as she could. "Sexting wouldn't work for me. I'd have to see it."

He wrapped up the remainder of his sub and shoved it in the bag. "Happy to show you, babe. Anytime. I'd even let you help."

She ignored the invitation and gestured at the bag. "Aren't you going to finish that?"

Shaking his head, he rounded to her side of the desk and dropped into the chair next to hers. Smoke swirled behind his eyes. "I'm hungry for something different."

Mia didn't bother with trying to be sexy. "Well, my lunch isn't different. Besides, I'm hungry, so you can't have it."

"Want me to tell you what kind of work we'll be doing today?"

Since that information had been absent from the description, she could admit to intense curiosity. "Yes. The scenario outline didn't call for actual work."

Kaelen got that smug look on his face that made her rethink finishing the sub. She was suddenly less hungry for steak. "I asked for a list of what kinds of toys you would and wouldn't allow instead of giving details about this part. I wanted it to be a surprise."

Mia lowered her half-eaten sub. "Seeing me here today wasn't enough of a surprise?"

He drew his thumb along her lower lip in what could have been a sensual caress, but it also could have been him wiping away sauce. "Seeing you here only made me wonder why I hesitated so long to ask you out."

Stones dropped in the pit of her stomach. She didn't want to become a victim of his charm. "Kaelen, please don't step outside of the scenario parameters." They'd agreed to avoid saying things of an emotional nature or making promises to continue the fantasy beyond that day.

He held up his hands in a gesture of apology and surrender. "Sorry. I won't go there."

"Why don't you tell me what work you have planned?" She rewrapped the other half of her sandwich. It would make a good dinner on her way to the airport.

"I'm researching the impact of sociological factors prohibiting men from using sex toys in erotic play due to the fact they think it'll influence how masculine they're perceived. You'll be asked a series of questions after each miniscenario."

The sociology grad student part of Mia's brain stood up and took notice. The woman who'd been disappointed by more than one lover lined up right behind her. What was it about men that made them leery of using electronic devices in bed? They used them everywhere else.

Of course, she wasn't opposed to the idea of having a job with perks that involved orgasms. She gestured to the door. "Give me five minutes?"

"Take your time. I'll get everything set up."

It took a little longer than five minutes because she couldn't use the bathroom when all she could think about were the various scenarios Kaelen had planned. She could really get behind a man who wasn't afraid to supplement his biological equipment with things that vibrated or pulsed.

When she returned, she found Kaelen pulling the sheets back on a bed that hadn't been there when she left. He turned to her with that half grin on his face and lifted his shoulder in a lazy shrug. "I found a Murphy bed. They said the room would have a bed, but when I came in before, I couldn't find it."

That explained what had taken him so long to call her into the office the first time. "How did you find it?"

"There was a note in the drawer with all the toys, which we get to keep, by the way. It had directions on how to pull out the bed and some warnings about safety features. You know, like don't jump on the bed because you can bang your head on the ceiling. And put these sliding things into the locked position. And don't forget the mattress pads."

Delighted to have a bed, Mia laughed. "Why the mattress pads?"

He swaggered over to her and pulled her hips close. "Because you're going to be that wet."

She was already pretty slippery. He dipped his head and gave her one of those slow, casual kisses that lit her fires. He was too talented with those lips.

"All right, babe. Give me a minute to wash these toys. There's a survey on the desk I need you to fill out first."

He disappeared with what looked like a fishing tackle box. Mia skirted the bed, which took up half of the office space, and looked at the paper on the desk.

It asked several questions about what she did to excite herself while masturbating versus what she did when she was with another person. How did she correct for maximum stimulation alone? Did she direct lovers to pay more attention to the areas she liked? They went on and on like this. The questions from Oasis had been informational. Kaelen's questions asked for an emotional interpretation.

Mia frowned at the questions. Until now, it had never occurred to her that she expected her lovers to read her mind. If she didn't tell them what she liked and what she didn't like, how would they know? And how could she balance that with not sounding bossy? Nobody liked to be micromanaged, especially not in bed.

Well, most people didn't.

When he returned, she handed the paper to him. "You could design a whole study around this idea."

He gave her a funny look as he set the plastic box down at the head of the bed. "Why are you still wearing clothes?"

Unwilling to pursue the reason behind his expression, she slid back into her role. "You didn't ask me to take them off."

He crossed his arms and lifted a brow.

She unbuttoned the tight shirt and shrugged out of it. The white lace demi-bra followed her skirt to the floor. "Are you going to undress?"

His smoldering gaze kept her pinned in place. She'd always giggled at descriptions of men with smoldering gazes, but now that she'd spent half a day in Kaelen's crosshairs, she had learned not to discount the power of a good smolder.

Like her, he unbuttoned his shirt first. Unlike her, he made a conscious effort to seduce with his striptease. She had to lick her lips and swallow to avoid drooling over his broad shoulders and ripped abs.

His pants fell down his legs, revealing the cock she had so recently come to know so well. It sprang from his nest of curls, hard and ready for another round. When he finished, standing before her in nothing but a plaid tie, he stayed put and let her stare. She was too busy enjoying the sight of his body to be self-conscious about the intense way he studied her body.

After a few long moments full of unspoken lust passed, he climbed onto the bed, arranging the pillows behind him so he could sit up. "Come straddle me."

Mia scrambled to obey. "Aren't you going to take off your tie?"

"I'm going to use it as a blindfold in a little while. First, I want to see how you respond when you can see the toy."

Unable to stop the analytical side of her brain, she pursed her lips. "Don't you think you should do the blind test first? That way I'll be more focused on giving you the data you want."

He slipped the tie, which he had loosened to get out of his shirt, over his head and handed it to her. "Blindfold yourself. No peeking."

Blindfolding oneself with a tie was easier said than done. The wider part had to go over her eyes, which made tying it a little challenging. Kaelen helped.

"Just sit there for now. I'm going to stimulate different parts of your body with the toys. I want you to feel free to give suggestions. I'm going to ask a lot of questions, but I'll try to keep them simple."

One hand closed over her breast. She felt his warmth, but even before her surgery, her breasts hadn't been sensitive or responsive. He massaged it. Then he pinched and rolled her nipple. She held her breath and wished for him to move on. He played with both breasts for a few minutes before his hands dropped away.

When they returned, he pinched a nipple between his fingers and pulled it, stretching the skin to the point where she felt a little tingle. Something soft closed around it. When he let go, a heavy object hung from it. He jostled the end of the thing, and it began buzzing. She felt the vibrations, but they didn't stimulate her sexually.

He did the same thing to the other one, but he didn't elicit a different response.

"Are your breasts not sensitive, or am I doing something wrong?"

One of the reasons she liked having sex from behind was that men didn't feel obligated to touch her breasts. Or if they did, they couldn't see her lack of reaction. Add in spanking, and she had enough stimulation to make the lack of response from her breasts unnoticeable.

"They've never been sensitive. Even nipple clamps don't do more than hurt." Though he'd clamped something to her nipples, the fact they didn't hurt made her think they couldn't be nipple clamps. "I don't know quite what you've done, but these don't hurt."

"They're soft clamps, meant for pleasure, not pain. I have them tightened as far as they'll go."

"Sorry. You'd get farther attaching them to my clit."

He cupped the sides of her face in his hands and feathered his lips across hers. "Don't apologize, babe. Does it have to do with your scars? Do you want to talk about it?"

"No and no." She wouldn't get defensive about her breasts unless he pushed the issue. She wanted neither sympathy nor pity. It wasn't like she'd survived breast cancer or anything life threatening like that. Next to what some women went through, her problem had been inconsequential.

He removed the clamps, but he didn't say anything. He circled her areolae with his thumbs. "On the plus side, I could play with them for hours and it wouldn't irritate or overstimulate you."

"Is that your plan?" She lifted a brow, but the blindfold ruined her attempt. She didn't even know if he noticed it.

"Some other time. But you did make a great suggestion. Lean back. Rest your weight on your hands behind you."

She gripped his legs just above the knee, aware that the position spread her pussy lips wider. He pinched her clit, and she sucked in air.

"Like that?" He pinched again. She couldn't tell if he was adjusting his grip or playing with her.

"Yes."

The soft clamp vibrated to life. Its weight stretched her clit, but it didn't pinch or hurt. The vibrations, closed around her clit like that, made her pussy clench in anticipation. A soft moan of pleasure, a completely involuntary response, sounded in the back of her throat.

"Have you ever told a lover you don't like your breasts touched?"

The blindfold made her less self-conscious about answering his questions. "No. I don't mind being touched. It just doesn't do for me what most men expect it to do. I tend to look for men who like asses or legs better than breasts." Kaelen's survey had indicated he found a woman's ass to be her sexiest feature.

His hands slid up from her hips, finding the sensitive areas on her sides. She breathed in sharply as a shiver shook her body. He played his hands over her flesh, caressing those sweet spots again and again. Then he pulled her forward, jerking her weight from her hands so that she fell against his chest. His mouth closed around hers, and this kiss lacked anything slow or patient.

He crushed her to him and increased the pressure of his hands as he moved them across her back.

The position also pressed the vibrating soft nipple clamp harder against her clit. She moaned into his mouth and ran her hands over his skin, mimicking the way he touched her. Shivers rocked her body and echoed through his. Or maybe they began with him and ended with her. She lost track.

He moved one hand up to grip her hair. He pulled, perhaps harder than he intended, and mumbled an apology as his lips trailed down her neck.

The vibrations seemed to magnify. She felt her clit swell, and she wiggled against the way the heat concentrated there. Tingles shot from the roots of her hair straight to her core. "No, I like when you pull my hair. Not hard, just like this. It… I… Oh God!" The knot of heat burst. A small orgasm pulsed through her body, originating solely from her clit. She shot to her knees, her bottom no longer resting on his legs and her body arching as he pulled harder on her hair.

"God, you're beautiful. I could watch you come over and over, but right now you're killing me."

The clamp slid off her clit. It had to have fallen off because his hands were elsewhere on her body.

His low tone washed through her cells, and he released his hold on her hair and her back. The hum of the clamp's vibrations stopped. The sounds of the tackle box opening and him rummaging told her he'd returned the toy, and now he searched for another implement to test.

She heard the ripping of foil as she returned to an upright straddle position. Kaelen urged her to lift, and he guided her onto his sheathed cock. The darkness made her hyperaware of sounds and feelings. His soft moan as she slowly slid down the length of his cock. The creak of the bedsprings as she shifted her weight. The rush of liquid heat as he stretched the walls of her vagina.

"You're in charge. Do what pleases you. Ride me like I'm a dildo." The sounds of sliding equipment told her he was still rooting around in the tackle box.

"Dildos can move. They change angles."

He chuckled. "I'm a stationary dildo. You'll have to tilt your body. Don't worry. You can hang on to me. I won't let you fall."

She wasn't worried about falling. She was worried about looking stupid. She was worried about getting off on his cock while he watched. What if he didn't enjoy it as much as she did?

His lips brushed along the line of her jaw. "You think too much."

She blew out a breath. "What if you don't like what I like?"

The trail of kisses raised gooseflesh as he made his way down her neck. "Are you really worried about not pleasing me?"

"Well, I don't want this to be boring for you." Mia had been bored during sex before, spending time counting cracks in the ceiling while her partner finished doing whatever he was doing. Boring sucked. He sounded amused, but that would change if she couldn't make him come.

He palmed her breasts, but his fingertips rounded her rib cage to feather caresses along her sides. She quivered, inside and out. "Mia, being with you has never, ever been boring. You feel like heaven on me right now, and if you do absolutely nothing, it's still just a matter of time until I explode inside you. The challenge will be making you come before I do." He slapped her ass, a move that had more sound than bite. "Now giddyap."

Throwing her worries to the wind, she rocked her hips forward and back to generate some heat. It felt good, but she would have to do that for hours before she managed to climax. She lifted, letting him slide out about halfway, and then she rolled her hips and pressed down.

Kaelen's body shuddered, and his grip on her breasts tightened. "You're so fucking hot, babe. You're making it very hard to be passive."

She repeated the move. "Nobody said you had to be passive. I thought you were testing equipment in addition to technique, not in place of." It took her three thrusts to get all the words out, but by the time she finished, Kaelen was lifting his hips to meet her as she slid back down on him.

The low hum didn't register until he stroked his fingertips along her ribs again, and they vibrated. Small pads attached to each of his fingers brought a different kind of pleasure to the sensitive places on her sides.

He swept his tongue into her mouth for a searing kiss. After she forgot how to breathe, his talented mouth traveled down her neck to find those places just below her ears that drove her wild. He pulled her hair in time to the rhythm of her ride.

Just as all the sensations combined and Mia teetered on the edge of the cliff, he pressed a vibrating pad to her sensitive and swollen clit. It was too much. Her cry turned to a shriek as the world exploded.

Immediately Kaelen flipped her so that she was on her back beneath him. Registering the firm mattress and the silky sheets, she relaxed, letting the force of her climax wash through her body. He thrust into her, maintaining the same gentle rhythm she used to prolong her orgasm. She wanted to meet his thrusts, but she had no control over her body. At last he buried himself deep and cried out.

She expected him to collapse on top of her, but he didn't. He thrust several more times before pulling out his softening cock, only to replace it with his fingers. Those vibrating pads drove her to the tip of another peak. She writhed and pushed against him, trying to escape an orgasm she couldn't control.

With his free hand, Kaelen captured one wrist and pressed it above her head. When she tried prying his fingers away to loosen his grip, he grabbed her free hand and held them both out of his way. She hadn't consented to being bound or restrained, so she didn't understand why he would resort to this. However, at the moment, she didn't much care. She didn't think he meant to do anything more than prevent her from pushing him away, and she really didn't want him to stop.

He fucked her with his fingers, massaging them around deep inside her pussy. The pad on his thumb stayed on her clit, and the one on the finger he hadn't thrust inside pulsed just outside her opening. He'd found a particularly responsive spot completely by accident.

Her body lifted and writhed. She had no control over the ways she moved, and for the first time in her life, she didn't try to temper her orgasm to preserve her pride. She knew she looked completely wanton and wild, and she reveled in it. That was what this whole fantasy was all about.

"Kaelen, oh, Kaelen." She repeated his name over and over. Sometimes it came out loud. Other times it managed to only be the movement of her lips.

He worked her faster, not stopping when she screamed, though he did slow his pace to bring her down gently.

She lay there, limp, blinded, and soaked in perspiration. Her body quivered and trembled from the aftershocks of the largest orgasm she'd ever ridden. She wanted to tell him she had nothing but respect and appreciation for any man with enough balls to use toys like that, but she hadn't yet regained the ability to speak.

The bed squeaked and dipped as he got up. The door opened and then closed, and she assumed he had gone to take care of the condom. When he returned, he flopped onto the bed, throwing himself so that he landed half on top of her.

He kissed her cheek. "Babe, in case you missed it, I had no problem coming."

She wanted to respond. Her mind formed ideas, images, and feelings, but she wasn't to the point where she could form coherent words.

"Speechless." He chuckled. "I'll have to note your reactions for my research, Ms. Calloway. I'll be honest and say I've never seen a woman move like that. Are you double-jointed?"

She made a noise meant to be a negative answer, but she wasn't sure how he took it.

"While I have you where I want you, we'll continue with this part of the experiment." He nibbled a series of kiss-bites over her collarbone, sending shivers in all directions.

Before, the blindfold had heightened her senses. Now she couldn't tell which end was up, much less guess what Kaelen was doing as he leaned over her and shifted. Little sounds—*pop, scrape, splat*—meant nothing.

He nudged her legs farther apart, but she didn't think anything of it until she felt the cool wetness of lubricant against the heat of her pussy. Forgetting the blindfold, she lifted her head to see. It didn't work. "What are you doing?"

By the time she finished her question, he had inserted a vibrator and turned it on so that it pulsed in regular bursts. Her body jerked. She wanted to push him away, but her hands weren't cooperating.

"Not ready. Gimme a minute."

"Shhhh." He smoothed her hair away from her face. "Research. Just relax. Let me do the work. We'll call this a thank-you for that awesome blowjob."

Her muscles might be liquid, but that didn't stop her pussy from responding to the urging of the vibrator. He increased the rate of vibration. She whimpered. He reached down and fucked her with it.

It felt good, but it was just too much. Having regained some motor control, she shoved at his arm. Even at full strength, she'd be no match for him. As it was, she didn't even interrupt his rhythm. Kaelen just didn't know when to give up. Stubborn asshole.

"Hey, that's not a nice thing to call the man who is rocking your world."

She hadn't meant to say that out loud. Her hips lifted, thrusting against the growing heat between her legs. "You're going to make me pass out."

"Not until you scream my name again." He claimed her mouth with a kiss that stole her breath and wiped away anything she might have said.

His heat pressed along her side, and he threw a leg over her thigh, pinning her in place. She burrowed closer, seeking the comfort of his scent and the solid feel of his body as he stripped away all her defenses. Hot and cold pleasure swirled and prickled at her breasts, belly, and thighs, circling her center until it converged. Desperately she clutched his arm, unable to temper the force with which she dug her nails into his skin.

He whispered praise and encouragement as the edges of her vision burst with color. She screamed as she climaxed and clung to him as she lost consciousness.

When she became aware of her surroundings again, she had no idea how much time had passed. Kaelen held her in the crook of his arm, and his legs tangled with hers. He'd spread a sheet over them and removed her blindfold. Mia inhaled the sweet scent of his skin and sighed. "I fell asleep."

He smoothed her hair away from her temple and kissed her forehead. "Passed out. Falling asleep implies boredom. Passing out means you had a great time."

Her hand rested over his heart. She flexed her fingertips. "I passed out, then. There was definitely no boredom involved."

She shifted her body, moving so her hip wasn't twisted, and his cock brushed her thigh. It seemed a little stiff, so she lifted the sheet to take a peek. It curved, long and hard, lying against his stomach. Definitely ready to go. "How long was I out?"

"Almost an hour. We still have a couple hours here." He lifted her chin and feathered a kiss over her lips. "Ready for the comparison test?"

She trailed her hand down his chest, taking the time to enjoy the feel of his muscles under her fingers. Wrapping her hand around his cock, she grinned. "I'm not sure you can outdo your earlier performance, but I'm looking forward to the attempt."

He thrust into her grip, even as he leaned away and reached into the toolbox. "As I recall, we start out with you in the cowboy position." He ripped the foil.

She took the condom from the wrapper and unrolled it over his cock, tracing the paths of his veins as she went and enjoying the way he shuddered under her tender care. She threw a leg over his hips, intending to sink down on his waiting cock, but he grasped her waist and held her above him. Her pussy clenched in anticipation, and she didn't like that he made her wait.

She glanced at his face and fell under the spell of his hot gaze. He sat up and wrapped her in his tight embrace, melding her stomach and breasts against his chest. He played his fingers up and down her spine. Kneeling up like this, she had a slight height advantage. Tilting his head back, she rested her fingertips on his cheeks and traced his lips with her thumbs. Knowing she would never get a chance like this again, she memorized every detail of his texture.

He let her explore for a little while, but when his eyelids fell to half-mast, he cut her forays short with a searing kiss. She melted against him, and her sigh turned to a moan when he guided her down onto his cock. She rocked on top of him, not bothering to replicate the wildness of their earlier coming together. This would happen slowly. She would savor every moment.

He moved beneath her, each thrust angled perfectly to rub against the place that drove her crazy. Before long, a light sheen of sweat covered his body, and they both trembled, fighting the inevitable. He caressed every inch of her skin, pausing at her clit to circle and press until she sobbed his name.

The electric sensations he generated converged, a tidal wave insisting on her acquiescence. She couldn't hold it off any longer. With a long cry, she came. Her pussy contracted hard, and he followed her over that cliff, shouting her name the entire time. He pulled her down and held her tight against him.

Chapter Seven

As they rushed around the place packing up the few things they had brought, Mia made some promises to herself. One: she would not let Kaelen know she'd spend the rest of her life fantasizing about him. Two: in her very next fantasy, she would be in the Slutty Boss role, and he would star in the role of Naked Assistant. Three: she was taking home the big purple vibrator he had used on her. No way in hell he was going to use that powerful piece of equipment on some other woman. She had an urge to lock him in a chastity belt so he couldn't use his equipment on other women either.

She straightened up the papers on the desk. The yellow binding of his paper caught her attention again. Though she really didn't have the time, she flipped it open and read the first paragraph.

When he snatched it out of her hands, she was on the second page. She tried to grab it back, but he rolled it up and tucked it away in his inside flannel jacket pocket. "Kaelen, you went through all the trouble of bringing it here. You might as well let me read it."

"This is your vacation. You can't do homework on vacation. Plus, there's no point." He handed her hairbrush over. She'd left it in the bathroom.

"It's really good. I don't understand why you would turn in such a huge assignment late."

"Let it go. Vacation. Relax. Enjoy." He held the door open for her.

She dug into her jacket pocket for her car keys as she crossed the dormant grass to her car. The sun glinted just above the tree line. "Stubborn asshole." She stuck her key into the lock. He slammed her door shut before she could open it more than an inch.

He leaned his weight on the car, but he pressed his body against her back. His lips grazed her neck. "Seriously, that's not a nice thing to call someone who just rocked your world."

He eased back a little so she could turn around. She inhaled, breathing his scent and striving to remember every detail of this perfect day. Before she could decide whether she wanted to apologize or defend her statement, his mouth closed over hers. He plunged his tongue inside and wrapped his arms around her body, crushing it against his iron muscles. He took, consumed, razed until only the limp shell of who she used to be stood there, trembling in his arms.

She took solace from the fact that he trembled too.

"I have a flight to catch. I'll see you Monday."

And just like that, he was gone. She watched his car disappear down the long driveway and tamped down the complex mixture of feelings that made her want to chase after him and beg him to not leave.

* * *

Kaelen forced himself to focus on the road ahead. Two days and nights in a resort with a sandy beach outside awaited him. Two days to soak up the sun, do some windsurfing, and troll the tourist traps for some cheap souvenirs to give his parents and his little sister.

Two nights alone in bed wishing Mia was sleeping next to him.

After a layover in Atlanta where he couldn't locate a place comfortable enough to stretch his legs, he was too exhausted to care about anything but finding a bed. A taxi met him at the airport in what he thought was supposed to be Bermuda, but was actually a resort on a private island, and took him to the hotel.

Check-in went off without a hitch, and his eyes were almost closed by the time he rolled his suitcase out of the elevator. Finding the room wasn't difficult, and thankfully the key card worked on the first try. He planned to flop onto the bed and fall asleep without even taking off his shoes, but a scream woke him up.

The lights in the room came on, and a woman crouched on the other side of the bed. Mia.

Shock rendered him speechless. She gathered her wits much faster. "What the hell are you doing here?"

She wore a silky nightgown with thin straps to hold it up. It came down to the middle of her thigh, and he had an urge to know whether she had matching panties. With her hair tousled and that feisty look on her face, she was an erotic vision in pink.

He thought back over his wish, and puzzle pieces fell into place. "You wished for a couple days on the beach too?"

She stared at him for a minute before sinking down to sit on the edge of the bed. "I guess they meant for us to spend the whole weekend together."

Kaelen parked his suitcase next to a wall and peered around the room. He hadn't expected anything too fancy. It was nice but not lavish. It had a kitchenette, a small dining table, a sofa, coffee table, and a king-size bed. This wasn't making complete sense. Some parts he understood.

"They didn't ask questions about this part, but they only gave us one bed." Then he realized she had been here for a few hours. "And why didn't they have us fly together? I had a two-hour layover in Atlanta."

She shrugged. "Maybe they went the bargain route on your wish."

He shoved his hand in his pocket for something to do that would make him feel less out of place. "I got it for free, as a thank-you."

"A day of fantasy sex and a weekend in the Caribbean. That's some thank-you. What did you do?"

Hefting his suitcase, he put it on the bed and opened it up. Might as well brush his teeth and get into his pajama pants. "My job. Look, I'm beat. What do you say we get some sleep and talk about this in the morning?"

She looked away and nodded.

* * *

She listened to the sounds of water running in the bathroom as Kaelen got ready for bed. This wasn't real. She'd been thinking about him, wishing they had the whole weekend together, when the door had opened and in walked the man of her fantasies.

When he emerged a few minutes later and approached the bed from the other side, she watched and wondered what he was doing. Then she remembered. One bed. She jumped up and grabbed her pillow. "Since I'm shorter, I guess I'll sleep on the couch."

He snagged her pillow from her grip and tossed it back on the bed. "It's a big bed. I don't snore, but I do tend to pull the covers when I turn. Just yank them back. I'll let go."

With that, he slid under the sheet. His eyes closed before his head hit the pillow.

"Kaelen?" She poked at his shoulder, but he was sound asleep. "Well, I guess that answers that question." He wouldn't be making a move on her tonight.

* * *

She woke in the warm cocoon of his embrace. He'd nudged his knee between her thighs, and he held her close with one arm. His bare chest pressed against her back, which wouldn't have been such a big deal except her nightgown had ridden up. Most of his arm rested on her exposed skin, but his hand had crept under her gown to cup her breast.

How many times had she dreamed of waking like this? She tried to stay as still as possible, but he stirred. He eased his hand from her breast, extracted his knee from between her thighs, and rolled away.

"I thought you said you didn't hog the bed."

His nervous laugh didn't lack for charm. "I don't usually. I must find you attractive."

More likely he'd just responded to having a warm body nearby. She closed her eyes. "You can have the bathroom first. I'm not ready to get up."

When she woke again, it was to the smell of fresh coffee. She opened her eyes to find Kaelen regarding her with that dimpled half grin. He held a steaming mug in one hand and a plate of assorted breakfast goods in the other.

"They were closing down the continental breakfast, so I snagged a few things for you. I didn't know what you might be in the mood to eat, but I've seen you make coffee. Two sugars, right?"

"Thanks." She sat up and rubbed the sleep from her eyes. He set the coffee on the bedside table and put the plate in the kitchenette. She stretched and helped herself to the coffee. Hot, with just a touch of bitter. It woke her right up.

"And I talked to the manager. They're booked solid, so we're going to be roommates for another night."

Mia frowned into her cup. She wouldn't mind spending the weekend with him, in or out of bed, but she hadn't shared that secret part of her fantasy with Oasis. No way would she have wanted to end up spending time with some stranger just because they'd screwed one another's brains out.

"I got the coffee wrong?"

"No. I was just wondering how they could have messed this up. They were pretty thorough with everything else."

He pulled the cord to open the drapery covering the slider. They had a balcony. "I think we can make the best of it, don't you? We have about thirty hours before checkout. I was going to go windsurfing this morning. Want to go?"

Mia shook her head. "I have no sense of balance. I'd rather just swim than spend time climbing out of the water."

He didn't force the issue, for which Mia was thankful. He called his good-bye through the bathroom door when she was in the shower shaving her legs. Finding it easier to admit to herself that she longed for his company and his kisses, she embraced her disappointment at the fact he didn't have a problem spending this vacation as if they were two people sharing a room by accident. Perhaps they were, but still. Maybe she wasn't so thankful after all.

In the original bargain, they'd promised this was a no-strings fantasy. Of course, she hadn't expected to act out her fantasy with Kaelen. But she had, and now she was confused by this need to be with him and act like a couple.

She spent the morning on the beach. Not really one for just lying out, she walked the shore and appreciated the natural beauty of the place. This was what she would have done if she had been here alone. Walking the beach, listening to the waves crash against the shore, and feeling the sand squish between her toes had figured prominently in her plans.

While she would have liked to try windsurfing, she just didn't have confidence in her ability to get anywhere, even with a few lessons. Not that she could have afforded them. All of her money had gone into paying for the wish, and that left nothing for extras like windsurfing lessons.

And what kind of job could someone do that made the fulfillment of a sexual fantasy a suitable way to show appreciation? It bothered her that she didn't know what he did for a living. She knew he'd served his country in the Army, and that he was two or three years older than her twenty-four years, but she didn't know anything more.

In all the times they'd interacted—and they'd interacted at least once a week—she'd never thought to ask a personal question. She had fantasized about a man she didn't know very well at all.

Perhaps the terms of the fantasy had been for the best. One day of incredible sex did not a relationship make.

She turned her attention to a flock of windsurfers sailing on the other side of the finger of land where she had wandered. They looked so graceful, skimming and dipping over the surface. A few of the more experienced sailors did tricks. Most people seemed content with the easier maneuvers that involved nothing more than avoiding a crash into anything else.

Mia watched until they began to head back to a base camp. The sun beat down on her head. She knew if she didn't get inside and get some water soon, she'd end up with a headache that wouldn't go away.

The cool air of the hotel room did a lot to lift the fuzzy feeling from her brain. She downed a bottle of water and took another one to the couch Kaelen hadn't let her sleep on. With no television in the place, she didn't stay down for long. She dug the papers she'd packed from her suitcase, in order to get some grading done before Monday, but she couldn't concentrate on them. She wanted to read Kaelen's paper, but he'd taken it from her.

She prowled the room. As she eyed Kaelen's suitcase, the image of him tucking his paper into his flannel jacket flashed into her mind. Without the smallest qualm, she opened his suitcase and took it out. She rationalized by telling herself she hadn't looked through any of his other items, though she noted he'd brought the sex toys from Oasis and more than a few condoms.

Those were leftovers. There had been no time for him to ditch those items before he had to board his plane. The sex toys she'd snagged were in her bag. If Kaelen hadn't been there, she would have made sure the door was locked and made use of them.

Settling back on the sofa, she sipped her water and read Kaelen's paper. In it, he proposed studying the correlation between a woman's level of sexual satisfaction and the frequency of the use of sex toys. He'd laid out a number of variables, both dependent and independent, to consider. It would benefit from peer review, but it was a damn fine treatment.

Mia was impressed at the amount of thoughtfulness he'd put into the paper. If he'd turned it in on time, it would easily have netted him one of the top grades in the class and perhaps an invitation into many different colleges for postgraduate study. The eight misplaced commas would be a problem with Brindley, but his ideas and his design were solid.

The door opened and closed. "Honey, I'm home."

She finished the last paragraph, glancing up only when his shadow fell over her. The saltiness of the water combined with the scent of sunscreen and sweat. On anyone else it might have offended her senses, but on Kaelen it made her want to draw him closer and taste his lips. The fact he wore long swim shorts and no shirt added to that urge.

"Did you get out of the room at all?"

Though she wore a bathing suit, she hadn't done more than walk along the shore. "Yes. I just came back a little while ago for some water and air-conditioning."

"Storm's rolling in. I was gonna shower and grab some lunch. Want to go down to the restaurant with me?"

She closed the report cover and set it on the table. His eyes tracked the movement, narrowing as he realized what she'd done.

He picked it up, flipped through the pages, and then threw it back down on the table. He parked his hands on his hips. "You went into my suitcase."

"It's a really good paper. Why didn't you turn it in on time?"

"I told you I was working."

"It's a brilliant idea. You've laid out your research strategy so well it would only take a few tweaks to turn this into a real study. What do you do that's so important you couldn't stay home and finish this?"

He smirked. "Don't you think your opinion is a little biased? After all, I put a bit of that theory into practice, and I think you enjoyed it."

Heat crept up her neck and bloomed on her cheeks, but she wasn't going to let him derail the conversation. "Kaelen."

"I'm a firefighter. We had a three-alarm blaze. They needed me."

Mia recalled seeing reports of the fire on the morning news. It had taken them all night to get the blaze under control. Fifty-two people were now homeless. One person had died, and three others had been hospitalized. The thought that Kaelen had been there, had likely been inside the building as it burned, scared the hell out of her. She closed her eyes to tamp down the after-the-fact worry.

"About the time class started, I was showering off a night of grime and soot. Then I headed home and fell into bed. When I woke up, I finished the paper and brought it to Brindley's office. Most of campus was deserted. I didn't expect to see you there."

He sat on the corner of the table, leaned his elbows on his knees, and combed his fingers through his hair.

She wanted to put her arms around him and hold him close. "I don't understand why you didn't say anything. You were busy saving people's lives. Even if he refused to take the paper, you had a pretty strong case if you wanted to challenge his decision."

He jumped to his feet and paced in an aimless pattern. She let him gather his thoughts.

"You already think I'm some kind of idiot."

Mia's head jerked backward as if he'd smacked her. In a way, he had. "I never thought you were an idiot."

"Fucking hell. There isn't a single time I've been up to your office that I didn't have to manufacture a reason to be there."

She frowned. Certainly he didn't need a reason to see Dr. Brindley during office hours, and her boss wasn't in the habit of sharing the details of meetings with her or anyone else. The man might be a hard-ass, but he had professional ethics.

"I fell for you the first time I saw you standing up in front of my class in that dark blue, shapeless dress with a sweater over it to make it more shapeless. I have no idea why you try to hide how unbelievably beautiful you are, but I don't really care. Less competition."

Her heart fluttered. She remembered the first time she saw him, how strongly he'd affected her. His smoking-hot good looks had certainly made him stand out, but when he spoke, she found she liked how his comments lent depth to the discussion. Sometimes she designed questions for the class just because she wanted to hear his opinion on the subject.

He flashed that half grin, but she could tell his heart wasn't in it. "I wanted to ask you out. But then you opened your mouth. By the time class was over, I'd decided I was going to marry you. We'd have two or three kids, your choice, and a house with a decent-sized yard."

Mia reeled, and her mind raced. He'd never asked her out, not once.

"Filling out all those questionnaires for Oasis made me realize I'd never have you, not after asking you stupid questions for a year and trying like hell to flirt with you. You never flirted back. You showed zero interest in me. You're too far out of my league. I'd resigned myself to having the fantasy."

So had she. "I thought you only flirted with me because you thought I could improve your grade in the class."

He faced her, his mouth pressed in a grim line. "I don't need Advanced Methods to graduate, and I don't need help getting good grades. I took it thinking I'd get up the courage to ask you out even though you didn't seem interested."

It had never occurred to her that he might actually find her attractive. The surgery to fix her breasts hadn't been until last summer. They didn't make a prosthetic bra that hid her problem, so until her surgery, she'd made do with a push-up bra and stuffing so the left one looked like it was the same size as the right. No man, especially one as good-looking as Kaelen, wanted to settle for a disfigured woman.

She rounded the coffee table to stand inches from his chest. Tension vibrated between them. "I still don't understand why you didn't say anything. Dr. Brindley was there. You could have talked to him."

"Maybe because I can't think straight when I see you. I didn't expect you to be there. When I saw you, everything I'd planned to say to Brindley flew out of my head. I focused on you and totally forgot about him. I'm not an airhead, but I can't seem to come off as anything but an imbecile when you're near."

He shook his head. His hands gripped her arms, and he pressed his forehead to hers. She shivered at the intimacy of the embrace and the desperation in his voice. Looking at their interactions with new eyes, she saw that he used cockiness to cover up nerves.

"I'm in love with you, Mia, but I don't know how to talk to you. Yesterday was the first time I ever relaxed enough to show you a different side of myself."

She stopped fighting the urge to touch him. Leaning closer, she slid her hands up his chest. "I liked who you were yesterday. I liked who you were Wednesday too. I liked that you flirted with me, even though I didn't think it was personal. I like that you look me in the eyes when you talk to me. I like teaching the classes you're in because I like hearing your opinions. I fantasized about being with you. But you're so far out of my league that I never thought you could actually be attracted to me."

He wrapped his hands around her wrists, halting her exploration. "It's more than simple attraction. I'm in love with you."

"You barely know me." And once he figured out what a freak she was, he would end the relationship, fleeing just like any other man she'd dated. Okay, maybe that was an exaggeration, but more than one man had ended his liaison with her soon after he found out about her breasts.

"I might not know what you like for breakfast, but I know you love Philly cheesesteak. You take two sugars in your coffee. You're smart, ethical, opinionated, stubborn, sexy, and short. I know how to touch your sides to make you shiver. I know how hot you get when I kiss you. And I know how to make you scream my name."

"You like short women?"

"I've had a thing for Sarah Michelle Gellar since I was fifteen, but you've got the number one spot, babe. She fell to number two the moment I laid eyes on you."

He kissed her, soft and slow, full of passion and tenderness. Mia pushed aside her doubts and all the reasons it couldn't work, because even if he changed his mind when they got back, she would have this weekend forever etched into her memory.

Chapter Eight

He scooped her up and carried her to the bed. Even after he settled his weight on top of her, he continued kissing her, drowning her in his version of slow love. She ran her hands over his hot flesh, luxuriating in the texture of his skin and the solid feel of him under her fingertips.

Until he captured her hands and held them immobile above her head. Breaking the kiss, he lifted his head and regarded her with solemnity.

She wiggled her hands, but he didn't let her move much.

He ignored her protest and searched her eyes for something. "I have a few questions before we make love."

She hoped he wasn't going to ask if she loved him. She found him attractive, addictive even. She hadn't lied before, but she couldn't utter the words until she was sure he wouldn't run the second he found out about her breasts. He'd noticed the scars before, though he hadn't commented.

"First, you said no oral sex on your survey. Did you really mean that?"

"I told you, that was because I was expecting a stranger. Oral sex is just so intimate."

"So that's back on the table, then? I can go down on you?"

She nodded.

"What about light bondage? I'm not into hanging you from the ceiling or anything, but I'd like to tie you to the bed frame every now and again."

She had the same objection to bondage. Not with a stranger. "Okay."

"And anal sex?"

Her eyes grew so large she thought her eyeballs might escape. "I've never done that before. I can't say it sounds like fun."

That half grin made a reappearance, and this time he meant it. "I'll work on changing your perspective."

"I'll try it, but you'll stop if I don't like it?" She waited for his nod. "I'll turn your paper in. I'll tell Dr. Brindley it was my mistake."

He shook his head. "I'll talk to him Monday. I seem to have overcome my inability to access my thoughts around you."

Transferring his weight to one elbow, he shifted to hold both of her wrists with one hand. With the other, he untied the bow behind her neck that held her bathing suit top in place. He peeled it down and looked at her breasts.

With one finger he gently traced the scar on her left breast. "Tell me about this. Tell me why you wear shapeless clothes that hide your luscious little body."

She tried to cover herself, but he wouldn't release her wrists. "Kaelen."

"No. You'll cover yourself and lock me out completely. I know how stubborn you are, babe. I can be just as stubborn when I really want something."

That had been the plan. At this point, she had everything to lose. If she told him nothing, her silence would damage their new relationship. He wasn't shallow or self-centered. She could find the courage to trust him, couldn't she?

After swallowing several times, she finally managed to speak. "I had surgery. Breast augmentation."

He continued tracing her scars, alternating between breasts. "Why? I know you didn't do this for vanity's sake. Otherwise you'd wear tighter clothes and low-cut shirts to show them off."

Though he didn't mention it, his gaze fell to her two-piece bathing suit, which covered far more cleavage than most one-pieces.

This time when she struggled against his hold, he let her sit up. She pulled her top over her chest. She drew up her legs, and he knelt on the bed in front of her.

"Mia."

"It wasn't what you're thinking. If it had been health related, insurance would have covered the surgery, and I wouldn't have had to save up for six years to pay for it myself."

When she didn't continue, he traced a path along her inner thigh. "I noticed the difference right off the first time I saw you after summer vacation, though I doubt anyone else did. You've spent a lot of your life working at fading into the background. I'm glad to hear it wasn't serious. I was so worried about you. I didn't want you to suffer alone."

And now she felt even more self-conscious. "They were deformed, okay? One was an A-cup and one was a C-cup. Our family doctor kept telling my parents it was normal, it happens to some girls, so my parents wouldn't help pay for surgery. They think I'm blowing it out of proportion, but they don't realize how much trouble I had to go through to hide it from everyone. You're the first person I've taken my bra off in front of since sophomore year of high school."

The hand on her thigh rose to cup her cheek. "So you split the difference. A B-cup looks great on you. They're the perfect size to hold in one hand, leaving my other hand free to do other things."

She batted away his hand. "You joke about it now, but six months ago you would have taken one look and never called again."

"In case you don't remember my heartfelt confession, I've been looking at you for a hell of a lot longer than six months."

"With my clothes on."

"Only because I lacked the courage and finesse to ask you out."

"Kaelen."

"Mia."

"You would have encouraged me to have the surgery."

He scratched his chin. "Probably. You were very unhappy, babe. You were thinking surgery would make you feel sexy."

"It made me feel comfortable enough to call Oasis." If she hadn't made that call, they wouldn't be together now.

"But not sexy. Tell me, did you feel sexy yesterday?"

She nodded. She'd felt more than sexy. She'd felt downright desirable.

"Do you feel sexy today?"

"No." Her frustration came out in her voice. If her breasts were fixed, why did she still feel like the same girl who had hidden her body with baggy clothes for the past eight years?

"That's because feeling sexy is about what's on the inside, not the outside. Yesterday you let go of all your inhibitions to play a role. I think the role you played let the real Mia come out and express herself.

"You put too much emphasis on your looks and not enough on what's attractive. I fell for your feisty attitude and your wickedly intelligent brain before anything else. Your pretty face might have drawn my attention, but it's what's inside that kept me coming up to your office to ask stupid questions for the past year."

"Wow. You sound like a shrink. Are you sure you're a sociology major?"

"Smart-ass. The sociology major part of me says you're hung up on this because society has taught you that women should look a certain way. You feel like you have to live up to some ideal. But in the real world, real men want real women."

"Again, you can say that because I look normal."

"Mia, if you took off your shirt and had two different-sized boobs, I'd probably be surprised. Then I would want to play with them for hours because that's how I am. I like you because you're different from other women. That would just be another difference. But it isn't one anymore, so I really don't know why it's still an issue."

Because the image of herself she kept in her brain didn't look any different. "Because I don't feel like anything's changed."

"I don't want you to change. As stubborn as you're being right now, I still love you. If you need validation of what your outsides do to me, I have that right here." He took her hand and put it on his damp swim shorts. Already semierect, his cock jumped and lengthened under her palm. "The only thing you need to change is your perspective."

A shaky bit of the confidence that had fled when she told him about her surgery returned. She gripped his cock harder through the fabric. "Maybe you could help me with that."

He brushed a kiss over her lips. "I could definitely help you with that. Let's get rid of all these clothes so I can start your therapy."

Under his appreciative gaze, she shed her swimsuit. She expected him to do the same, but when he stood up, he crossed to the dresser and opened a drawer. Neither of them had unpacked. She peered after him, the feeling of being sexy dampened by his puzzling behavior.

He rummaged around in the drawer. The scraping sounds of things sliding out of the way surprised Mia. She hadn't known anything was in there.

At last he returned and threw a length of nylon rope on the mattress. Mia eyed it uncertainly. "You want to tie me up now?"

His dimple peeked out. "More product testing. This time I'm going to bind you and blindfold you. Then we'll have to do it all over again with the blindfold off."

Mia blinked. He hadn't covered all the variables. "Then again without the blindfold or the restraints? I don't think it'll matter by then. I probably won't be able to move."

His grin grew. "Lie in the center of the bed."

Eager for this experiment, she centered her body on the mattress and rested her head against the pillows. Kaelen grabbed her ankles and slid her halfway down the bed. Mia looked back at the headboard. She didn't know if the rope was long enough to cover the distance. Before she could question the position, Kaelen lifted one of her legs and kissed her instep. He rested her ankle on this shoulder and ran his hands up her leg, bending down to reach all the way to the top.

Her breath caught, and she hoped he would touch her pussy. He didn't.

"I'm going to do something a little different. Don't worry. I'm pretty good with knots, but there are scissors in the drawer if we need them."

Mia nodded, unsure if she was playing the role of slutty secretary again. Then she pushed away the idea. It didn't matter.

He bent her leg and positioned her foot on the mattress. Then, with a series of precise movements, he wound rope around her thigh and her ankle, binding them together. When he finished, he checked over his handiwork. "You have to tell me if anything is too tight or if it's cutting off your circulation."

The rope was thick enough that the individual strands didn't dig into her flesh uncomfortably and smooth enough so that it wasn't scratchy or abrasive. Mia wondered whether he would bind her hands. She waited for him to tie her other leg, but he didn't move. She glanced up to find him staring at her expectantly.

"Did you hear what I said?" He slid his finger between the rope and her flesh, testing the tightness.

"Tell you if it's too tight? Yes. I will."

"Wiggle your toes."

She did, and he watched. Apparently satisfied with what he saw, he bound her other leg the same way and made her wiggle her toes again.

This position didn't make her feel overly restricted. It just didn't feel like bondage if her hands were free. She imagined him between her legs, his thick cock filling her pussy. She wouldn't be able to wrap her legs around him. Would she feel bound when it came time for that?

He pushed her legs open a little more. The cool air hit her pussy juices, and she shivered. He came around the side, holding her open with a firm grasp on the rope. It tugged at her skin, but it didn't hurt. "Give me your arm."

It didn't take her long at all to figure out he intended to bind her wrists to the ropes holding her thighs and ankles together. She held her arm out to him. Minutes later, she felt truly bound. Her wrists were tied in a way that forced her legs to remain wide apart. Kaelen had unrestricted access to every part of her body.

Then he put the padded blindfold over her eyes. He brushed a kiss against her cheek. "What's your safe word?"

She moistened her lips at his husky tone. "Oasis."

The bed dipped as he shifted. He didn't bother hiding his movements, and she was able to approximate his position. So when she felt his fingers tracing her wet folds, the sensation didn't surprise her. She knew exactly what he planned to do.

"So wet. I'm going to make you scream."

He didn't give her a chance to reply. Heat from his tongue seared her clit. She wished she wasn't wearing a blindfold. The image of Kaelen with his head buried between her thighs wasn't one she wanted to miss. She moaned and called his name.

He flicked and sucked, kissing her pussy with complete abandon. Sharp pulls as he sucked harder had her thrusting her pelvis closer. Wanting to wind her fingers through his hair, she jerked at the ropes holding her wrists in place. She struggled, but the action was deliciously futile. Tension curled in her center, and she came in a gush of cream.

Between her legs, Kaelen moaned. The vibrations prolonged the feelings of pleasure flooding through her bloodstream. He lifted away, taking his body heat with him. "You taste so fucking good. I think I'll have some more."

Mia shivered. She shifted her face toward the sound of his voice, but she had no idea where he was. Then she heard the hiss of a zipper, and she knew he was getting the vibrating equipment from his luggage. Or hers. She hoped he was going for that big purple one in her suitcase.

"Wiggle your fingers and toes for me."

She showed him that her circulation was still good, and then she felt his lips kissing a path down her neck. He nibbled on her earlobe, and a kittenish moan squeaked from the back of her throat, a completely involuntary reaction.

"I love the little noises you make." He whispered his declaration against her skin, searing it into her heart. He ran his hands over her skin, caressing the spots on her sides that made her quiver. A sweet blaze burned inside and out.

He made his way down her body and resumed his position between her legs. The sound of a vibrator caught her attention. This time he didn't use his finger to tease her folds. She had no way of knowing which vibrator he used, and within seconds, she didn't care. By the time he added his mouth to the mix, her entire body trembled.

"Kaelen, oh please, Kaelen!"

She expected him to take her over the edge, but he lifted his mouth away and turned down the speed on the vibrator. She moaned a protest.

"We already know how you react to this toy. Time to use something new."

New? What else was there? They'd played with most of the toys in the cabin. Those they hadn't tried were just different sizes of the things they had used.

The next sensation wasn't something she expected. Coolness smeared over her anus, and she realized he was massaging gel into that tight muscle. She clenched. "You'll go slow, right?"

"Yes. And if you don't like it, I'll stop and do other things that'll make you feel good. Relax. It won't hurt. I promise."

The shock of the unexpected touch faded in the face of increasing pleasure. Kaelen massaged in slow circles, and the vibrator in her pussy buzzed faster and harder. Something hard slipped into her ass. She was sure it felt larger than it was. As he'd promised, it didn't hurt. The beat of the vibrator in her pussy combined with the fullness in her ass to add a new dimension of sensation. Sharp points of pleasure tingled from her scalp to her toes.

When he closed his lips around her clit, the orgasm washed over her. She screamed. She arched, and she might have lifted from the mattress, but her bindings made it difficult to move that much.

He turned down the rate of vibrations and sucked her clit lightly, bringing her down gently. By the time he'd slipped everything out, she felt like a pile of jelly.

"I'm going to wash up a little in the bathroom." He brushed his lips against her inner thigh. "I'll be back in less than a minute, but call if you need me before that."

She mumbled something, but she couldn't decide on exact words or really get the sounds to exit her throat. He chuckled, and she heard his footsteps as he crossed the room.

Her wits hadn't quite returned by the time he came back. A warm cloth pressed between her legs. She felt a little self-conscious about having him clean her up. If he untied her, she would see to those details herself.

He kissed the inside of her knee. Her legs trembled. Holding them up like this, even bound, taxed her muscles. Or maybe it was because of the orgasms? She didn't have time to process the reason because he dragged a finger through her open pussy and pressed down on her clit.

"I love watching you get wet. I think next time I'm going to have you use the toys on yourself."

Mia licked her dry lips. "What are you going to be doing?"

He licked a path up her stomach, between her breasts, and along her neck. If she hadn't been bound, she wasn't sure she would have allowed him to do that. Something about being stuck in this position gave her permission to let go, to let him do whatever he wanted, and to enjoy everything.

"Watching." He closed his mouth over hers and plunged his tongue inside. At the same time, he lined his cock up with her pussy and thrust hard. She gasped, even as she reveled in the way he filled her.

He swiveled his hips and ground against her clit, and the gasp turned into a moan. He thrust and pounded. She writhed, her legs spread as wide as they would go and held there by his weight. She struggled against the rope, wanting desperately to hang on to something, mostly Kaelen. But this position stripped her of all choices. Not only did she have permission to let go, she had no choice.

An orgasm spiked through her system. She screamed, and her vaginal muscles clamped tight. His rhythm faltered. He thrust slower and breathed harder. She thought he might come, but he seemed to have been pacing himself, not giving her a moment's respite.

In no time, he resumed using faster, shorter thrusts. Though the pulsing of her climax had yet to fade away, she didn't think she had it in her to come again. Every part of her body trembled. She felt boneless, unable to move. The ropes no longer mattered.

Her pussy burned with heated juices, and he fed the inferno with every inch of his sweet friction. His body slapped into hers, over and over, forcing her higher up that cliff. She wanted to speak, to moan, to beg, but she had lost control of her voice. Behind the blindfold, her eyes were open so wide they ached, but she couldn't close them. Stars burst in the darkness, and she recognized the sound of her screams.

This time Kaelen joined her. He thrust once more and collapsed on top of her useless body. She felt cherished and safe. As consciousness faded, she finally admitted something important to herself.

A little while later, she woke to find herself untied. The blindfold lay on the table next to the bed, and the pale pinks and purples of dusk streaked the little bit of the sky she could see through the gap in the curtain.

Kaelen lay next to her, holding her close with one arm banded across her midsection. "Welcome back."

"Back?"

He chuckled and planted a kiss on her neck. "You passed out an hour ago."

She had nothing to say to that. Four orgasms had the power to do that to a woman.

"I'm glad you're awake. I'm hungry."

"Hungry?" She planned to ask him where he wanted to go for dinner, but he slid under the sheet and pushed her legs apart.

The sore muscles of her inner thighs protested, but she ignored them. Given enough time, she would get used to being as physical as he wanted to be. She pulled the sheet away so she could see him this time.

He parted her with his thumbs and licked with long, slow laps of his tongue. She trembled and gripped the pillow under her head, crying out when he added two fingers. He thrust them against her sweet spot and sucked her clit to the same rhythm. His moans of pleasure vibrated against her pussy, and she came, the soft waves breaking gently over her body.

Kaelen slid off the end of the bed and stood, his cock hard and ready. He dug in his suitcase for more condoms. "It's a good thing I took these. I hoped to convince you that, at the very least, we needed to use these up."

Mia giggled, a gleeful sound she hadn't heard herself make in far too long. Yet she'd already done it twice in his presence. His answering smile and the smoldering look in his eyes reminded her of something she neglected.

"I love you, Kaelen."

He sheathed his cock and settled between her legs, his weight resting on his hands as he hovered over her body. His cockhead waited at her entrance. "Oh, you're in for it now."

"In for what?"

"The long haul." With that, he eased home.

She smiled up at him. "Take as long as you want."

Epilogue

Six Months Later

Mia sat on the top of her suitcase and urged the zipper along its path. It squealed in protest and moved less than a quarter inch. The doorbell to her small apartment buzzed, so she gave up for the moment and ran to answer it. She'd spent the past semester toying with the idea of giving Kaelen a key.

Their relationship had progressed fairly quickly. The first week back had been a little awkward because they had decided to keep things quiet until the end of the semester. She had tried not to look at him more than usual, and he'd seemed extra restless as he sat in class. Then finals had redirected their energies for a short time. By the time the next semester began, they'd reached the point where they automatically assumed they had plans together unless they had to work.

She threw the door open, and he dragged her into his arms. The past few nights had been lonely. When he was scheduled for those long shifts, days passed before she could see him again. He kissed her until they both gasped for air.

"Are you about ready, babe? Our reservation is for nine, but I thought you'd like to work up an appetite first."

"I need help with my suitcase, and then we're good to go."

He turned her around and slapped her ass. "You just want to get me into your bedroom."

Normally she would agree. But tonight was their first romantic weekend together since their Oasis vacation, and she wanted to get him alone in the hotel room. They had been methodically testing out his sex-toy theory, refining the parameters of the study the fun way. However, he lived with four other guys, and she had a roommate. Privacy was sometimes hard to come by.

He eyed the bulging suitcase on her bed thoughtfully. The lid curved over the contents, and the edges of some of her clothes stuck out. "It's just for one night. What do you have in there?"

She smiled. "All our favorite toys."

He flipped open the lid, lifted her clothes, and peered inside. She'd put them into plastic baggies and lined them up in neat rows inside her suitcase. The little dimple near the corner of his mouth deepened. "Yep, most of them are there."

Since she'd packed everything she owned, she didn't know what he meant. Had she overlooked something? "What's missing?"

"How about this?" He reached into his flannel shirt and pulled out a pink leather paddle with a heart shape cut out of the center. A white ribbon wrapped around the handle, and a matching bow was perched at the top of the heart.

Moisture gathered between her legs, wetting her panties. She could already feel the sting against her backside. "Oh, Kaelen."

She thought he would claim a kiss or ask to try it out, but he sat on the corner of her bed and studied her somberly.

"I gave my notice at work. My last day is in two weeks."

A pang struck her heart. He still needed two classes for this degree, but she graduated next weekend. The doctoral program at the University of Michigan to which she'd been accepted wouldn't begin until the fall term. "Why? You still have a semester left."

He nodded. "I know. I'm going to take my last two classes this summer. With the compressed schedule, I won't be able to make my shifts at the fire department. I saved up enough to cover rent and expenses." He ran his hand through his hair. "I heard back from the grad programs at U of M and Eastern. I've been accepted to both on the condition that I finish my undergrad degree first."

She squealed with glee and launched herself at him, tackling him with more force than she'd anticipated. Luckily he could handle it. He rolled them both until he was on top.

"You don't mind me following you?" His teasing grin returned.

She had hinted and prayed, but she had thought she would have to suffer through an entire semester living on the other side of the state. "I can't tell you how happy I am. Congratulations, Kaelen. You worked hard for this."

He tucked a strand of hair behind her ear and nibbled on her neck. "I'm going to need your help looking for an apartment." He nipped across her collarbone, leaving behind gooseflesh.

She fanned her fingers through his hair to keep his attention there. "Or you could just move in with me." She hoped he was as ready for the next step as she was.

Her strength was no match for his. He easily broke her hold and lifted his head to study her with those gray eyes that turned her knees weak. "Go to sleep next to you every night. Wake up next to you every morning. I'd like that, Mia."

Emotion welled in her chest, and words failed. He grinned and feathered a kiss across her lips that showed he understood exactly what she meant to say.

Michele Zurlo

I wear a lot of hats for someone who doesn't like anything near my head. I'm a wife, mother, teacher, and when I have spare time, a writer. My childhood dreams tended to stretch no further than the next book in my to-be-read pile, and I aspired to be a librarian so I could read all day. Alas, that dream faded when I got a social life.

Years later, I happened upon a free laptop that didn't come with games of any kind, which I figured was a good thing because I didn't have that much free time to throw down the Minesweeper Black Hole. Staring at the brand-new computer, I thought it would be a shame if it went to waste, so I decided to write a novel. Once I started writing, steamy, sensual stories poured from my fingertips, and now I just can't stop using that laptop. I hope you enjoy reading these tales as much as I enjoyed writing them.

Read more about Michele and her books at http://www.michelezurlo.com

Loose Id® Titles by Michele Zurlo

*Available in digital format at http://www.loose-id.com
or your favorite online retailer*

Re/Bound

* * *

The SAFE WORD: OASIS Series
Yes, Justin
By My Side
Out of My League
Wanting Wilder

Available in print at your favorite bookseller

Safe Word: Oasis
Contains *Yes, Justin; By My Side;* and *Out of My League*

CPSIA information can be obtained at www.ICGtesting.com
Printed in the USA
LVOW120045270213

321795LV00001B/180/P

9 781623 001698